SEX CHANGE

Alan Goldfein

As always,
to Ute.

About the author

Alan Goldfein has written for *Time, New York, The Village Voice, Commentary, Playboy, Oui, Satire, Beyond Baroque, Cimarron Review, Colorado Quarterly, Forum, Florida Quarterly*, and *The San Francisco Chronicle*. He is the author of *Heads*, and has been anthologized in a Random House Collection, *On the Job: Fiction About Work*. In the 1970s, Alan Goldfein received the Mark Twain Society Award and a New York State Council of the Arts award for fiction.

During an extended stay in Germany, the novels *Jews and Germans/Germans and Jews, Europe's Macadam/America's Tar, Let Us Now Praise America, The Black Wife*, and *The Guidance Counselor* were created.

Alan Goldfein has taught economics at the University of Maryland, history at Carnegie-Mellon-University, and writing at Berkeley. He has also written numerous episodes for television series, such as *Knots Landing, Perfect Couples, Bodies of Evidence*, and *Paradise*.

I

Until he married no one knew—or at least few did. He, and then his wife, close-carried what became their secret, which was sometimes poison, sometimes elixir. Arthur Becker and his wife Anna were still the husband and wife that they had been before the marriage, and so in some ways the exchange—or, considering their unique sexualities, what they considered an exchange— would not be an exchange, as it had been prompted by how they had behaved for years in their own special time tunnel. They had known who they were and weren't. They had studied-up on themselves, they could even make each of them the other. But this marriage business for Arthur Becker, that came later.

Not that he had one now, but *Arthur Becker had been born with a vagina*. Just as he had been born, not Art, nor Arthur, but Marta. And as years came, there came scrimpings of little upper body strength, quite little—especially in the self-surveillance and determined self-pumpings-up of a boy whose father had been quite the admired local athlete. Arthur's shoulders were too narrow for tough-boy games like football or soccer; his hips were too broadish for wrestling or for track—some kids mocked him by pointing out that he had "child-bearing hips", as if he didn't know—in the mirror there they were, those skimpy "bumpers", he called them in sorrow (and in a regret which, his parents told him, there was no need for him to have); those "bumpers", they extended-out beyond the vertical drop-line finitude of his narrow shoulders—in various mirrors, obsessive-hunted mirrors, Artie just couldn't but see those hips as betrayers and traitors, and little did he know that many women, mostly models and actresses, felt the same about their own pelvises, as if those darned "eagle-wings" had on their own gone-to perversely launching and spreading-away on them. . . . Needless to say, Artie Becker hated this unfair victimization by Nature—he remained afraid to say 'by God'. He just wanted to be a boy. That's all! Was that too much to ask? He *was* a boy! He followed boxing like a boy, he thrilled at knockouts, especially thunderous dead-cold one-punch ones; he read about war and history and politics—he knew Alexander the Great and Napoleon and Eisenhower; he was on first name terms with all the brand-names of all the cars and the companies and nations that produced them—he was good at math (although not at shops); girls' close presence got him boy-squeamish and even antagonistic. So steeped in misery could Arthur find himself at times that he wanted, at those times, to rip himself apart, tear out his "Jewish lox with a tomato slice" female organs (which, spread-legged, he had inspected as best he could on as many numerous occasions as he had stared at his hips-and-shoulders' "perversities" in his bedroom mirror), how could he throw-out and forget his hopeless hopes and dreams of, somehow, achieving maleness and . . . and *what?*—no he couldn't imagine himself accepting himself and becoming a *girl: throwing himself away, his Real Self, so as to become—well, to become just what he sadly was!* . . . Of course Arthur's tormented gloom tyrannized his mother and father to the extent that the most prevalent sound about their house, and one that fell from lord-knows-where, within-without, was no-sound, quiet—even when they spoke their sentences seemed to be coated in a purdah, a sacramental silence, and one wherein fermented that great cloud of resentment that Arthur had hovering over his parents, his weapon for their having created him. And this cloud, it weighed-down to such an extent that—and Arthur swore this—he wished that his parents were dead, sometimes he did, this even when he was as young as five years—this wish gave him evil chills, shivers. (It must be said though that as Arthur grew older that deadness wish against his folks fell into the dark slow murky turbulence of his unconscious: it dissolved-away as Arthur did grow to have sympathy for his parents—it dissolved; while his torment did not.).

But Arthur played with boys, he did do that—and only boys, boys exclusively—when they would unbolt their critical guillotines and let him. Marta Becker, or rather Arthur Becker, slender as a slice of crackly unleavened matzoh (and this was his own unfortunate self-image), skill inheritor of his ex-jock dad's genes, he could toss a football yet with a perfect spiral, and far

3

too, in street games, speedy and dodgy as a cat he was always the anointed quarterback—*if* the game were "touch", no way for him in tackle, he'd be "broken-up into like smithereens". And, amazingly, he was ambidextrous and he was blessed as super-coordinated, so he could drive either left or right in basketball, and like the great Mickey Mantle of old he could bat in baseball from left or right as well, although he was not strong enough to be expected to hit any homers. But those athletic moves of his were sorely put to the test, assiduously strained in the bathroom, as he had to plant and balance himself in a straddled thigh-V over the toilet in order to urinate, for he had sworn to himself that he would never, *never*, sit to pee. . . and afterwards, to deal with the unavoidable spray that he (or, well, *she*) made manifest, he'd clean up round the bowl; on his knees with many layers of toilet paper, he'd do all the neighboring checkerboard bathroom tiles. Indignant but determined, a good boy as a maid (and his family had a maid!) he just *did it*. And did it and did it and *did it*!

Damn-damn-damn, he had that accursed *vagina*!

But, damn, I am a boy!

Later on he would learn that the professionals called his situation *gender dysphoria.*

Big words for a big secret that was a big transgression—at least for him it was. Big words that made you hate all big words, intellectual words, he'd hate them as if they were creepy lies, coward-substitutes for feeling, decent honest feeling.

And he always suspected that every other kid—every other boy anyway—*knew it,* knew the whole deal, knew of his misery, knew of the great treacherous mistake plastered-onto his body. Arthur saw other kids,

as he saw it, as seeing-through-him, and almost immediately too, a finger-snap, a lite-bulb. Gawking then at
his secret. Natural to gawk—he didn't blame them, he'd
have gawked himself. At home, along with making
from instructions model-to-Mars-rocketry out of plastics, creating, from instructions, model aerodynamic
trains, out of plastics, he created, once or twice or
thrice, out of *plastic*, the model penis (with no instructions save his book research), that penis which he had
been so unbelievably cruelly denied. He would then
take his "cock-mockup" and place it onto his vagina,
first as if to rectify Nature's malicious mistake; and
then, once it occurred to him that he could do this
"thing" that was a ridiculous comic insult amongst
"good" people, and that it didn't mean what it pur-
ported, he *did* it: he fucked himself. He of course did
not realize this at age eight, but he had created a dildo;
except he did not utilize it for pleasure, no way—rather,
he guessed, for punishment. He slipped, or he joggled,
his "homemade dick" into the unwelcome pulpiness of
his vagina. And sometimes he did it soft-like, but sometimes what came about from him was more like action
with a vengeance.

He had no siblings. It occurred to him, even at his
pre-adolescent age, that his parents did not wish to
press their luck on the bearing of yet another trans-
person—although of course he did not use that social-
science word even in his thoughts—he did not even
know it. It also occurred to him that his parents did not
have another child because they feared that if they had a
"normal" son or daughter, that sibling (although of
course Arthur also did not think in that word's terms),
that sibling's normal existence might humiliate him

further, he their *un*prodigal non-normal son, their existence might have his parents love him less. And less and less and less. (Immediately upon his demanding that his parents dispense with 'Marta' and go with Arthur, or even Art, or even Artie, they who had blindly named him did obediently transform what they called him). His father Mark was a broker, a partner with Baltimore's largest and most prestigious firm, Vander-Diggins. Mark Becker oft-times just about pranced about their house, because he saw himself as quite important, quite special—although, when alone, he had cried about the misfortune "bombardiered-upon" his son—and therefore onto himself. Arthur's mother Elaine dealt in real-estate, and she was the "tough monkey", the realist (she often lied to potential buyers about the faults of houses she wished to sell: that was just her justified way of succeeding, of practicing good-business in the American-favored way)—and unlike her husband Mark, Elaine never cried about Arthur. Perhaps, as the boy had come from her womb, she saw the "travesty" as so much her fault, even subconsciously, so it was beyond admittance and beyond remorse. They were a family with "mucho money". But they were also a family of two adults who, when they were not staring at their son surreptitiously and sympathetically, had difficulty staring at their son, "he" their one-and-only, staring him straight-in-the-eye with truth, when they were thinking about what "truth" was. Because what was truth?—was truth ugliness? Was truth suffering? Was truth a random nothingness—an island? Was truth a joke played on a young boy who was also a young girl. Was truth something that made his parents feel guilty, inordinately so, unfairly so, as if by the innocent intermingling of their semen and egg they had caused this, let's face it, miscarriage. And worst truth of all for a young boy-or-girl-or-boy-or-ad-sorrowful-infinitum, was the truth that poor Arthur experienced even more guilt than his parents did: He had so let them down, hadn't he?—especially his father Mark. Mark Becker had been the deity of his time, at least in the Jewish Baltimore of the Fifties-Sixties. He had been a star lacrosse player at the University of Maryland—he had played the position of attack, and in THE college sport of the Middle Atlantic and the Ivy League. Mark had been instrumental in Maryland's defeat of Princeton and Johns Hopkins and Rutgers—he'd been cheered like crazy, even by "the goddesses", the gentile girls, the *schiksas*, he'd had coeds galore, his future had been assured, such as immediate hiring by the "upper class" (usually non-Jewish) firm of Vander-Diggins, and his near-immediate rise to as much of a star as he had been on the lacrosse field. No wonder this demigod pranced as he walked, without even knowing it. And no wonder that both he and his son felt such insurmountable blame for their having let each other down—and further blame for feeling so much blame. Arthur actually wished that he possessed the gumption to just tell his father, square with him, how sorry he was for "he" being he, as he was after all, except in wish, a *she*. And Mark actually wished that he could accept his son (or daughter; or son-daughter; or daughter-son), but accept he could not—no matter how fervidly he tried. When Mark Becker laid eyes on this child who was the undeniable emanation from the secretions of his own prized body, he seemed to wither within himself: he did not prance and strut as he had on the athletic field or in the elite offices of major corporate stocks and bonds—his back bent, he slumped, that prized body of his felt tsunami-shorn, it even ached when, at Trader Joe's, he lifted cartons of the special Gerolsteiner mineral water that Elaine so prized. He even went into therapy to deal with this, well, abomination (he just couldn't escape that word) that life had viciously, indifferently, thrown at him, *at him!*—and so devastated him as to have had him resort to that abominable word "abomination" *for his son!* . . . Truth also ought be said that "rectifications" such as surgery and hormones were not yet appropriate, not quite yet. "Rectifications", such as they were, were quite dangerous and subject to mistakes in the process of "genital reassignment", or "gender affirmation" or "gender conformity"—"making a penis is no walk-in-the-park" (quipped one sadistic-comedic surgeon putting-on the ominous declarative voice of a hanging judge); an operation would have to await adolescence, at least. For at that later age Arthur would be more able to more maturely decide who he wanted to be. Perhaps he would come to see "the female" more favorably and then decide to remain a girl. *But how can I REMAIN what I never was!?*—Young Arthur swore that to himself—and to his parents—he would *never* wear a dress and put on lipstick, and he would kill himself—he swore he would—if girl-breasts started to grow and push their way out from his chest like dog-snouts and he would have to wear a *bra*. And if he did not do away with himself, then, he swore, he would cut *them* off, those "pests of breasts", all by himself. At his age of eight he denied the existence of God.

"God is there," said his father Mark, who did not believe. "Things happen for a reason."

But Arthur could see in his father's eyes the creedless sickness of it all (he never saw his father cry—Mark hid that "weakness"), and then Arthur would see in his father's eyes, the eyes of a man who had for years resided within a narcissistic bubble, the grim acceptance, the accommodation, to life's twistings that made it just about impossible for him to embrace his "son", to kiss his boy-girl who was craving a daddy-kiss. Mark would watch Arthur being embraced and hugged by his wife Elaine, but that didn't help him with his doing the same. He wrung his own neck for that. He made excuses—"The boy keeps shifting up and back in my mind to a girl, and then up and back more, and so I don't know *how* to kiss the, uh, my, kid; I don't know who *I* am in the whole damned rotten *deal*."

Arthur's mother Elaine told Arthur: "It will all work out. I know you don't see that now, but you'll see. Things have a way of that."

Arthur's parents wanted to give him more advice, but they could think of nothing but such trite words.

There were even moments when Arthur's father Mark had to resist his making outspoken jokes and wisecracks, such as 'Hey, you can lead yourself while dancing,' or unintended ones like, 'Artie, I can barely hear your feet when you walk into the living room.'—for such ironies, while they might have helped Mark, would have just about destroyed his boy-girl son-daughter, whatever.

Arthur sometimes resisted these, what amounted-to, aborted hugs from his father—who did sometimes make approaches towards such closeness, after he'd wrestled himself up to it. Arthur perceived the difficult energy involved for this man, the torturous tightening in his father's athlete-body, but it didn't matter. Arthur did not want to hurt his father, as much as he did not want his father to hurt him.

When they went to restaurants or to movies it was okay. Losing yourself was okay. Sitting between your parents silently, even if as an implied prisoner, a resident of another world (that sometimes reflected-back upon your world as a cheat of a world), that was okay.

That was okay!?

And it was okay for Arthur—in a way—that there was, for him, a right-sport—if you could call it that. The only "sport" in which he could compete problem-free as a male, and with uninsulting males—well, semi-uninsulting—and hope to be adept-at and competitive, was pool. And so, Arthur spent a great-deal of after-school time at Bonnie's Parlor, which was not a beautician shop—Bonnie, the owner, was a woman. Arthur, with his specially custom-made Palmer cue, which his father Mark had bought for him from his friend Jim Carey, the best pool player in Baltimore (who had, once or twice, beaten the great Willie Mosconi), Arthur, "he" with his broad girl-ass (not gone uncommented-upon now and then by losers), "he" bent over felt table after felt table, "he" learning to stroke with smooth confidence especially at 9-ball, the gambler's game, "he" a natural it seemed at putting "English" on the white cue-ball so that it could do its duty of stopping-cold after connecting with the object ball, or retracting a good "halfways" back and up the table for the next-planned shot, "he" knowing almost by instinct (as a girl might?) where to lay that cue-tip left or right or high-left or high-right or low-left or low-right, so as to put the necessary spin on, first, the cue-ball, and then, consequently—as a physicist would know—the opposite consequent spin on the object ball, so that it might come off the rails at angles unbelievable and sink into the desired hole, and etc etc etc—so that Arthur, by age fourteen, could win, weekly, in the neighborhood of one hundred dollars, which did impress his father Mark, as much as it depressed his father Mark, and the same impress-depress lite-cloud dark-burdening Arthur as well, for he surely did not wish to become what they called pool-hustlers and hangers-on in Baltimore, a "dirt ball". Well, not fully—not merely a dirt-ball, and a broad-reared cunt-rumped one at that (with his multi-Kleenexed cod piece leaning and squishing on the mahogany edge of the beautiful table, and with him, Arthur, when he felt hostile-confident enough with his winnings, to wriggle his "girl-rump" in insulting losers' faces)—but what damned choice had "he", winner-Arthur? . . . He who, as a "winner", was aware at every moment of his "winning" as his losing, of his sinking the 9-ball into any one of the six Brunswick table pockets, that "he", defeating boys, and defeating *men* too, even bulldozing some of them, was, within himself, a boy, who was feeling, not all, but too much, still too much, and without portfolio, a *girl*.

His athletic moves, so bizarrely momentous, as if accomplished by a spirit-ghost of himself that was more himself than was the outward skin of himself, this double-feeling (which never left him, which was always there), this eventually got him to thinking-about, and then finally led him to, acting—this ought be mentioned now, although it came later, this love of being various, different people who were not, remotely, "poor-handi-

11

capped" him. Because of his sexual sensitivities, his ambivalences, and even his rage-hostilities, Art Becker became one hell of a perceptive actor, and a subtle one, that cannot be denied. He played the sexually irresistible Richard Katz in the movie version of Jonathan Franzen's *Freedom* and he portrayed the sexually resistible rogue Mickey Sabbath in the movie version of Philip Roth's *Sabbath's Theatre*—although these starrings of his were plastered deeply into his dreams, not his Reality: it was just so easy to see himself, possessed as he had been of labia and vulva and clitoris, top-billed in these two movies, as there was nothing to contradict him in his grand-fantasies, such movies of such novels never having been made. And, by that time of his life-dreams, he also was *not* so possessed of "the wrong gender"—he had, as it were, divested, or was on the way—the quite long way. He had begun the hormones such as testosterone, there would be surgery, which was dangerous—it is very dangerous, very risky, to create, from labia and clitoris, a penis. So surgery was off off off in the future. And there was the consequent deepening of his voice. And there was weight-lifting, a great deal of that. There were, not implants, but shoulder paddings and a chest vest that was near as thick as the Special Forces ones that were bulletproof. And there was psychotherapy, first psychophilosophical, then behavioral and bio-feedback. And a will that was tremendous. Art Becker's will was unbeatable, in the arduous venture of becoming—what he thought was—his true self. *("God, does it have to be so hard!")*.

*　　*　　*

And of course there was that one prime area in which the young Arthur Becker had his difficulties, couldn't but have had them. This was not in his movie-depiction-deceptions but rather in the flat-out arena, the no-dream-warren of real life: the *women* neighborhood. "He" *wanted* women, "he" day-dreamed of women, and most especially (for a while) Natalie Wood, for she was not a sexpot, she had a voice that was sweet and even naive and trusting—Natalie wouldn't laugh at Arthur's "predicament", she would instead worry with him, she would huddle with him, and the two "lovers" would try to work-it-out. Thus this desire of Art's for girls and women fell mostly, deeply, imprisoned, in the area of romance, not in sex. And he had learned this fate early-on: In high school, in Baltimore, before he had grown-up to a maturity where he was sure of his station in life, he was just simply stuck with the stubborn, brutal salience, the "nitty-gritty", the "skinny", that he had no penis—no way around *that* one—staring (sidewise) at a urinal he could merely experience a contempt born of incapacity (he'd even heard a few *teachers* making fun of him); in the locker room of Forest Park High, the very same school where his parents had been hero and heroine—although he avoided the school pool as if it were shark-infested (doctors' notes required)—he was forced to camouflage as if he were a double agent (which of course he sort of was): this by way of tissue paper in his jockeys, same as he did in Bonnie's Parlor pool room, and sometimes he bulked-up with excessive stuffings not unlike the cod pieces that men wore during The Wars of the Roses and The Hundred Years War, and that to this day male ballet dancers employed to augment themselves on stage. And then there were those difficult harsh raw-skinned periods of detachment where he spoke to no one, not parents, not friends (he had one), not even teachers—so that when, in one case, he received an A on a test the teacher wrote across the paper in thick red ink "Who Are You?" And on dates, by age sixteen, even with, especially with, girls—"whores"—who had "reputations", Artie read-up in advance: the endocrinologists wrote (as much as Artie could comprehend), that fetal testosterone would eventually "teach" the grown boy to "go mount", while fetal estrogen would lead the born girl towards a grown-up back-arching reflex (lordosis) set-right for being mounted—which "knowledge" did not help Artie one bit: he was forced by his "incapacity" (and his way-over-his-head science-reading) to just hump while on top and while clothed, this with an artificial energy that felt stupid, so he "pleasured" those supposed high school "whores" with his finger, all the while observing in his dates' abstracted eyes and downturned lips that combination of enjoyment and disappointment that he himself knew all too well from living life all too poorly.[1] (One "whore" shut his "act" short by way of the neck-slicing CUT!-gesture that a pissed-off movie director might employ). No, it is impossible for a supposedly "normal" person to imagine how Artie was forced to only *imagine* penetrating a girl between her legs, to only *imagine* her screams and squeals that—*he*

---

[1] A compounding complication was that Artie had skim-misread the endocrinological article, and on two fronts: (1) it concerned rats, not folks; and hyenas; (2) estrogen, in ample amounts, could lead a female to go mount—a male. It is doubtful, however, that estrogen-mounting prowess would have caused estrogen-escaping Artie to go raving at Good News.

imagined—would come with his God-given male domination and that he imagined all other boys enjoyed. Yes, he had wondered what it would have been like for a boy with a hardon to enter his, well, "pussy"—but such travesties-of-sex were perversions, disgusting, they almost made him throw-up. But "almost" is only almost: Arthur had to *know;* for one, curiosity; and two, if he were ever to be absolutely certain that sex-change would-be/*should-be* in store for him, he simply had to experience the dread-anathema that females did—how could you so love being *penetrated!?:* Arthur could not bring himself to provoke, to act girl-sexy and wriggle his ass (which was, he'd noticed early-on, becoming fuller than those of his would-be brethren) and maybe blink his eyes in that fake-comely female way, and all the other things they did (which turned *him* on), so he had to await Scottie (Skip) Cutter, who was quite possibly the most perverse student at school, and perhaps the most perceptive:

Cutter was a sinewy stringbean with tattoos all over, in an era before such body-brandings became The Thing; he had no friends and appeared to pride himself on that—and, because he was lightning fast, he could duke-it-out and defeat even guys on the football team. And Scottie-Skip seemed to sense the mixture that Arthur was, his painful-enough infusions of hostility said so. So, one afternoon when school was out, he waylaid Arthur behind the Shops shacks and huts (Arthur had gone there to retrieve a radio he had been working on for three years to nothing but a chaos of junk-failure), and Skip acted-upon what must have been his savvy theory: He pounced on Arthur, he pulled down his pants, he cranked-away with what kids called his "stick" until it achieved the desired stickness and inserted that hardon of his—which Arthur never even saw—into Arthur's "cunt", going in-out-in-out-in-out, until his white stuff (which Arthur considerably envied—oh he knew what semen was!), that dripping jelly entered Arthur, some of it dripping out like nose drops when you had a cold. "You come?" Skip asked. "Come where?" Arthur answered, believing that the question might have to do with whether or not Arthur would accompany his schoolmate rapist to some other place where they could do *It* more (and also knowing full-well what the question meant). "I've got to go home," Arthur had replied, and Skip had just grinned in a kind of well-proven triumph and disdain. And Arthur had taken the Number 5 Baltimore Transit Company bus to his home-stop, now fully aware that being "prey", being anchored and plunged-into, was absolutely not for him—with but one little minor exception: the truth was that during the "action" with Skip, his Thing, Arthur's clitoris, it had gone hardening-up, almost against Arthur's own anti-clitoris will, as if this "thing" of his, this accident which was inside him, and which was, to his way of thinking, also outside-of-him, a kind of betraying-partner-enemy, was giving him pleasure—and how could it have behaved in this girlish way? And indeed, that night in bed, and many nights thereafter, he had fingered himself, in-out-in-out-in-out, imagining doubly: that he was Scottie Skip Cutter *and* that he-she was also the basic She. Sometimes he had arched his back and pumped-away with his rear end, not quite knowing whom he was being. At moments then, this masturbational imagining was pleasant, erotic, and at the very same moments it was torment, it displayed his own emptiness, his own wrongness, his own vile misplacement in the universe—how could this birth-insertion of his that was false and that he despised act-up with an internal "erection" when all the things it stood-for were to him anathema?—this was absolutely Hell. . . And Hell was also the tribute that Arthur now had to pay for Skip's silence. In addition to doing his math and English homework (for instance summarizing *Silas Marner*, interpreting bullshit Puritan poetry so it made even remote sense), and translating from their French workbook, Arthur had to give Skip one dollar every day, which meant that *he* went without French fries and Wednesday pizza slices and deserts at lunch. . . It was not until Arthur's junior year at The University of Maryland (where he had of course not joined any fraternity—although he had been rushed by three or four "frats", the lower-ranked unknowing ones, Jewish ones: well, he had become rather handsome, if in a "frailish fine-boned [what they thought-of as] English upper-class way" [and then within a year, he had evolved again, towards the "lookage" of a sensitive-faced Osama bin Laden, although he was shorter than that handsome terrorist by some four inches]), at university he realized that, by wanting a girl, he could be considered gay faking-it, and by wanting a boy (*which he did not!*), he could be considered gay and not-faking-it, for, as he came to learn, the gender of a face is processed by the amygdala within 150 milliseconds, and so what could he do but curse The Joke of Existence, and go trying to undo that Joke by finally working-up his nerve and getting naked, slowly, completely, naked, for a trusted girl who he considered (tried-to-consider) his girlfriend—and she was horrified; and though she tried to hide her distaste at seeing her one-nighter "boyfriend" in possession of the very same sexual instrument that was her own and that she had already experienced the excited and anticipated filling-of, she had no choice but to suggest that they be FRIENDS—she swore that she would not reveal his secret—and soon after, because she disliked her own distaste for her "friend", the friendship found itself dying, and leaving Arthur with only himself as his friend and contempt as a concept (and reality) of which he'd become one great-miserable connoisseur. He had learned in Biology 101 and in Chemistry 101 that the human organism was all cells, molecules, atoms, hormones, etc, which, miraculously, if you weren't an evolutionist—or even if you were—these microscopic nothings came together to produce a "normal" human being—who could get laid and who could be liked. And yet, with no malice aforethought, these little thingies had come together, in the sorry case that became Arthur Becker, to amalgamate into a cockamamie mismatch that fooled the fucking 150 millisecond amygdala and thus said Arthur-cockamamie you have to live with this unfair bullshit of physiology—unless you're brave enough to brave the surgery that you swore (to yourself) that you could-would brave—and which, one, might not work-out, and, two, might well fucking *kill* you. . . The irony was, however, that, as has already been implied and said, girls did finally come to find Arthur attractive and desirable, because of his manner which was (as has already been implied and said, what would come to be seen as bin Ladenish), he just was softly intelligent and unaggressive—pure, in a sense; and because of his handsomeness: though slender, he was six feet tall, with wavy dark hair that seemed "exotic", maybe Spanish or Arab, and those intense dark eyes; his nose was lean, thin-spun, with a bump, a nice one, a vulnerable one (again, like bin Laden's nose), it was unintrusive, uninterrogatory, unpushy; his lips always seemed to be pursed, when his upper lip was not risen in the manner that many attractive girls employ to exhibit endearment. He was, as one girl said, "a darling"; another, "a dish"; another, "a sweetie-pie". Another: "cock-suck bait, if there ever was one." . . . And all of these observations did find their ways to him.

Despite his bizarre (but unbizarre) attractiveness, and because of the abysmal frustration it caused, as he could do nothing with it—as his father would have, and as his father (still) did (Arthur was pretty sure of this)— Arthur saw himself as committing suicide. He was a "freak", he'd be doing "the normal world" a favor. He imagined the ways of suicide—hundreds of times he envisioned himself as swinging from rafters with his bedsheets taut about his neck; the "leap-to-freedom" from the nearest Baltimore harbor bridge (which one he could never decide-upon—maybe the farthest bridge, way out by the Chesapeake, would be better, to stifle people's talk and his parents' pain); pills—too *feminine*, the last stigma, his curse, must he even end himself in the effete-fey way that he had been wrongly brought into this world—which had *caused* the curse? He imagined, he imagined, he pictured and he imagined— and it was like as not his endless imaginings and their fluctuations that taught him the wherewithal to try and become a member of the only profession that so perfectly fit his fluctuating position in the world: as mentioned earlier: an actor. . .

II

But before that theatrical realization could come about at the University of Maryland, first came what Arthur would exultingly refer-to as The Arthur Becker Rebellion—and it was one to which in later life he would come to owe a debt; one of substance and righteous resistance and stubbornness and gratitude. There had come a time at the university when he had had enough of mocking looks and mocking words and even his own masochistic self-mockery and self-abnegation—for if it is the case where just about everyone is having sadistic fun at your expense, you may come to reason, and maybe justly, that they are right, these people: you are a joke, nature's joke, put perhaps upon this boring Earth for others' delighted and delirious ridicule, and edification too. And right or wrong he had had enough, he'd get even, or at least so much even as could be managed. As he was not nearly strongly-built enough to challenge guys, and with hopes of beating them up, he decided that he would deprive them, not of their masculinity, which *he* did not have—

and which he wished *they* did not have—but of Things: Things they coveted. Things that gave them pleasure. Things that had cost them a lot, in money and time and in the development of various abilities. He would become a thief. What was more romantic than a thief?—especially a justified one. A thief beloved-by the audience. Examples: Clint Eastwood, George Clooney, Brad Pitt, John Travolta: Even imagining that there would be an approving-admiring-applauding camera on him as he performed his "dirty tricks" (he couldn't stop imagining this camera) Arthur would be a vindictive (but honorable—somehow) filcher of bicycles and records and CDs and books (usually the megalithic Pynchon paperbacks that were all the rage and which they, his ridiculing enemies, not a one of them, did read beyond five pages) and sportscoats, and jock-shoes, which self-dubbed "Underground Arthur" figured he would sell, cheap, to the local College Park used clothing store.

"This is not a good idea," advised Doctor Jack Feder, the psychiatrist that his father Mark had acquired for him. Doctor Feder was located in Baltimore, so every Wednesday Arthur got into his used Plymouth convertible that his father Mark had also gotten for him—obviously as compensation for the boy's un-speakable unfair sufferings—and that had helped render Arthur a speed-demon back to Baltimore, and a self-mocked spoiled brat, and therefore even more of a sufferer—and Arthur had sped the thirty miles back to Baltimore and its downtown Medical Arts Building, where he met Doctor Feder. The psychiatrist was a self-promoter-aggrandizer and even a liar, an easy habitual liar to suit, supposedly, truthful purposes—usually grandiose ones—he (self) rumored to have been at one time a buddy of Doctor Ludwig Guttmacher's, who had been a pal of Doctor Robert Lindner's, who had written *Rebel Without a Cause*, who had been an acquaintance of Wilhelm Reich's, the maligned and hokey (and greatly believed and followed) supersex orgone box inventor, he who had been a friend (semi, and guarded) of Hannah Arendt herself—who had written about "the banality of evil"—and who had been a lover of the unbanal but not unevil (he'd not been un-Nazi-ish) and not unbrilliant Martin Heidegger who, in addition to having known Hitler had also known Einstein who had also known (well, met him) Freud. Thusly, this Doctor Feder, who by intellectual-historical substitution (and intellectual-historical bullshit) knew-em-all, he talked to Arthur, and he talked and talked, as most-important Feder, most self-justified, he was no listener. (Examples: "Arthur, there are things that are easier done than said;" "Arthur, you are enjoying a very low opinion of yourself."). And he kept-up surveying Arthur with the densest aim of significance, a scriptural significance, as if he were assessing how to navigate the "boy's" abstruse sexuality of female attributes and male wants and characteristics, and do it without compass or astrolabe—or any shred of affection or empathy. Or, for that matter, interest.

"Arthur, you've been given a good swift kick in the old knickers by nature," Feder also said, "but don't kick back, not in this juvenile delinquent way of stealing. This will only serve to make you lower than your victims, your victimizers. You know, in this country parochialism reigns, we are a primitive land, very un-cultured, we're Babylonians—and you've become the brunt of this American know-nothingness, American cruelty that believes it's goodness. Still, Arthur, don't kick-back your kickers, it'll only cause a fecal hurricane[2]—those shtunks are idiots."

"Then how, how will I, well, kick back?"

"Good question. I'm not against, per se, kicking back. But in more subtle ways."

Feder was not tall, not short. In a way, due to his arrogant and uncontainable personality, due to that Biblical tonnage he carried, and to his penetrating cavernous eyes that seemed primordial (but forced as such by way of their protuberance, as if they were being flexed) you saw the five-foot-seven Jewish man with tight-clung beard and bulgy ears and brush-like hair (*an older Jewish man with a full head of hair!* thought Arthur—*incredible*), you saw Feder as any height you wanted him to be—and Arthur saw him as a shortish-tall. And as a demon who was as decent as he was a demon.

"Have you considered hypnosis?" Feder said.

"Hypnosis?"

"Instead of theft. The mind is the greatest property of all to steal. To have one in your control is to be a giant, like myself."

"Yourself?"

"To hypnotize someone, especially an enemy, an adversary, will have you walking on air, on a cloud. You will feel, Arthur, what you have not felt until now—as if you are a *man*."

That 'as if': Arthur could have choked to death this psychiatrist—who obviously, like everyone else who might be a well-deserved prospect for Arthur's hyp-

---

[2] shitstorm

nosis (if he could be, unlikely as it was, a hypnotist)—
like everyone else, this "doctor" was a bastard ridiculing bigot of sex.

"You"—Feder must have caught note of Arthur's
enmity and decided to work on it—"*you will be a
Man.*"

Doctor Feder handed to Arthur a paperback—
HYPNOSIS ON SELF AND OTHERS—he had written
it. But it looked self-published due to its flimsy paper
and oversize photo of the pompously glaring-eyed
Feder with his seemingly boundless capacity for
encircling any object, human or otherwise; he glared at
Arthur as he glared on the book's cover, then he gave
the poor girl-boy a copy, autographed it and asked for
two dollars, "cheap" ("Your father Mark will be only
too glad to fork-over the extra sawbuck, my child, and
by the way your father Mark—full disclosure here—he
sees me, as his 'doctor', as a consequence of his guilt
and sorrow and failure at, well, Arthur—I'll pull no
punches—his participation in having you."—which sad
fact, *his father a mental patient*, Arthur hadn't known,
and which made him sick, literally—he threw up later,
down on Reed Street, after the session). "Your father
Mark," said Feder, "he has read my book, and he has
admitted to me that it has helped him—in board
meetings, and with clients." (Arthur later learned that
this self-promotion was a bald-faced lie.)

Arthur read the book, which he found to be an arrogant fount of egocentric hokum:

> Giving the Eye: an ironlike wire will drill into the
> subject's will and render him [no 'her', as
> Feder was not a modern man] subservient
> and eager to yield and to confide.

Intensity: Lunge the facial muscularities towards
gravity: this is a no-monkey-business acute
necessity, as hypnosis has been employed as
an act too often on the stage,with cohorts as
subjects; such association must be total-
swept from the subject's mind.

Speak the Speech: slowly and with depth; a high-
pitched Squawkiness of the vocal chords
will only serve to create distrust and nervous
diminishment within the subject or (sic)
object.

Discernment: Choosing the jury box: the subject
ought to be well-scrupulous chosen for their
propensity towards subjection: Look for:
shyness—one who droops downwards a
great deal; trust: one who regards you and
others with revering eyes; one who is prone
to neither the too jovial nor the too
depressed; both attitudes and characteristics
are defensive and avoidance-prone.

(A stockpile of etceteras passed-over here).

Aside from the obvious clichés, and the artificial
easy-does-it fungibility, Doctor Feder's book was so
poorly written it would have received, Arthur specu-
lated, in English 101 or Psych 101, an F. . . Nonetheless, Doctor Feder's personality was so similar to that
of the model hypnotizer in his book (and possibly
because, without Arthur's knowing it, he had hypno-
tized Arthur?) that Arthur actually fell to attempting
this magus's advice. What, after all, had he to lose? For
the poorly thought-out alternative of theft he might be
caught and arrested, and then, godsakes, incarcerated—
and with his problem: oh, he did picture himself in a

jail cell, forced to drop his pants to shit (another problem, caused by the anxiety due to his physical indisposition, was irritable bowel syndrome) and thus be revealed to drug dealers and muggers and other criminals (okay, *accused* criminals) of zero empathy (*niggers!*—Arthur, a liberal, was no liberal-lover and with little in the way of liberal tendencies—he blamed his own liberty-deprivation for that), he'd be revealed as a "voodoo man-with-a-pussy-cunt". The upshot of that distinction being obvious. So, no theft. Hypnosis.

But how? The potential subjects for Arthur's overwhelming venture of mind-capturing were, by the very nature of their consideration for these trance-reprisals of his, those who had in one way or another made a belittled mockery of Arthur; yet such prospects were, by their very cruel and inconsiderate-cold and aggressive natures, the least-likely subjects of hypnosis, especially of Arthur's amateurish apprentice skilless-ness. To try and numb and then transform these insentient soulless spirits would be to waltz blindly through a minefield of his own making—and these miscreant curs would probably get back at him with even more viciousness. For example, there was Marty Frame. "The Frame Man", who played lacrosse as had Arthur's father Mark: Frame who was vice-president of a FRATERNITY (all of which had rejected pussy-built Arthur), Frame who had befriended Arthur so as to borrow the Plymouth convertible of his "daddy's baby 'goy' or 'birl' " so as to drive down to Durham, North Carolina so as to "lay my sticksome rod" on some tarheel chickita, and then Frame who would keep Arthur's car down South there for weeks at a time (Arthur missing his psychiatry sessions in Baltimore),

Frame operating with sheer charming guiltless aplomb and absolutely no apology, this damned Marty Frame who called Arthur "chum" but who also called him "crinoline-boy" ("Hey, I'm only fucking with you")—though of course Arthur wore neither crinolines nor panties. . . *FRAME!* Arthur stared at and into the cortex of this manipulating false friend rogue, he stared with all the grim majesty with which Doctor Feder had stared at Arthur (i.e. Step One)—and zilch: Marty Frame wasn't even aware that Arthur was "giving-him-the-eye". . . *Don Jacobs!?*—what about Don Jacobs! He who so often managed to jut his right index finger up Arthur's (clothed) ass-crack—*and in front of people, especially girls*—as the Jewish crowd seemed always to congregate at The Wall, a brick divider between The Rosenbaum Business Building ("Jewish Engineering") and the goyische Stuart Arts and Sciences. Jacobs would coax-out imprecations such as "Wriggle, baby, wriggle" and "Don't let me go stink-finger for naught." Jacobs was so impervious and oblivious he didn't even know that Arthur was attempting his desperate mind-control. And the impregnability of these two characters to Arthur's woeful efforts made that woe of Arthur's a tornado.

"I can't hypnotize my adversaries," Arthur told Doctor Feder, and Feder, who was many things, including a pretty obvious shrinker-hustler-grifter, grinned with a glorious secrecy which may have meant any tricky thing, positive or negative, just flatly said (sort of hypnotically) "Then, okay, steal."

"You mean it?"

"Action beats inaction, son (*well*, thought Arthur, *at least he calls me 'son', not 'sweetheart' or any other girl thing*)—stealing's better than nothing, m'boy. You can't go to the administration of your school like a crybaby and whine that 'the bad boys are mistreating me'—that will only make it worse, for you yourself. But you've got to do *something*."

"What if I'm caught?"

"Do not mention *my* name." Feder made a joke out of covering his eyes with his palms and semi-ducking behind his desk as if he were Groucho (and he did look a bit like Groucho). "Hey, *I* don't want to go to jail. I'm serious.

"Arthur," he added, climbing back up to desk level, "you are not an easy, uh, boy, to help."

That 'uh': Arthur knew it was out of the sheer frustration foisted-upon this sheerest of frustration-undeserved egotists.

"But please," Arthur said, "please don't tell my father—about the stealing, if I do it."

This time Feder closed his potent eyes—which Arthur took to mean *trust me*.

And Arthur "cased" the university, especially the frat houses that had rejected him. He saw bikes, roller-boards, U of M caps, loose shoes and boots at the borders of outside, concrete, basketball courts, where the players had put on athletic shoes in the afternoon and then forgotten their real shoes, he saw packages just delivered by Fed Ex or UPS or whoever—maybe music instruments were within—what a haul! What payback! How well-deserved too! But discovery is reality—it defeats fantasy: Arthur had a conscience. Despite all, he was decent. He could not steal a thing. . . Back then to Doctor Feder:

"Arthur," said Feder, "You know, uh, boy, you could live this way the entire rest of your life."

"No!"

Feder broached again his evil-victorious smile.

"So-then: How does a man who is not a man and who wants, desperately, to be a man, *be*-a-man? The question is both rhetorical and not."

Arthur sat, waiting, and the truth was—the discomfiting truth—with potent Doctor Feder, Arthur did tend to feel female—or whatever feeling female was, it must have been that.

"I don't believe in surgery," said Feder.

"I was thinking of it."

"I could see you thinking."

"Please, I can't continue to be what I *am*."

"I believe," said Feder, "that every creation has an adaptability, within, to *be* that creation."

"I don't know what that means. You don't mean 'a girl'. *God*."

"I am not a religious man. No Daniels in Nebuchadnezzar's lions' dens for me. No Ovid "Metamorphoses" of mean-jawed hyenas into sweet-tooth doggies. No Abrahamic sacrifices. Moses was a 'mother' who beat-out and conned-out all his competitors. Any number of cocksuckers might have climbed Mount Sinai if they'd had the right PR and got a good start."

"Doctor Feder, I don't know what all *that* means."

"It means the spirit of the biological, *as* biology, not as spirit."

Feder now adopted his usual lean-back air, as if he were investigating every minute crack and fissure in the ceiling; a bit farther backwards and he might have tumbled-over. He looked like a man who used-to smoke a pipe and percolate perceptions to his love-himself delight, and a sixth sense talked-to Arthur, it swooped-in: 'Being a psychiatrist inflates a man to the heights of the colossally creepy.' "Arthur," said Feder, "I have thought a great deal about you: you know, you have been gifted a potential, for variety: Of feelings. Of sensations. The whole sex-spectrum. You may be too young to realize it yet, all of it, both the male and the female. So, perhaps you ought to relax, let yourself steep for a time, store yourself up like a good wine improving in an old brick cellar. What I'm saying is, you might work on your variety, which is the primordial, or could be. And that, that *inside* knowledge as it were, it might well come to please you. You will find that you will *know* how to touch a woman's body, as your own, which you only now see as male; you will know how to caress it, the woman, how to kiss and *love*—as you know yourself in your male wants. And your appreciation of this self-spectrum, Arthur, coming from it, your being woman while you are, within, being man, you will have, what? enwreathed the male *and* the female, and you will *appreciate* what you will be— such *ecstatics*—a tripling of yourself; and then, in appreciation of your manied self: Self-*love*."

" 'Girl' feelings? *No!*" Arthur would have climbed over Feder's great desk and slugged the slimy trance-man—except for his being too intimidated. However, he did manage a rather brave, "This is bullshit!—your talking *hermaphrodeity*!"

Feder grinned, his entire face an agglomeration of his supposed super knowledge.

"You do know, Arthur, that in early modern times on the stage boys played girls. They 'understood' girls' feelings. They 'appreciated' them. They may well have 'coveted' these 'girl feelings' so that they wished to hold onto them when they became men—and many of them did, throughout their lives."

"Now you're talking *homosexuality!*"

Feder leaned forward: "Supposing, Arthur, I should now reach over and take hold of your testicles."

"I'd . . . "

"No you wouldn't."

Sitting still, awaiting some moral, some further finalizing metaphor for himself and his queer-beaten future, Arthur still felt as if he could choke this ostentatious dogmatizer who seemed to be blowing-up now, expanding beyond mere psychiatry, beyond art, beyond normal human feeling and understanding—and sympathy. Feder was inhuman.

Feder said: "And you may *not* know that the opposite of what I've just said is also true. In the early nineteenth century the "divine Sarah", Sarah Bernhardt, *she* played Hamlet. So, my dear Arthur Agonistes, why not *be* a Hamlet who goes beyond Hamlet, who does our dear famous deep Hamlet one-better and unconfuses himself by incorporating the *female*, which all men do anyway, as that is why we *love* them. Why not prance the stage of life upon which you find yourself, through no faulting of your own, prance the stage with your *gift*—which *is* a gift: You press and you absorb. You stab and you surround. You pronounce *while* you understand. You photograph quick shots and snaps of posings while you paint with deep assiduity—you lie and you truth tell and you blend them to a higher thing: a woman-man for *all* seasons. You want to be a man, Arthur, but you can be *better* than a man. Arthur, I

exaggerate for effect, the effect of serving Truth—
which is what *you* should do. So, Arthur, considering
your gift, I *envy* you!"

"And I *hate* you! Go to *Hell*!"

But even as he swore in his bombast of negative,
within this desperate onslaught of denial, he feared that
all his negations were as spurious as were his fate's
inevitable female flits and flutters. . . Outside on Reed
Street he considered jumping in front of the next car
that passed along fast enough.

The only place where Arthur Becker had been truly
comfortable in all his youth—at least for moments—
had been summers at Camp Solstice, which was located
in Maryland's small strip of the Appalachians—not so
far from the Presidential retreat of Camp David—and
which was devoted to the spirits of the transgender
young. But even there, where gender seemed to melt
away in the mountain trail hiking of forests and
canyons, where all the kids played at the same sports,
where no child mocked or tormented another, where
malice seemed unknown or forbidden, even there a
sadness could pervade: it was in the over-grandiose
ways that these societal rejects overexposed themselves, as if they were actors in some benign but yet
hysterical chaotic play of jubilation and salvation
performed on another planet—this behavior was to
proclaim their supposed unembarrassed liberty, their
de-chagrined "happiness", but it also exposed—once
again—their sorrow at their exile, their abnegation of
"society", their separation and abstention. . . In second
place for Arthur's comfort-in-the-world, after the
"sensitive" Camp Solstice came the college to which he

transferred once he realized that if he would be anything at all in this life, if there was even a chance of that, for role-changes would be the norm, and would be praised, this was possible if he could be a thespian: thus, CMU—Carnegie Mellon University, in Pittsburgh, which had one of the few highly-rated drama schools in the nation. There, this abnormal boy, or girl (he had not yet at this stage had his surgeries), he might gain a school-respite from school-disdain, there he was not abnormal—or, anyway, not nearly so much as he had been at the University of Maryland. At CMU he observed any number of males who appeared to be walking in female ways, even some sashays, and a few, but very few, girls who walked like roughneck guys. And Arthur himself, even with his vagina and his morningly hard-taped breasts which, although quite small, had begun to show their swellings against his tapings, their birthright intentions, and his finelined face that did not require shaving, he wished—when he wished it at all—to be walking with "the dudes", among whom were two fellows who you just knew that, by their easy demeanors of confidence and their frequent wisecrackings, they would be successes in the world of acting. These two were Ted Danson and Albert Einstein, who, once he reached Hollywood, changed his last name to that of his mother's family, Brooks. Perhaps it was just that these two future winners were seniors when Arthur entered school—their minds were already on the West Coast—so they paid Arthur no attention, even when he tried to hustle himself up to them, even when he tried to be ironically funny like Albert Einstein (Brooks) or to walk with the sympathetic superiority (and indifference) of Ted Danson. Or perhaps it was just that Arthur was trying too hard, he smiled broadly, too broadly, when he came near them, he even looked as if he had things to say, which he did not—he even came to believe that these two knew his "secret", they had intuited it by way of being the campus topnotchers—which thought of Arthur's was ridiculous—even supernatural.

After a time, though, Arthur found on campus a new attraction, the one most perfect for himself, there was no doubt: This was in the faculty personage of a man named Cadeau Courir—quite the unlikely moniker indeed (Arthur had had French, two years: he knew that the admired man's name meant Gift Runner—it sounded like an American Indian's cryptonym.). Courir was a mime; he was CMU's Professor of Mime, such an absurd-pretentious oxymoron title—and he was reputed to have performed all over Europe and in New York and L.A. And in no way was he even slightly reminiscent of those annoying agitprop mimes in fierce whiteface you saw infiltrating the streets of big cities, those annoying surreal caricaturists with anger camouflaging the comic, they who "copied" you as you walked, belittling you (and *themselves*, incidentally), with the lack of respect (and privacy) every person does deserve. No, this was not Cadeau Courir. In addition to teaching the beauty of movement Cadeau Courir performed weekly in the auditorium of the Drama Building, for all at Carnegie to appreciate and to learn from, even if by the cellular entrée of osmosis—even some engineering students did attend. He was slender as a rail, Courir was, his entire form seemed to have been etched or traced or lithographed with well thought-out lines and few curves, and although such a composition might be expected to convey harshness and sharpness and danger, as, say Mick Jagger's choppy anatomy did, Cadeau Courir's did not. Instead, a distinct kindness projected-outward from Cadeau's raw-rooted features with his salient veins, he was a moving monolith of generosity-projected, as smooth in air as a dolphin in ocean, and he seemed to recognize the vulnerabilities of everyone and to caress them with his softnesses; at once he appeared as a vivid refutation of the blocks-and-tackles of daily life as it was daily-lived while he sculpted-out life's magnifying, tran-scending, possibilities. And he did indeed seem to tread upon stage or upon the pathways of the campus as if he were slightly, ever so slightly, well, walking-on-air. Or clouds. Oh he was better than a dolphin—Arthur thought so. One might have had brought to mind Fred Astaire, except that one did not upon seeing the man expect him to ballroom dance and chase-in-yearning after a dancing-away Ginger; he was simply *he*—and his voice really was so soft, as a consoling preacher's might be—and it was so decidedly southern. Dignified southern, attracting southern, ancient southern, even *acted* southern, as aristocrats are presented in movies set in Charleston or Savannah. In a way, Cadeau Courir was trite, like a fairytale, a cunning self-concoction; but wasn't everyone that, minus the cunning part; and in a stronger way Cadeau Courir seemed an ultimate goal of perfected, civilized, virtuous, human life. . . And, of course: Arthur wanted to be like Cadeau Courir, who he was sure was not a homosexual—although rumors of that sort couldn't but circulate about the university.

By the way, Arthur hated homosexuals, he rather de-spised them, and he knew why: his hatred was because many students, and people in general in his life, saw him as one—and there was no way to convince them otherwise. What would he do, what could he do: strip off his clothing and show just who he was, "pussy-lips and all": he not a goddamn queer but something more perverse, more weird, more mocked, more sideshow circus-bait: what the "professionals" called a transman (didn't it sound like a ticket-collector on a train?), and this as technically as he was a *non*trans *woman*. Woman-equipped, woman ready-to-roll, but *woman who would not roll in the woman way!*—Holy Hell, by this time he was already *menstruating*. In his dorm room, before litting-out for his classes, he now had to—before stuffing in his ample Kleenex cod-piece—insert his Tampax (which he could only acquire in the same surreptitious way that too-young guys got some bum to go into a liquor store and buy them beer: he chanced his way to the borderline of The Hill, Pittsburgh's black ghetto, and, confronting the likely homeless first Negro man who did not look as if he might kill him, Arthur explained that the package he desperately wanted was for his girlfriend, he got the unfortunate [for five dollars: Arthur still received from his rich parents a good guilt-allowance], he got the black man to purchase the giveaway blood-absorbent[3]. . . But back to the famous mime Cadeau Courir: obsessively, Arthur Becker practiced The Cadeau Walk, he tried to exemplify the cloud-lofted Cadeau-liftings of arms and

---

[3] It should be mentioned that Arthur did not, ever, experience what is known as PMS—but that absence may well be due to the fact that he could not distinguish such an upsetting syndrome from the upset of his basic syndrome—as he considered it—of his abnormal being.

hands, the lilted holding of his narrow chin, the dolphin-waving arcs of his midsection, even the way his blue-white Nike shoes (Arthur did study the shoes), they touched heel-and-toe to ground. As some people work and work on their Tai-Chi motions, Arthur Becker mimed the mime's slow-acting airless-air-filled grace, which seemed also to be his personality. With his small (but growing) breasts well-taped and his Venus mound clutched tissue-tight, *not panties for godsakes*, but a size-too-small black jock strap, Arthur first worked on the infamous allegorical Marcel Marceau prison-pattings of his hands against The Invisible, along with the accompanying grimaces of life's strained despair and hopelessness, the struggling of his shoulders, the bent pressure of his thighs and hips, he becoming a-man-in-a-world-cell—after all, what introductory mime suggestion could be, for him, more true? And he practiced this air-patting so much, so fervidly, that he could just about see in full-fledged actuality that bricked-up wall of life before him, which indeed Cadeau Courir had first prescribed to all students, step one, and to which he of course gave that landmark French mime full credit.

"You are very good, you take it so much to heart, you truly live it," said Cadeau in the classroom. "You are a mime quite natural."

There were mumblings in the classroom. Discrediting Arthur, for sure—and that he saw as a sounding-scene that could well, ought well, be, by many mimes, mimed.

And as Arthur worked on the more advanced mimetic motions and stillnesses, as if by conquering them he might walk into a wholly new world, a pain-presenting world that in reality held no pain, there was a certain troubledness that had entered the great mime's face, so that Arthur was not sure if along with the obvious complement of Arthur as a "natural" had come a concealed meaning. He saw such intense observation in Cadeau Courir's estimation as Arthur leaned to tug on an invisible rope that should have belonged to him but was being used by some invisible other to pull him in a way he did not wish to be pulled; as Arthur imagined himself falling down a hole that had just opened up before him, a black hole, so to speak; as Arthur climbed a rope the frayings of which burned his hands and arms; as he escaped a fire, running while in inexplicable frozen step; as he flailed at imaginary wasps and yellow-jackets while ducking from their attacks; as he reached for (another imaginary) hummingbird.

"But you know," said Cadeau to Arthur," this mime, it is primary while it is secondary. It is like poetry, and as with poetry, while it shows the deepest, unless you are The Laureate himself, you cannot live from it. Mime is like a skeleton of acting, as it is of living. It is the forensics of acting. But because it shows too much while it shows too little, it is not, alone, true acting. As with poetry, it is not a novel."

This latter lecturing took place in the mime's office, to which, out of concern, he had invited his best student, and thus his most worrisome, Arthur. Arthur, who had such great difficulty in staring at the man's pure-elemental face, that he constantly glanced out the room's windows, into Schenley Park, where some students were necking—and where, could you believe it?—well, this was an "advanced", a "liberated", an "uninhibited school"—a boy and girl were fucking against an oak, the boy humping as if to knock-over the thick tree, that boy doing what Arthur could not do—and Arthur, for a moment, was not sure, not really, if the boy and girl had been set up by Cadeau Courir for Arthur's benefit, or disbenefit: they were fucking *mimes*.

"But," said Arthur, "I don't wish to be famous, or successful. I just want to be a mime. It is so far in my life the only, authentic. . ."

"You are a very sensitive boy," said Cadeau.

This observation annoyed Arthur. He had been told this too many times, far too many—this was the reason why one of his most prized mimes was, unlike with other boys who faked playing the invisible non-guitar, those jerks (why didn't they just learn to actually *play* the actual *instrument*!?), Arthur's favorite mime had become that of a boxer, with his superfast one-twos he imagined he could beat the best of them, like, in this era, the rocklike Roberto Duran stumped by the lighting-handed Sugar Ray Leonard. He now closed his eyes and saw himself boxing, as if he hadn't heard those Cadeau warning words of his "sensitivity".

"Well," said Cadeau, with that irresistibly tender-elegant southern accent of his. "I cannot stop you from your miming aspirations. As much as I would like to."

As great as he was at what he did, when the mime had spoken in warning of what in effect seemed the puniness of mime, was Cadeau Courir speaking of his life, his own, of his self? Of not making something out of nothing?

"You really would like for me to . . . quit?" asked Arthur.

"Not to quit. But to recognize, to know in your heart, that this is not, can never be, the main thing, your main thing." With his aqua green eyes Courir penetrated Arthur's own so easily, so candidly, so uncounterfeited; but was this intense enveloping of Arthur full-authentic or a habit, a routine—another mime that The Mime could no longer in his life *not* perform? "So you should recognize," said Courir, again softly—again mime?— "that you will not become lost, forever insisting on what you know, or will come to know, is only what it is. A shadow. A shadow of a shadow. This way of being will drag on you. You will be living the life of a substitute."

"You mean empty?"

"There is too much 'empty' in the world. And worse, 'empty' believing that it is full."

Leave it. For your own sake, ask no more.

As with anyone, it was no easy thing for Arthur Becker to pull himself away from what he was, from his authenticating discovery—or what he thought was that. Even this pulling-away was, to him, a mime, as, as he came to realize, this abstract imitation of symbolic behavior that he had become obsessed by was really not his amelioration but his attempting to accomplish, and by unnatural means, the feat of walking, laboring, struggling, aspiring, failing and succeeding, as would a man. A real-life man. And as he was now twenty-one years of age perhaps the time had come for him to be exactly, unremittingly, that. A Man.

III

Arthur spoke with his parents:

"It's time," he told them by the pool at their capacious ranch home in Stevenson, that nouveau-wealthy Jewish suburb of Baltimore. "It's well past time."

The intense, burdened eyes of his father Mark said that he knew exactly what Arthur was speaking about. The surgery. The change. His father was not disappointed. He had always wanted his "daughter-son" to make the change to son-son. What father wouldn't have, Mark justified his approval to himself, although he understood well how much pain would be involved.

Arthur's mother Elaine simply repeated, "It's time."

She had not had a daughter. She understood what being a girl was, would-be, if a girl truly was a girl. Likely it had hurt her more than it had hurt Arthur's father that for all these years of adolescence the "boy" had had to live a lie and dream a lie and suffer that lie. She had blamed herself, although there was no blame to be had. She had blamed her DNA and Mark's, which was like blaming the moon and the oceans' tides. She had wanted blame, as if by wanting it it would not be heavily thrown on her.

By the pool, in his one-piece bathing suit Arthur exhibited for his parents the various modalities of mimes that he had learned, mostly of forms of manliness. Why did he do this?—especially after the warnings of Cadeau Courir about mixing and mistaking mime for life. He wasn't sure why he did this, and he experienced his own resistance to it as he did it—was this display to show how he would be after surgery? To dramatize in order to augment truth—especially a truth that might not come to be. All surgeries were not successful, the percentages were not so great—lord knew what sort of disquieting freak he could become. But, now by the pool, Arthur mimed: Arthur stretched and reached into the various positions that to his mind were the statuesque effortful workings of manliness, done now without effort. He even threw in a few recollective workups of some machismo types he'd known (and wanted to be like): slashy Skip Cutter, who had raped him in high school; Ted Danson, with his superior quiet walk of condescension; and, of course, the graceful-kind-and-spiritual-manly Cadeau Courir himself.

Neither Mark nor Elaine understood. What in the world could such posings have to do with becoming a man?—a person operating in real life Why should their son be so hung-up on making of his existence nothing but a caricature? But Arthur's parents told him that they were proud of him. And though they were deigning-down (they couldn't help that, it was just simply built-in), nonetheless they were proud as well.

"I won't miss my vagina," Arthur said. "Nor my breasts."

His parents nodded confusingly. They knew that what Arthur said was true, but still these were such strange words to come out with and announce. Life could be such a strange whirlpool in which to tread water awkwardly and energetically so as to live beyond the merest treading of water, to live peacefully— somewhat.

"I am eager now to get it done."

"Johns Hopkins," said Mark, "is quite possibly the best hospital in the world."

Johns Hopkins was surely the most famous institution in so oft-ignored yet populous Baltimore.

This is my last chance, thought Arthur, as, accompanied by Mark Becker, he walked up the wide concrete pathway and then the broad steps of Johns Hopkins Hospital. Now, that great institution is located not in the bucolic setting of North Baltimore where Johns Hopkins University impresses all who pass by on Charles Street with its colonial architecture—some of it actually as authentic as Jefferson's Monticello, but smackdab in the East Baltimore ghetto made nationally infamous by that hit TVshow *The Wire*. Instead of the luxurious and impressive Mount Sinai Hospital on New York's Fifth Avenue, just north of the Metropolitan Museum and The Guggenheim, renowned Hopkins Hospital centers that dilapidated and unlivably drug-ridden redoubt with some four square blocks' domination of Victorian darknesses and crevices that seem to whisper loudly BEWARE ALL YE WHO ENTER HERE!—and Arthur reacted as would have any normal human being: *I could stop and turn around right now. As a woman, with my height and strength I might have been a* *heroine. I still could be, if I don't go through with this male changing. I could be a great female tennis player, better than Billie Jean Moffitt*; I could be champion in that hexagon of no-holds-barred female fighting; I could be a statuesque model. But I would be such a hypocrite, an unfair inauthentic winner, a fraud, a super-fraud—I would hate myself for all my life. And all the women who I had defeated would hate me too, as a cheater. As a great Something, I would be a greater Nothing. I would remain a freak, nothing more than that.* But there was also to consider: as these were the days of America's Vietnam intrusion, America's bombings of Hanoi and incinerations of the Mekong Delta, such "crimes" were the "accomplishments" of MEN, there were no women directing this destruction against which Arthur had demonstrated in Pittsburgh while a student. *Do I wish to become a fully-fledged part and parcel of that sex that is responsible for such arrogant inhuman unjust devastation!? Do I?! Am I Lyndon Johnson and Robert MacNamara all wrapped up in one!*

He knew that he was stretching the point here, arguing politically in an area—his own private gender-life!—in which politics did not enter. Unsureness leads astray.

With his father he sat on one of the uncomfortable plastic bucket chairs in Reception and filled out frustrating form after form after form, and felt as if he were signing his life away, while Mark Becker held him at the shoulder, at the arm, and, as so rarely, at the nape of his neck, pulling the boy's—*the young man's*—head on

---

* She became who she had been born as, Billie Jean King, after accepting her sexuality.

and over toward his DAD.

He took a one year's leave from Carnegie Mellon in order to go through with "The Great Transformation". His reason, or excuse, written out to the Dean of Liberal Arts, and written out by him with no assistance from his father, was the rather gargantuan and grandiosely metaphysical (but thoroughly true, while thoroughly laughable) *"I wish to contemplate the world and my place within it, with no intrusions nor complications induced by the distractions of what is called school-work, no matter how necessary for later life they may certainly come to be."*

To rid himself of The Curse of menstruation, Arthur began receiving testosterone treatments, first as pills, large tablets, in order for his body to slowly adjust without great debilitation—and this "inauguration" he could do at home. Each morning, upon awakening, and one hour before having his cereal, and never forgetting, and inebriated by the illusion that each downed pill was a promise as well as a beautiful blue penis in miniature, he swallowed what was really a quite large all-day capsule—and he experienced no side effects, which, as listed in the accompanying information sheet as provided by the pharmaceutical company, might have included: dizziness, nausea, constipation, diarrhea, a diminishment of the immune system, a susceptibility of the brain to infection, baldness—etc. Then months later, at the hospital, Arthur required infusions, which were of course of greater capacity, and he watched the first drippings of masculinity enter his bicep, which in his imagination he saw at moments, as in a cartoon, as his dissolving vagina (and he couldn't help but grin). For a few months, however, he did miss that bloody, embarrassing, menstrual draining, that liquid visitation, as it were, from another, deep, universe, but also, as it was, a preparation for the giving of life to another. So, he was losing that possibility, that capacity—and it did provoke second thoughts, usually in the middle of the night. But at least he no longer had to insert Tampax, and he was glad for the freedom and "cleanliness"—and abandonment of absurdity, *for him*—of that operation. He was losing, he was gaining. Yes, he was engaged by thought and afterthought and afterthought, and even careening counter-thought. But (or 'and') he continued on: And he began to observe that his cheeks and above his lips and down below, on his chest and *all about his damned breasts* (which so far stubbornly remained as icons of what was and what might have been) hair grew, sometimes merely strands, sometimes only filaments, in some spots these curly burrs—and at night in bed, while he continued by manipulating his clitoris to masturbate over *women—and only women*—like Natalie Wood (her sweet purity), he too often made the mistake of looking down and seeing those increasingly hair-swirled tits of his shaking to-beat-the-band as he fingered himself—and he felt, while having his orgasms, a betrayer, a dirtier, of those beautiful women with their beautiful vaginas, which, beautiful, had never been remotely how he had perceived that vagina of his own. And that betraying-dirtying attitude he was coming to feel very frequently, as the testosterone was more and more stimulating his libido—and this bothered him and it *did not* bother him, it pleased him. *I am a hairy ape-ette*—that was his newfound opinion—and he didn't mind clinging to it, as his voice was lowering, deepening—some men calling on business for his father Mark even made the mistake of addressing Arthur as Mark after he picked-up the receiver and went "Hello". But because he did not as yet have a penis (which was in the offing, *definitely it was, (did they have to work-it-up individual special, tailor it like a rich man's suit!?)* he kept asking the surgeons *When!* as well as the Hopkins specialists in endocrinology—he just couldn't bear living much longer with no penis—he was even embarrassed now to strip down to swim in the family pool, where his father Mark and his mother Elaine might get these awfully surreal ganders at the half-baked concoction that he was, with all this *hair* (it really didn't amount to all that much)—even though they knew that this was all the process, all their "boy's" desire.

Arthur, the lonely boy, did have that one friend, thank God. Joseph Lerner had gone with Arthur from Kindergarten through to twelfth grade and had been the smartest kid in all those grades. Joseph had attended Duke University and was now a med student, not at Hopkins but at the lesserly regarded (but still of decent repute) medical school of the University of Maryland, also in Baltimore. Joseph was geeky, seriously so, he always had been; what with his unfair for a juvenile heavily wrinkled face and bent back at the thorax from scoliosis, and his neck that was already dangling a premature turkey-wattle, he looked as if he were an old man when he was sixteen, so he was a fate-recipient who understood fate's cruelish mockery, and so he could be trusted: And so, at ten years of age Arthur had gotten naked for Joseph, he'd had to do such for someone outside his immediate family, and far enough away from his uncles, aunts and cousins who were no more to him than plain old public people. Thus Joseph had been permitted to bend to examine Arthur's vagina, rather close-up, Joseph fearing pessimistically that this was the only chance in all likelihood for him to ever get to intimately see one ("I'm gonna be bald before I get balled"—his own miserably-funny line); Joseph quite bewitched by the preposterous (and silly) absurdity of Arthur's "It" being situated right there in the centrality of his buddy-boy-pal's anatomy, and then Joseph's taking a chance and reaching-out and touching it, and then catching-on as to why the cool kids referred to the fissures and riddling beckoning undulations, unsightly as they might be, as in totality a dead-ringer for a tasty taco—Joseph looking-up from his kneeling position to see, it seemed, if his buddy Arthur's face and total boy-being were still Arthur's *real* gestalt and no masquerade trick that was being played on him, Joseph trying with his smartest-kid-in-class gray-matter to symbiose and synthesize his friend Arthur's undeniable boyness with what was (in the books) his opposite that required skirts and all kinds of mysterious under-stuff but was obviously now *not-no-opposite-at-all*, Joseph with another and another and another bewildered look back up to Arthur's face as if for reassurance and reassurance and still more of that, that this was not *The Twilight Zone*, that wise substantial-voiced Rod Serling would not come suddenly out of the screen of Arthur's room TV, proclaiming a profound whatever about human origins and reproduction and desire, and Joseph, then, reneging on his original exchange-promise to play in front of Arthur with his own penis, that *normal* thing, flip it about a bit—he just couldn't *do* that!—and Arthur deriving from Joseph's "betrayal" what would be his future level of trust from, towards, both man and girl.

"Don't tell," Arthur had requested. "Don't tell on me."

And Joseph had of course been bursting to tell. Telling might have stood a chance of getting him liked—by the same kids who didn't like Arthur.

"Kids'll believe you're lying."

"Hah."

"Kids'll believe you're lying!"

"I won't tell."

Joseph had grinned, a strangely disturbing grin, as if the secret he now held, by its colossal grotesquerie, would, once out of his revealing mouth, substantiate the crazy un-animal truth—and certainly relieve some of that pressure that always lay on himself for being *the* renowned, uncontested, school geek.

So, one-decade later: Joseph was now on the way to physicianhood and Arthur was still not yet in what he liked to call "the promised land of dickdom". They had not seen each other in some time. Joseph gave Arthur the once-over, this took place in Arthur's room at his parents' house, he still being on-leave from Carnegie-Mellon. Arthur's room was chock-full on the walls of male-types he would have liked to have been, had he not been burdened for so long by a vagina and female-articulated body: Various makes and manners of male bodies surrounded the two young men—all in their signature cants. James Dean, leaning forward on a Harley Hog; Sinatra singing while leaning with his cocky-sharp masculinity; Bob Dylan, leaning, with harmonica between his lips and his microphone; and, this was crazily unexpected, the harsh physiognomy of the murderous-looking actor Jack Palance. One might have thought that Arthur was a closet "homo", or was, once he'd become a man, aiming in that singular-same direction. True there were also a few Playmates from *Playboy,* but Arthur had included these not only to please himself and his urges but to comfort his parents as to his future sex-direction once he achieved his future sex. (Which such tape-ups did not fully do). Actually then, the tape-ups of James Dean, etc, and of the centerfolds commissioned by Hugh Hefner, were on the walls for reasons thoroughly justifiable. Both the males and the females were models. The males were models for emulation—a wide panoply of the men Arthur could mime in privacy as he decided what sort of man he would be (as if psychological inheritance, and the genetic, gave him the least of choices in such a matter—although deep-down he knew that they did not); the females were (obviously?) models of desire. And there was the fact that the testosterone inflow was making it believably (if semi-remotely) possible for Arthur to begin to see himself as those ideal men on his wall: his maidenly body-fat was redistributing from the female pattern to the male—his thighs were slimming-down, as were his hips and buttocks—it seemed that all such soft mass was relocating at his abdomen, and just waiting there for him to create a washboard stomach by doing a zillion situps with barbells balanced on his shoulders—was it his imagination or weren't his forearms and biceps going lean and hard, not leather, but intimating it?—that would be just great . . And once he saw Arthur naked, after so long a time of separation, trusted Joseph Lerner understood. "Oh I knew," he said.

"You did?"

"Not really, but in a way."

Arthur gave out with a friendly, and even confident, harrumph.

Joseph asked: "You're going through 'the change'— no? You decided. Congratulations."

"So you approve."

"Of course. Wholeheartedly. Did you think I might not?"

"I had my doubts."

"Why?"

"The way we were."

Joseph certainly understood that statement, but by narrowing his eyes in irony as if he did not, he magnified, at least for Arthur, his complete understanding and remembering.

"And how was that?" he asked, "how we were."

"Hard to explain. Mutual jealousies and envies, I guess. In different ways. We were both so weird."

Joseph shook that off by giving his eyes over to the pantheon walls-of-the-impossible-desired. He asked—

"So, do you shave now?"

"It's not easy, but I'm starting to."

Arthur said this with a pride that was also, somehow, an embarrassment.

"Mostly though just now I'm needing only to use a little fingernail scissors. Snipping here and there."

Joseph smiled. Amusement? To Arthur it looked as if his old just-as-weird friend, now a med student, was trying to be not-just-as-weird by adopting the paternal.

Arthur said, "Don't smile."

"Well, I guess a bra could cover up your hairy bosoms."

"I will *not* wear a *bra*!"

Uneasy and trying to put Arthur at ease, while definitely bearing some hostility within himself—and knowing it, and not knowing exactly why it was there after all these years, it all was too complicated—Joseph found himself coming out with: "Hey, you should see some of the nothingburger numbers I've seen in the books at med school. And some real-lifers. Now, if you want to talk about freaks—"

Arthur answered: "I am *not* a freak!"

Trying again, through his own dis-ease, to put Arthur at his ease, Joseph said: "Look, guy, *I'm* a freak, sort of. You've known that. I've been one a long time."

Arthur just answered: "*I* won't be a freak for *long*!"

Now Joseph was offended, and now Arthur felt guilty for having hurt his only friend; but considering his own lifelong pain and the further medical treatments that were upcoming, what else could he have said! He hoped that he would not lose Joseph, who had also been cheated in a way by life, his being a geek, an aged-old-man-looking-geek with broken-looking back; so Arthur was definitely afraid that such friend-loss might come to pass: he would lose this intimate, the only one aside from his parents. Well, he told himself, Joseph hasn't suffered as I have. But of course he did not know that.

Anyway, being a serious medical student, Joseph Lerner had little time now for hanging-out in Arthur's weird-decorated bedroom as if they were under-developing eight years olds. He had indeed suddenly discovered, and for a second sudden time, that he did not like his friend so much—not like he had (and hadn't) all through public school. They weren't "dweeb-twins" anymore—or they wouldn't be once Arthur went through all the required medical-sex conniptions and concoctions. Occasionally however Joseph would call Arthur to see how he was doing. He did seem sympathetic, especially if he did not have to face Arthur. He never asked anything so crude as *'Did you get your dick yet?'* But that telephoning was now about all they had.

And, speaking of calling, of the telephone, Arthur's voice found itself getting deeper than it had already become at the time when one of his father's colleagues had mistaken him on the line for the powerful, impressive, sturdy, leader of men, Mark Becker. Arthur was becoming huskier in vocal chord just as he was becoming huskier in the cordwood of his corpus. This of course did not happen in a day, or even a collection of weeks, but over more than a few months' time with that augmented testosterone coursing through his veins and arteries and thyroid and pituitary, through his entire being, through his beating heart, one could say, as if that male hormone were lit-up and visible, as if it were a cartoon presentation—no, as if it were a dramatization that might have been made most striking by the graceful swimming motions of someone like Cadeau Courir. One could hear those pristine distaff tones of his that Arthur had always lamented begin their descentful journey towards the guttural scrunch that his parents might have associated with someone like Marlena Dietrich or, well, Al Pacino. And Arthur listened to himself with such stupendous approval, he was even tempted to make a recording, but he considered that too vain—and maybe even too comical. Oftentimes though when he took walks alone he spoke aloud to himself in that new deep voice, or he even sang—he liked singing. He was a jazz and standards fan, which artistry was by now out-of-place in the late Sixties, but still his favorite singers were Sinatra and Joe Williams, two baritones. They had previously, obviously, been out of reach for even the remotest of imitations by Arthur—he had sounded to himself more like Billie Holliday and Ella Fitzgerald (at best)—but now he was closing in on those idols of his, those resonant-potent roaring-cocky romantic men. Oh the girls-and-women he would now, soon, get! . . . What he first got however was Joseph Lerner, on one of the few dwindling times when Joseph was to call, asking, "Mister Becker, may I speak with Arthur?"

"You are," Arthur said. "It's me."

"Are you *trying* to speak so low?" asked Joseph.

"It's natural. It's *me*. I don't have to try."

"God," said Joseph, "a voice, a larynx, when you can't see the person, it transforms the pictures in the mind."

"Does it make it more difficult for you to deal with me?"

"Just maybe this first time—I hope."

Translation: Absolutely.

And Arthur did get it—or maybe he hoped—that due to his losing of his freakishness, his diminishment of such abnormalities, and the promise of more lessness to come, his freakish friend might well feel freakland abandonment, freakland solitude, and so, envy, and so be becoming, even, Arthur's enemy. Human beings were that way, more than they liked to think. No, Arthur could not believe such an ugly, selfish, solipsistic inhuman-human thing—except that he did believe it. When you are born with a distortion, a severe distortion, you know (and hate) the supposed "truth of

the civilized", the supposed credos of the undistorted—
there is a reigning morality alright, and that is
amorality. No, it's amorality believing that it is very
moral. And what's more "queer" than that! At least
such cynical reflections kept-up their poppings into
Arthur's mind—just at the time when he ought to have
been Mister Uncynical Optimistic. Why!? Just as, in
one of his dreams, in more than one, that whole cadre
of public school kids who had made fun of him, who
had tormented him, in the gym locker room, in the
schoolboy toilet, they had got in his dream(s) their just
deserts, their comeuppances, by seeing him become
famous as . . . as what?—even the dream(s) recognized
that they were only dream(s), a child thing, revenge,
and it all got too image-garbled (as dreams do) to
provide any comeuppances. . . It did occur to Arthur
that as he became more adult he might however
develop a tad more sympathy for Joseph than he ever
did have, and for all the cadres of the cadres, sure they
all had problems (even if they didn't know it yet)—and,
yes, he did equate becoming more adult with becoming
more a *man*. Joseph, after all, he would remain appearing like a wrinkled old man right up until the time when
he became a wrinkled-old-man.

But, no joke, real monkey-wrench in the works:
Testosterone may work phonetic wonders, but not with
breast tissue—that does not readily decrease. And
Arthur had not anticipated this foul-up. Fortunately for
Arthur he had not been "blessed" with "big boobs", he
had been, as he liked to joke, an A-minus cup. But A-
minus was still what it was for a young man, especially
as it was paradoxically beset and beleaguered by swirls

of his new (and much coveted) chest hair. Arthur's parents said nothing about this, no humiliating comments came from them—but Arthur did imagine what they must have been thinking. He himself now saw his tits as gophers or moles poking out of smooth grassy ground, not so unlike what he saw so much of on the shores of Chesapeake Bay, where he often rode his bike. Alone. The only quick solution, the doctors told Arthur, was binding, and they gave him a thick black cotton strip, which resembled a sock, a very long one, and elastic, which he wore underneath his shirts—and he kept away from stretch nylon gauchos and the like, which women often wore to show-off their breasts as larger and more seductive than they were. But this incessant requirement of binding soon created breathing problems and back pain—and not only that: the black strip, to Arthur, seemed to indicate a sexual quality, a sort of hidden erotic instrument that, in his fantasies, he might just whip-off like a stripper does with her slight coverings to torment pathetic males in bars. And this was, subliminally (and actively), having him feel feminine, moreso than he had even *before* he had begun the whole feminine-divestiture process. This damned black strip, it was making him, unconsciously (and at times not so unconscious), walk with a bad-girl tauntingness, it had him experiencing his body as more curvaceous—it affected, again, his dreams, wherein he was miming prostitutes—and, sometimes, *enjoying* it. He actually sensed what it must be like to be an alluring-tormenting stripper. And why was he plagued by such mimings?—he knew why: because he had The Female yet within. The Female Within was pulling him back.

Damn the stubborn irony holding-out within the unironic.

Just like Reality to do this! To keep doing it!

No, this had to stop!

Mastectomy!

What would be trauma for, say, a woman with breast cancer, what would cause her to struggle with her visions of self as a woman, what might be unspeakable and dreaded-darkness, was for Arthur Becker manna delivered down from sunny heaven. Ah, the removal of his breasts. And because Arthur was blessed (in his mind) with smaller breasts, he qualified to have what is called *periareolar*, or *keyhole*, surgery, which uses lipo-suction and does not require any repositioning of the nipples, which would be necessary with a double-incision mastectomy with free nipple grafts, which would mean that the nipples would be resized, re-shaped, and then replaced in the proper masculine position on the chest. Both surgeries were considered major, as with all transgender surgeries, and in most European nations the patient would spend one week of observation in the hospital; but as America is a land where almost all products and services are overcharged, sometimes by as much as ten times, such as hospital costs, Arthur was released that very day. Insurance would not pay for an overnight, not in America—any chance that American insurance companies could avoid serious deliberation that would indicate that saving a person's psychological sense-of-self and was thusly about as great a medical treatment as could be, these firms rejected, calling it cosmetic surgery—that there was their great Out, and they summarily took it. But fortunate for Arthur, his father Mark, as a senior partner in Vander-Diggins, could handle the inflated American charges. Just about. . . But neither Mark nor Elaine ever mentioned the extraordinary expense to Arthur. Not once. . . And although Arthur was aware of how much money he was costing his family, he had little conception of how to graciously and comfortably say he was sorry for the expense, or how he appreciated the sacrifice. His surgery was necessary, as would be future ones: he could not live as the cheated person he still was. So he had, he had definitely on his bucket-list, aside from surgeries, the bureaucratic: he filled out a pile of forms and faxed them in, thus changing with a pridefully thick check mark from F to M his birth certificate (even though he had yet to receive his penis), his passport (which he had never used), his driver's license, his Social Security card, his health insurance card (necessary even though he was still on his parents' policy)—etc etc etc etc etc.

As everyone knows, surgery, *surgeries*, cause pain: Subsequent to them Arthur took opiates like Oxycontin, like, even, Delaudid, and although he had at first feared these drugs, feared the translucence and trip-slipping-away of Reality that they might precipitate, feared nausea, feared vomiting, feared perhaps the panoramic bamboozlement (that some people praise and crave), and feared addiction, it turned-out that if he did not love these prescribed meds he at least took considerable pleasure in them. As he put it to his primary care physician, he at times flew in-between planets and galaxies, he saw single stars separate (likely they were two stars to begin with), he was Superman released both from Krypton and from the binding body of Superwoman; and he imagined that once he returned to

Carnegie-Mellon's drama school he would be easily the best student actor, he would escape any spasmodic episode-flashes of his unfairly glue-stuck past, he would develop mimings that transcended any that even Cadeau Courir had developed, for his works would link the male and female and therein project great knowledge of human behavior, and do it with spontaneity. As reward, he would receive the most desirable women—and usually he imagined strong ones, physically so, those just about his size. About this he was not sure of the reason, but the fact that Arthur was advised to sleep on his back until his wounds healed, this seemed to put him in a position more amenable to fantasies of weakness, even of submission (He joked to himself that he was having "unprotected masturbation" [and he laughed, to himself])—but his clitoris seemed to be enlarging; and, sure, wasn't it supposed to go the opposite way? Well no, the doctors told him: testosterone expands the clitoris too, as in the first months of pregnancy, it was just a penis deciding, as it were, which way it ought to go. But so much indeed did Arthur relish these medical-induced "trips" of his that he reported daily to his father that he was in terrific pain—even when he was not: acting (or miming) the pill need, he would embrace his own chest as if smothering his great pain (a side-effect of this self-embracing was the scraping, the coarsened roughing-up, of his now flat chest, this too was caused by the male rawness created by the testosterone—but Arthur endured that rawness for its intimation of strong male things to come—*and* for his drug[s]). This exaggeration went on for three whole weeks, until Arthur's father Mark wised-up, contacted the surgeon and Arthur's GP, and was told to take those bottles of pills, immediately, from Arthur's ever-crowding nite-table. Mark flushed the vials down the toilet, and Arthur did not know if his reaction to that "deprivation" was a "normal" addict response or the oncoming magnification of male-emotion, but he had flashes, along with his Superman ones, of beating his father with his bare hands—which his father had never once done to him.

Guilt here, but enjoyment too of this "perversion".

And the diminishment of Arthur's "girl bottom", he decided, had not gone far enough for him. He felt unbalanced with that "balloon" down there that he'd always felt that he had to carry around. And now to his mind it was a caboose, an ox-cart, a plump soft sofa pillow. It was absurd. It was comical. "Yes," said the doctors. "Hormones can only take you so far."

"I want a small guy ass," Arthur said. "Tight and muscular. Like for jeans."

Surgery again: He had his ass "cut down to size," only a few "slices" required at the outsides. As his hips had narrowed a bit from the hormone treatment, his "new" rear-end even fit more perfectly. At least he thought so.

But this surgery did mean that now he had to sleep on his belly for a week, which he hated. No fantasies would come while sleeping on your belly—at least no dignified ones. And he received no opiates. All he got were Advil and Tylenol. He understood, he felt dis-trusted, but he could have killed his dad. Strangely, the distrust that he sensed coming from both his mother and father, this invested in him a reactive potent feeling. As if he were a worthy-worrisome enemy. As if he were Mister Rebellion, as he imagined most boys had been in their teenage years, and he had not been. Now, at twenty-one, he was a late-bloomer. But not, he decided, by so much. He could redeem his loss. He had *balls*—which, physiologically speaking, he did not have, as yet. Nor, to this date, "a dick".

So then, the tour-de-force: And Arthur had a choice: *Metoidioplasty* or *phalloplasty*. Metoidioplasty consists of releasing the clitoris, which Arthur experienced as having been enlarged by the testosterone, so that it did extend out farther than "normal"—for a girl. It even resembled, or so Arthur considered, a penis, albeit a small one—certainly not one to be considered, Arthur joked to himself, a "cock" or a "tool"—which was, you bet, what he wanted. ("Dear God," he used to pray at night, although he did not believe in such a guy sitting up there at the top of the universe, "give me a good dick—for all I have suffered I *deserve* a good dick."). With Arthur's already enlarged clitoris, he was told, his urethra could be extended and rerouted through the new penis that he would be receiving (this in a moment), so that, for one thing (and a not-inconsiderable thing) he could stand up and pee. (Once reestablished at Carnegie-Mellon, he would immediately picture the picture: he could blithely and proudly approach a urinal and guy-indifferently do his business, unlike how he had always done in school, ferreting himself away in a closet-toilet stall like a, well, like a "pussy". And he'd known that there were some guys, sadistic ones, who had the goods on him and had, from their positions at the urinal, smirked at his "coward-secrecy"—and some scum had stood on the neighboring stall toilet seat and peered-over at Arthur "relieving" himself, while the bladder "relief" was obviously not much of a relief, psychically.). And anyway: with metoidioplasty, however, "the new man" does not receive much of a remarkable (urinal-worthy) penis—much less coitus-worthy, even though testicular implants are supplied.

The hell with that! You only live once! I've gone this far, damnit, I will go through the whole route!

For some reason, as for so many other reasons, Arthur considered that great creator and reflector of human imagination, his teacher Cadeau Courir. That phenomenal man was precisely what a mime should be, what a dedicated mime should aim for, just as *a penis, if it's going to be a true penis, should be the best penis possible!* Arthur opted for the phalloplasty, where a respectable penis is constructed with skin from other parts of the body—if it's the forearm, the "tube-in-tube" technique is used, while the patient's skin is still attached to the arm it is kept vital until it is moved to the pubic area. Like a mom-and-pop shop that has not done well, the vagina is permanently closed-up; and a scrotum is built-up out of existing tissue. And this procedure is not *an* operation; it is a series of such. But, if the patient reacts well, his new penis *will be* sensate from the attached new nerves that have been trans-planted from the arms and even the sensitive regions of the neck. You even get testicular implants and an erectile prosthesis—"We throw them in," the doctor joked.

Arthur laughed. . . The best course within this nerve-wracking anxiety of transformation was certainly to laugh.

"But the whole deal, it has its dangers," the surgeon added.

"What's the worst that can happen?"

"Aside from the tissue-thinning and possible fistulas, where openings develop so that blood escapes from—"

"I'm going to do it anyway. I'm young. I'm strong. I've got a whole life to live."

"You get cocky, that's the other danger."

Again, Arthur laughed.

"I'm trying to be funny," the surgeon said, "but I mean it. There are psychological problems, or possibilities. To make up for all the years of your being deprived you may now become exhibitionist. To put it mildly, a show-off. You've written in your application for surgery that you're going to become an actor. Well, I can't imagine a more apropos profession, and one possibly *less* appropriate as well. The future can be dangerous, before you know it while trying to be what you want to be, you become something else. You really have to watch yourself."

"Believe me, I will. I've watched myself all my life."

"I believe you, Arthur. And I hesitate to tell you, but medical ethics deems that I do tell you. As you'll be an actor, you'll likely want to be as authentic as you can be."

"You bet."

"There are two more surgeries, if you wish them— some men would like to keep, what-can-I-say, *reminders*."

"Huh?"

But Arthur guessed:

"Getting rid of the cervix, my ovaries and fallopian tubes."

"Hysterectomy and oophorectomy. You'll have to wait at least a half-year for these, while the rest of you heals." The surgeon then repeated Arthur's phrase 'getting rid'. It seemed to amuse him.

But Arthur couldn't imagine those 'some men' who would have liked keeping their reminders of having been women, as what?—beloved souvenirs. *Between their legs!? Out!* he thought—*Out with the wrong thing!* He had heard some actor at Carnegie-Mellon proclaim that too. Or something like that. Was it in Shakespeare? For a drama student he knew so little drama.

"And now," said the surgeon, "you will have to learn how to be a boy: walks, talks, struts, slangs, all our ways that the girls see as crude and immature"—he winked as he slapped Arthur on the knee—"but that we boys love and can't do without, and the girls love too."

"I already know all that," said Arthur. "I've *always* been a boy."

The surgeon's expression of dubiety was very irritating.

"What do you think?—I wanna be some kinda *hermaphrodite?* I've *always* been a *boy*. All my ways are and *were* boyish. They always have been. You should see me throw a football spiral. I am one hundred *percent*."

Couldn't the surgeon *see* that Arthur's 'ways' were intrinsically boyish? As deep-in-the-flesh-and-bone as 'ways' could ever be.

"Will I *now* get an erection?" Arthur asked. "After these last surgeries. That's what I *really* want to know."

"Some can, some can't," said the surgeon. "It's trial and error, sad to say. Sometimes, well, that old new erection is stubborn as a"—to be more amusing than threatening he decided on the comic " 'mule' ."

"Arthur, he said, "You'll know and you'll feel soon enough."

The surgeon seemed almost angry at Arthur, or at least a bit put-out. When Arthur swore that he had always been boyish, heart and soul, if not penis and muscle, the surgeon had had that under-the-bone feeling based on his experience in this sort of procedure and the personalities of those people upon whom he had operated, that although Arthur was not lying he was just protesting just too much. That Arthur really had not known exactly who he was. Well, this was not surprising. The surgeon had learned in his profession that people were not one thing, and, amazingly-but-not-amazingly, they did not recognize the other things that they were, and from which they could not escape. He wanted to say things to Arthur, but he decided, again based-upon his experience, that he did not really have to: Blatancies and subtleties exchanged places within every human being—and then under cover of living, the exchanges exchanged again. They were ongoing. Arthur would learn, by way of his own coming experience. . . And perhaps delusions did not really matter.

Arthur received his penis, in its incipient Stage One anyway.

IV

Because the surgeon had asked Arthur to wait and "let lie fallow for at least one full month, no less"—and authoritatively measuring each cautionary word with a staccato stamping, Arthur obediently waited. He did not masturbate for fear of wearing out a new, and really not quite finished, instrument before it had even begun its wearable life. But during that interim, which was to him intolerably long, he had so many erotic dreams that it required a great will to forestall on any follow-throughs. And after that month passed, he hesitatingly asked his trusted (but ambiguously trusted) (and now also ambiguous) friend Joseph Lerner, who knew young women from medical school, if Joseph might find for him someone. Arthur himself knew no one who might be right for him, even remotely so, since he had been away in Pittsburgh, and in his high school and University of Maryland days, especially after his one miserable mockery of a failure (with a girl who was not a high school "whore" yet who would try anything with any guy, or just about any variety of same) where he had lain himself and his dammed accursed vagina upon the girl's awaiting vagina, as if this were some exotic rite of sisterhood—and she had cried (were her tears for Arthur or for herself?—for she had truly liked Arthur), and Arthur had been too leery and fidgety to again attempt anything so absurd as to repeat that episode, so poor and empty and devoid of normal human behavior as it had been—that girl, that nice girl, she had never, not once in school, been able to again look Arthur in the face, except with such a miserable sadness and, it sure looked like, pity.

With what certainly resembled reluctance (and a cautionary sarcasm) (and a kind of cunning obtuseness) Joseph arranged a meeting for Arthur with Anna Bass, a second year med student. They met at The Checkmate, a coffee house on Charles Street that was now just a plain old coffee cafe full-up with old ladies and chintzy chandeliers and mirrors and sofas for the most part, whereas in earlier years it had served as the 'in' magnet for local beatniks and "hipsters" who'd sat on used-chipped wobbly chairs at used-chipped wobbly tables, and who'd thought of themselves as the real cool jazz and Buddha-spirit imitators of Jack Kerouac and his "cohort"—and certainly not the obscenely same-named, the travesty-same-named, the evil-jokiness-of-history same-named, but completely opposite, hipsters of today, who were mostly techies and business grad students eager to one day become just like Arthur's polished father Mark. The wall speakers did not play Woody Guthrie or Bob Dylan or B.B. King or John Coltrane—or even Standards like, say, "Fly Me to the Moon", that might be considered remotely, subliminally, decently, lascivious. Instead, there came the vocal "stylings" of Steve Lawrence and Edie Gourmet and Rosemarie Clooney and Andy Williams. . . Anna Bass was Joseph Lerner's choice for Arthur because she was a very sweet girl, everyone thought so. She hoped to become a physiatrist, not to be confused with a psychiatrist—a physiatrist worked with the development of people's bodies, diagnosis and improvement; they prescribed exercise more than they did pills or surgery. And they understood physical fragility as well as physical strength. Anna, thought Joseph Lerner (who by the way, being a shy fellow was himself going to go into pathology and research, keeping himself away from any interactive personality problems that might redound to a physician who was human), Anna, thought brilliant-shy Joseph, was perfect for Arthur—at the very least as just a date, an initial starting point, a training exercise. . . She was already seated in The Checkmate when Arthur arrived, and from Joseph's description he knew that the young woman he was staring at, while she was intentionally, shyly, staring away, was this Anna. He thought to turn-tail and run, but having been for so long a rejected boy (or whatever he had been) he certainly knew rejection as well as Cadeau Courir knew miming Everything, and he could never be the cold indifferent wielder of such rejection-suffering. So, he approached:

"Anna?"

She nodded, in an unsure way—it looked as if she were working on the solution to a difficult problem in mathematics—and Arthur considered that perhaps she too was considering a quick jump-up and escape.

She was not ugly. She was not unattractive—exactly. She had short pixie-cut brown hair, a high forehead above her natural brows, large brown eyes that appeared frightened at one moment and like expanded magnifying glasses the next, enlarging the object of her sight—for good or ill, for joy or for suspicion, or for fear. But those eyes were sweet. Absorbing eyes. Her nose was rather tiny, as if it had retracted, having faced a great and maybe stinking dinner, perhaps a raw ortho-dox Eskimo repast, which she did not wish to eat. But that withdrawing nose was not comical, nor was it critical—it just seemed that if you were to draw such a face as this Anna's this was the nose that you would be obliged to describe—and you even wished to touch it, much like you might tap lightly for affection on the nose of a pup. To just touch-tap, as if to say 'I am no danger to you'. Her mouth was not brightened by lipstick, and it also was not large. . . But this Anna's neck: At minimum, it was muscular; the build-up of tendons and wizened cords was obvious, as were the veins—the combination of these made it impossible for Anna's jaw-line to present itself in prominence, as it does with most women, so that one might even imagine the precision delicacy of the woman's skull; at once Anna's neck rendered Anna's head by contrast small-ish, as it gave one the immediate sensation of its being a museum pedestal for her full face. Extending out from Anna's shortsleeve navy T-shirt that read GOLD'S GYM (which was located almost directly across Charles Street from The Checkmate), were these Anna-biceps and forearms that were—what can one say!—unfeminine. They—Arthur could not think of any other word—bulged; where you might admire or fear such on a man, on a woman's arms they gave warning; and confusion. And at their end, their finalities, were hands that certainly were not built for medical surgery, but that would be tailor-made for, well, butchery, or log-carrying, or the limb manipulations involved in physiatry. Anna's hands were not meat cleavers, no, but they were the hands of masculinity; as much as—thank God—Anna's chest was one of femininity: she had large breasts, and the bra she wore had those breasts extending fully (Arthur's thought: "Power bazooms"). As Anna was seated, Arthur could make out no more of her, but he certainly wondered if his friend Joseph had intentionally arranged this meeting so that Arthur might confront someone of as mixed-sex as was he. Or as—as he had by now trained himself to believe—as he *had once been*, but was certainly, absolutely, definitely, *no more.*

Fucking blind asshole Joseph. Trying to do well, trying to help, he insults me.

Or was he even trying to do well?

Emotionally, Arthur went this-way-that, all-over-the-place: *This girl, this woman, she has a physique that I've wanted for myself, and I've tried to fake, and now that I have a penis and testosterone I'm going to have my body make its way to be like hers, in certain parts anyway. . . No, that's ridiculous. No, it isn't. And she's so nice, she's sweet, I can see that, and her voice is tender and even musical in a female way, so while I want to get to be like her in my bones, I am drawn to her as my opposite, I find her desirable and undesirable, she is poison and she is elixir—and she is just a GIRL.*

I am drawn and I am repelled.

He could not believe that just after they had ordered their coffees he flatly came out with it and asked her, and firstoff boldly, egregiously, the following: "Anna, are you trans? Transgender."

"My God," she said, "No. I am me. And I'm not a Lesbian either."

He hadn't even considered Lesbianism, so obsessed was he with what he considered the more hormone-inspired dispositions. He went with—

"You have all your, well . . . your parts, and—"

"Gee, thank you," she interrupted.

"Oh," he said, "I didn't mean anything mocking, cruel. I just meant that you don't have any, you know, wrong ones."

" 'Wrong ones' ?"

"Like you're satisfied with yourself. You're satisfied?"

She went shaking her head as if determining if this character sitting before her was from this planet. "Arthur," she said, "this is weird, what you're asking, what you're saying. I'm a girl. I'm a woman."

"Then . . . ?" He went trying to communicate—somehow!—without the communication aid of his eyes, of his further deliberate inspection—his great interest in her sweetnesses being attached, being projected outward, from her super muscularities. And as she observed his oblique-embarrassed scrutiny her smile combined into this merger of the sweet and sour, along with the disbelieving—and also, surprisingly, the sympathetic. As if she had to take care of this child, walk this babe-in-the-woods out of the woods. But it was also as if she were a child herself, or an adolescent.

"I work out across the street," she explained. "At Gold's Gym."

"Ah. But why?"

" 'Why?' "

I know I'm being an idiot. Why can't I just stop!?

She went again with " 'Why?' " Her magnifying brown eyes appeared to swallow him up with amusement and disbelief. She shrugged with a kind display of delight. "I do weights because I love to do it. That's all."

"And you're not—?"

"You already asked that, you dope."

She'd said that cutely, as would have any girl who liked the person she was sitting with, for whatever reason, even if he was more than a touch naïve—or because he was.

"I won a Pose Down," she said. "The women's one. And I do *not* take anabolic steroids."

"Ana- huh? A Pose Down? What's that?"

"Well, I suppose I can't be too mad at you for not knowing. Few people do. About the woman part, anyway." She explained the ins-and-outs of Pose-Downs, where men and women in competition flex their muscles on a stage—and on television!—into "well-sculpted representatives of the human being race. The best."

"Oh," he said, "you mean like Arnold Schwarzenegger used to do." Arthur quickly gave her another once-over which he tried to camouflage by covering his lower face with his coffee cup and sipping unstoppedly.

"Yes, just like Arnold Schwarzenegger."

Irony compressed her lips, and now she did, to Arthur's appreciation, develop a female jaw line.

"There are many women who build up their bodies," she added. "We are not freaks. Though it's true that some people seem to think so."

'Some people'. She meant him? That word, "freaks",

it certainly disturbed Arthur, who had of course always considered himself a freak and was now, he had resolved, working his way out of freakdom—or anything falling remotely within the freak-neighborhood.

"But," he ventured, "if a woman is a woman already, why would she want—?"

"To 'ruin' it?"

"Yes, I guess."

"Why does one person like steak?" she said, "while another is a devoted vegetarian."

"And that's it?"

"That's it. I think so."

"Do your fellow students in med school make fun of you, ever?"

"No. Not that I have observed." She looked away. "Okay, a few. Those jokers. But I can handle it. I almost *like* it, to tell the truth. It substantiates me as what I am."

Whatever she is.

Well, this was a far cry from how Arthur had experienced his earlier life in this school and that. But then again this Anna, she was speaking of med school, not high school. The students were mature, they were intelligent, they saw all kinds of things laid out in the beds of hospitals. And it was clear from this Anna's narrowed expression, which she had fought for as long as she could, that she was becoming a bit put-out by Arthur's questionings. . . . But now she admitted, once again, "Yes, yes they do, some fellow students do— they can make fun of me—girls and guys. . . and to heck (she did not say 'hell') with *them*."

"Good attitude."

"Thank you."

Are we playing a game?

Was Joseph having sadistic fun at pairing us—saying mirror mirror on the wall, I'm you—or was he serious? Serious that she and I were twins?

But she wasn't born the way she was now, like me. She decided to lift weights, to Become. I couldn't decide to, what? unlift weights. The heavy-ass weights of screwball wandering hormones.

Anna now told Arthur that in Biology at med school she had read that "Biology loves variation and differences while society is dumb and hates it and is scared by it—the whole incredible maze of it." She said that it was all still indeterminate, not only by gender, like what is man and what is woman, but even by "species specificity", like many plants and animals can be both male and female, and that in some species it's males that do the giving-birth, and *some species have more than two genders* (Arthur went "Huh-How?" and Anna raised that Huh-How with the hyena, as female hyenas are tough and attack *lions*, and those females can have *penises*); Anna added that despite all the scientific investigations and even MRIs into which they shoved dogs and wolves (after training them and then still yet drugging them for the required MRI tunnel stillness), that research-biologists could not be sure where doggishness left-off and wolfishness began, or vice-versa. "A dog is a wolf is a dog—to *this* day, even *with* evolution." She clapped her hands in some version of victorious substantiation about all this, and she went, "ta-*da!*" (Some of the old ladies in The Checkmate turned to look at her, at them.), then she went on about how gradation, "prismicity" "spectricity", was all the world—she was such a smart, a brilliant, a *thinking*, girl—a proud prismic muscle girl: Gradation, she said, indicated the truth that we humans, we didn't begin as God's creatures, or even advanced Neanderthals and Heidelberg Men, but as rats, well, scurrying rat-like *things*—"how about *that!*"—and then "we flowered, we bloomed, to catlike beauties, like leopards and jaguars, and then to 'brainy' early monkey-like creatures, they picking ants and mosquitoes off each other's backs, like decent charity, like reciprocity, like *socialism*, if you really want to know, and then we're off and running to Human Man, not that *we're* the *End*"—"so," she said, "me with my barbells and my dumb-bells and my girl-wants and my girl-being, which I love having, *make no mistake about that*, I am an *Evolution*, a *process*. And so are *you*, Arthur. . . " Then she looked to the Checkmate ceiling, as if there were inspirational writings inscribed there between the old-lady pleasing chandeliers: "To quote Carl Sagan, the physicist-astronomer, 'We are made of star stuff'. I'm a star, *you're* a star."

Arthur could not conceive of any way to continue their conversation, if he even wanted-to—he had always shied-away from such explanatory books as Anna had just consized for him, as if they (and she) were trying too hard, and they tended to make him feel worse about himself than he had felt before he glanced at them. For godsakes he was not Mendel's pea. It was so incalculably strange to be sitting with a woman who wanted to make of herself a man, a brilliant man—even though that was precisely the process in which he himself was engaged, desperately engaged—while she was *not at all* trying to make of herself a man. She loved being a woman. Just not a woman as your usual people considered womanly. *Why!?*—this question was still not answered to his satisfaction, even with her reportage on biology and the identity of dogs-and-wolves. A man might, after all, *do* something to become a man, like lift weights, *add-on* something—which this Anna was doing. While a woman, a *normal* woman, didn't have to do anything—she was what she was. Unless she decided to *not be* what she was, which was a woman, with all those beautiful enticing things, their woman attributes, their shapes, their walks, all their lyrical ways of expressing and gesturing—which, true, Arthur had rejected for himself (it was too *queer: imagine, she could become pregnant, this Anna, which, horrifying to think, no, stupefying, until recently I could become as well—and I wonder how she feels about such a condition for herself*)—there they were, all those woman-things, which Arthur desired to possess, not within himself, but *for* himself, *for* his *pleasure*, once he had become a full-fledged Man. Arthur was confusing, he admitted that to himself (at times, at thousands of times) and Anna, was confusing, she wanting to remain a woman while not wanting to *be* a woman—as far as Arthur could make out her wants. For godsakes you would never see any girls like super-sturdy Anna Bass lined-up in bathing suits in the Miss America contest. That would be—Arthur was sorry to think—hilarious. Perverse. A sick joke. Anna was nice, no two ways about that, but she was certainly, especially, confusing. (Within himself, however, in the back of his mind, Arthur could not stop imagining how he might mime an Anna, perhaps explain her in that way, that caricatured Cadeau Courir way, that way that did not use words). . . And despite his confusion Arthur did feel a certain closeness to Anna. Sitting across from her, it was as if they belonged together, while they surely, also, did not. It was neither brotherhood nor sisterhood that Arthur felt that they might feel towards each other—certainly, absolutely, not that sisterish last, and certainly, absolutely, apparently, not that first, *brotherhood*—if he could believe Anna's words, which he *did* believe. It was an intimacy of neutrality Arthur felt here, an emotion of neutrality, an emotion of no-emotion that yet remained an emotion, all a possible impossibility. Anna was muscle-city, yet he felt protective of her, although he imagined that if they were attacked by thieves here in The Checkmate, she would probably end up being *his* protector. No, *protectress*. But more, Arthur thought of what they had, just immediately, in these instances, split-seconds, as a feeling of, sort of, love. Really, love—as much enigma as split-second stabbing by elegant disappearing fingers that had grown-out from your own hands. Mime City. Trick photography. A neutral, objective, pairing, this identity, like maybe, what? Siamese Twins—not back-to-back, but facing. The surreal goes real. Like as if Balthus and Grant Woods had paired-up on a project— The Transatlantic Gothic. And Anna's sweet face, sweet womanly face, strong as it was, that had a lot to do with that—what better word could there be?— "love".

They took a walk, up Charles Street, towards Mount Vernon Place (which was a circle), which was centered by Baltimore's Washington Monument, which was only slightly shorter than Washington's Washington Monument, and was a circular obelisk rather than the triangular one some thirty miles to the south. And which had a giant sculpture of George Washington at its apex—it

was an old joke in town that the artist who had created
this George, revolutionary uniformed as he was, had
made his right arm rather outsized-long and shaped the
forearm part so that it curved down and outward from
George's cape-coated midsection—this from the
southern viewpoint, which was how Arthur and Anna
were approaching it; it was as if Washington's arm
were a super-long penis, which would have been appropriate for The Founder of Our Nation—and it seemed,
if it seemed like anything, to be bent-down in the act of
peeing (perhaps on a rainy day it did, in a way, pee, a
leak of pee—probably a million "Balamorons" had
thought this). And was this arm-penis a mistake?—who
knew? Perhaps the sculptor had been commissioned to
make the penis this way, or perhaps he was an art-wag,
or maybe not even American. And, considering the
mysterious sexual nature of gender shapes that was at
the center of consciousness of these two young people,
both Arthur and Anna couldn't but stare up at George
Washington's mega-cockeroo—and refrain from saying
one word about that extensive thing.

But, well, Arthur did imagine Anna with a penis. He
couldn't stop it. This "creation" of not God's or
nature's but of a deprived sole's mind, this "augmentation" which was a lie, an illusion, a perverse mental
construction—which he had tried to fight off by
closing-up his brain—good luck there; that faux Anna-
organ was the bitter determined figment of a man who
was envious of a woman's manliness, but not to the
ultimate point of departure where she wanted any
damned penis—she had after all been in possession,
and apparently proud possession, of a vagina, and for as
long as Arthur had been in possession, and shamed

possession, of a vagina. And this imagining of Anna's imagined penis, it posed quite a problem when they went to Anna's small flat nestled within the matrix of the downtown traffic flow at the University of Maryland Medical School—which was where she had invited him, and where he, ambiguous *he*, had not been, with ambiguous *her*, ready to go at all.

His reasons were obvious.

But were they?—they were not obvious to Anna. For, without much ado, *any* ado, as if it were prescribed by the Dean of Med School, this med student stripped off her T-shirt of GOLD'S GYM and step-slipped out of her jeans; and although, true to her being a girl, her hips were hourglassish (moreso than his had been [when he had been a girl], and they were so hourglass-ish just even above her incredibly exorbitant Gold's Gym-made quadriceps) and her breasts were beautiful and firm, with quite large aureoles, and although she wore panties (of a pastel blue with cute curlicues about the elastic waist) and although she seemed to have stepped out of the purest girl-egg, for she was almost hairless, and although Arthur experienced a kind of resonant tingling-outwards such as he had never quite experienced before—for his ex-vagina had, when it had been induced-to by his fantasies of say, Julia Roberts, his ex-vagina had reacted with a sort of sensation of drawing-in, a reaching and a pulling and an in-folding, a housing-of, as did petals if you tendered them—so although Anna did display so many female attributes now, Arthur's now-penis, unschooled? went less than (what he figured for) "manly". His ex-vagina had always experienced that ached wanting, that called-for receiving, rather than any giving, it had welcomed an entering rather than demanded an entering, a well-rubbed intrusion, even if that intrusion was ached-for as well. But this "giving", this vibration that Arthur now experienced, it was not accompanied by a stiffness, it was rather more accurately a *sitffishness,* an imitation of life, you could say (*he* did, within—along with the self-soffing "dead man walking")—Arthur's penis did not achieve the full hardon he was now praying-for—it was bent a bit, rather like George Washington's peeing-like penis atop his monument, which of course had been not our first President's penis but his overproportioned bent arm. In any case, Arthur was loath to unzip and undress and show himself, which he did do anyway— well he *had* to, to be a "man"—he displaying then what he also considered a "lukewarm instrument". It was a mimed erection, he heard himself think, *papier mache,* not the authentic prick—unless mime was more authentic than was reality. . . Which maybe it was, being deeper, being more philosophic, being more aware of the smart ought as well as the bumptious-immediate "is". . . Also, his "undong dong's" hardness, what there was of it, it was concentrated down in the base of his penis, rising-up no farther than midway—this was the sort of "erection", he imagined, that maybe a masochist would have, a pig's-belly hardon, not a stickman's, not a full-fledged driller-in. He hated that "base" mini-erection.

"Is it my muscles?" asked Anna staring straightaway between Arthur's thighs as a doctor would, or a callow med student. And then staring away, towards his feet.

"No," Arthur lied. "It's not your . . . muscles."

"Then what is it then?"

"It's that"—and this claim blurted-out, as if of its

own free will, as if it were an organic thing, a biota with blurting speech—"I love you." Even he was surprised at himself.

"You 'love' me? But then your, you know"—she kept her head from looking at it—"it would be hard, wouldn't it?"

"I don't know. It's a different kind of love—I guess."

"A different kind of love?"

"I don't know. I don't *know.*"

Anna had begun shaking her head and lifting her shoulders, and her cheeks rose up toward her eyes, as if she could not understand some difficult med school explanation, or doubted it. Arthur noticed that with her shoulders' rise her breasts had risen as well, but due to her muscularity, they seemed caught in a kind of half-way lockdown by those armored-up tonalities of hers, they had Arthur imagining an iron shield, like knights wore in the Crusades to protect themselves from disbelievers like Jews and Arabs.

"Are you much experienced?" asked shy Arthur, boldly.

Anna shut her eyes for some moments, then re-opened them. " 'Am I much-experienced?' What a question. I have to plead the Fifth Amendment."

"You're not much experienced. I just feel it." He felt it because he was glad of it. He was relieved by it.

"And you had to say it, huh? Okay, no, I am not— much. Guys aren't overwhelmed by my body. My ..."— she had now turned to giving herself an oblique once-over, one quick proprietorial scanning—"my duality. Guys just aren't into it, bigtime. Or, you could say, in a way, they *are*, overwhelmed. Reverse-overwhelmed.

Just like you."

"I'm sorry."

"Don't worry about it."

"But then why do you keep up your weightlifting?" He hesitated, but decided to continue: "Aren't you worried," he asked, "about ever getting, you know, married?"

She grinned, as if facing a child's dumb question; then she soured-up that grin: "I don't worry about such things. 'Marriage.' People—women—they shouldn't worry about such things. That's weak. Is that, marriage, the goal—*your* goal?"

"No," he insisted, lying. Marriage really was his goal. Having been deprived of 'normalcy' for so long—and really still not there yet at undeprived—having felt his antipathy towards that other unachieved best-world of 'normalcy' beat and swell within him as his great secret enemy, he yet, truly, definitely, wanted Normalcy's ultimate companion, its embrace. Its Love: Oh dear *Normalcy*.

Standing there naked, the two of them, how ridiculous this standoff, this at best exploratory talk—and she spoke: " Weights. Lifting. Grunting. Straining. 'Why do I *do* it!?' Artie, haven't we already been through this, a half-dozen times! Is it so offensively terrible for a woman to want to be *strong*!? To be able to, like, carry her groceries and things without a *man's* hefting it all—and for that matter, although you don't have to be a Venus-Aphrodite to *do* it, to fix things around the house, to maybe build a tool-shack or whatnot, to hammer boards real flat and good."

"I guess it's not wrong. It's fine."

"You 'guess'."

Arthur noticed now that even under her arms Anna was hairless, she had shaved there scrupulously. She was a woman, that was her identity through and through. As much as he wished to abjure all confusion and just Be Normal, Anna wished to abandon all gender-jumble and just Be Woman.

Standing there naked, Arthur tried to will his penis into its full-fledged stiff-strengthening. *Miming* an erection! Force of mind but apparently not of eros. But truth is, he was nonetheless proud of this humble accomplishment of its tingling, and *in a woman's presence*, as unfulfilled as that mere tingling was, as dubious as it was. As has been mentioned, he had been with women before, but only when he'd been hampered by his vagina—and it had never gotten, well, woman-wet, not in the least. Of that non-femalishness he'd also been proud, it had proved to him who he was—or rather who he should be. But all that was water under the bridge. All that touching and pressing by vagina-upon-vagina such as like what people mostly did with their lips, kissing—two vagina's kissing while the brain of one of the vaginas was, his, had always been, discouragedly praying for the alchemy that would turn it, extend it, transform it, into a dominator of a kiss, a bomb that was atomic rather than conventional—an instrument that *fucked* as a fuck should fuck: a PENIS. Couldn't good grace just, for once, for *once*, kick the stinky shit out of bad grace?—and render Arthur capable of, God forbid, banging a woman into ecstacy? But here in Anna's flat it was a whole new situation. And a whole new predicament.

"I could take the bull by the horns," said Anna, like an offering.

Arthur understood, vaguely, and he was shocked: Anna was such a shy polite young woman, but after all she was a med student—she had seen it all, hadn't she. And she had even won a PoseDown—the very fact that she had entered such a competition spoke volumes about her energies and her ambitions and her boldness, subdued as it could present itself at times. She could take the bull by the horns.

Arthur's instinct, believe it or not, was to cover-up his penis with his hands, as if warding-off some anticipated sucker-punch thrown by a bully. But he fought that defensive instinct, absurd as it was in this case. He sure as hell did not wish to be on the receiving end, like a dumb moronic helpless bull fending-itself-off from being taken by the horns by a female pica-dor—but you bet being on the receiving end was exactly what he wanted. And he found himself wondering too if perhaps his operating surgeon had been too optimistic in telling him that it would only require one month for him to be penis-prepped and penis-set. Ready-to-roll for action. It was now six weeks. Again he tried to will his "bender" into a "stiffer", which was the noun that he had invented long ago, and which was of course his life's greatest desire, since he had become first acquainted with what was resonant between people's legs. *Stiffer, damn you, stiff!*

And anyway: it would have been pathetic, and squirrelish, and girlish, to fight off this girl's reaching for his penis—which she did, which he did not fight off. They were even still standing there in Anna's small apartment in central southwest Baltimore, with its view of the harbor's edge and the permanent docking there of the (supposed) very first Clipper Ship, and some cannons of Fort McHenry, where America's national anthem, *The Star Spangled Banner,* had been written in 1812, when the British had attacked; and where Arthur affixed his gaze, as it would have been ridiculous, even medical-patient-like, to just look downward and watch while this surprising Anna did her helpwork—which was, after all, itself, an attack.

And one which was unsuccessful.

"Let's just lay down on the bed," said Anna—which they did.

For the most part, her flat had posters on the walls of body builders, both male and female. Arnold Schwarzenegger hung, Lou Ferrigno, who had played The Hulk, a magnificently muscled woman named Sally Motley, and Oliver Sacks ("He used to work out with Schwarzenegger," Anna said, "few people know that."). There were a dozen or so books on a small, narrow bookshelf. Mostly medical. Physiology held sway. Dishes were piled-up in the kitchen area sink. You could smell broccoli—once you tried to not-concentrate on the attempted sex.

"Let's just rub all round each other," she said. "Let's just make the best of us, as we are. We'll do what we can."

Wise, mature—so that offering rang to Arthur. A bit mothering, but so what.

They did what she suggested.

Arthur's penis remained at its accustomed quarter-mast.

"You just don't like my type," she said.

So, she wasn't so wise mature. She could fake transcendence over disappointment, or try to actually experience that transcendence, but ultimately a person lives within the boundaries of their desires and expectations—a person who is not a saint. Her words had gone higher-pitched, her head had made these fretful turnings of mere inches.

"I like your type," he said.

"You like my type? You even said 'love' before. Then . . . ?"

"That's not it, liking, what the problem is."

She rose-up on one elbow to listen to what promised to be an arduous unburdening of a revelation that might hurt.

And because she was such a sweet girl, and obviously understanding, he told her the truth about himself. Aside from his friend-like friend Joseph Lerner, she was the first person, the first peer, he had ever told—and he told her so, which got her to changing the subject with a quip (that he didn't get) about D.H. Lawrence and men and their friendly lovings. But, aside from not knowing word-one about D.H. Lawrence he also wanted to get on with it, his telling. After all, the few girls who in the past he had lain on top of (there'd been two), they had just learned by the misbegotten experience, stifled the sort of facial amusement one might have exhibited at the zoo while watching the antics of monkeyshining spider apes, struggled their expressions into those of hurt-swollen eyes and cheeks of sympathetic pain, and then said nothing, zilch, and Arthur, fallen then deep-down into the deepest well of life, had never bothered to explain. Why bother. And he knew that he could never resort to one of those plastic penises (the *crème de la crème* brands complete with unsaggy testicles) that they sold in adult book stores (protected within glass cases as gun stores did with their handguns)—aside from the immorality and inauthenticity and the riddled-warped-crinkled ugliness of those Big Things (Big *Solid* Things too) there would be the dilemma of getting some grubby man outside the slimy store to go in and buy the "instrument" for him—and then that using of one, even if he—SOMEHOW—got away with it (which would involve some body-twisting trickinesses for sure, some penis-is-faster-than-the-eye Cadeau Couririshnes), that would be wrong and phony and immoral and a disgusting travesty (and likely painful) for which he would hate himself beyond measure. . . As he told Anna Bass his "secret", his "truth", his body shivered as if it were freezing, no heat was on. He even felt as if his body might give out, fall away from him, and he might pass out.

Anna heard Arthur out, and said "Oh I'm sorry."—which did not seem quite enough, so she added the helplessly emphatic , "I am *so* sorry."

More comfort than sexual, she rested her strong thigh on his new penis. Her thigh was so muscular, so etched by sharp lines and practically loaves of sinew. Her thigh was so impressive, so beautiful—and so wrong.

Arthur said, "Don't be sorry about it. I'm glad of it all."

"You *are*? How could you be?"

He closed his eyes, as if he had secret strengths, as if he could withstand anything—anything life threw at him. He near fooled himself with his own "manly" act. "It's taught me a great deal."

"You understand *me* then," she said, "and all I've done with myself. Though you just may not think you do. . . Or care." Despite that she did not wish for it to be, despite her honest sympathy for him, her stare had gone accusative.

"You're not a trans-person," he said. "You've had no surgeries."

"Yes—I mean No. But—well, you know."

He answered Yes, he did know, he did understand—but of course he didn't.

She rubbed her thigh along his penis.

It remained as half-sleepy as it had been.

"Inert," she mumbled, as if to herself, upon discovering in the woods a wounded fluffy jackrabbit.

"You know, Arthur," she said, "you oughtn't mention your surgeries so grandly, as if you've fought in Vietnam and won the congressional Medal of Honor for bravery. That pride is only going to hurt you and keep you down and swelling inside yourself, instead of outside yourself, you know."

He knew she was right. He also knew he couldn't stop doing as he did. At least for now. Maybe in future times. . . "He" was him.

"Lay on top of me," she said, "but on your side a bit. Can you?"

He didn't understand but he did it. This position was a bit untenable, especially for someone so unpracticed as was Arthur—so, being weak in this unaccustomed way he quivered and shook some as he worked at maintaining his balance atop Anna while astride.

"Now I can try again," she said.

"Huh? *You* can try again?"

She worked on his new uncompleted penis. She caressed, she stroked, she pulled softly. She could not get it fully hard.

"Arthur," she said, and very softly, so nicely,

"Arthur, try to get it in as is."

"As is?"

Like a man trying to be a *man* by doing too many pushups, he was already wobbling from keeping himself viable at this new halfway position, his left arm was hurt and weakening as if he might collapse beside Anna into the bed's thick foam—and breathing heavily; this despite the workouts with weights that his endocrinologist had advised, and his surgeon as well, and that he had been doing religiously; his left arm (he joked miserably to himself, it was just like his lame penis). He felt so damned weak and trembly—but he did as Anna wished.

"Just try to stuff it in," she said.

"Huh?"

"Well, you know, like a marshmallow."

"Like a *marsh*mallow?"

"I hope you're not offended."

Of course he was offended—how could he not be the hell offended!, but he tried the stuffing stuff, squeezing his penis between his thumb and forefinger, pulling, pushing at its underside, as he managed to land his "instrument" about maybe an inch, tops, within Anna's vagina's lips—even her wetness could not help so much. Even her reclining further up high on her back so that her vagina was now fully presented, facing as it was up towards the ceiling of her flat.

A considerable amount of grunting and groaning was going on—it was all Arthur's.

"Damnit, *again*!"

"Again?" asked Arthur.

"You think you're the first *failure* with me?"

Arthur said not a word. By now he could no longer

sustain himself in that awkward position that Anna had suggested.

"Men *fail* with me," complained Anna. "You're not the only one with a cross to bear."

"Then it's not just me?"

"You're just the first that was a girl."

Now *that* was mean. Anna seemed to not be the sweet girl that she had been until this moment.

"I am *not* a girl," Arthur swore, "and I *never* was."

"Have it your own way. I'm sorry and I'm not. Sad is sad is sad. There's enough sad in the world to cover it like burning lava. You're a drop in the lava bucket. *I'm* a drop in the lava bucket."

She now sounded philosophical, moreso he was sure than she wished to be. Actuality beat the philosophical, especially when the actual was staring you in the face, slapping you in the face—so you might have thought. So she really had gone mean. . . and Arthur certainly understood. . . Not that understanding is forgiveness. It may well be just the opposite. That, the world knows too.

Arthur said, "Anna, I've been thinking you were different. I've been seeing you as different, I mean in a good way. Special."

Anna said, "*And*, in a bad way—tell the truth. Being who you are, you should know better. Arthur, there's just so much a person can *take*."

"I know that."

"You don't. You think you do, but you don't."

Arthur wanted to start getting dressed. But getting dressed was an action, a reality, not a philosophy—it could even be seen as an offense. In Anna's bed, sunk in it, he was paralyzed.

"Arthur," Anna said, "I know what *you* need, it's just come to me—in a flash: You need a woman who had started-out life as a *man*, full physical, full internal, and gone through troubles like you have, but different, opposite. You're a transman and what you need is a trans*woman*. I'm sorry. I've just now got so furious, and I shouldn't have got furious, and *serious*, but I *have*—I just can't contain myself, even knowing your weaknesses and your sorrows, that your fault is *not* your fault, not really. But what I just said, it's true."

And despite all that Arthur had gone through, in living, in the vortex of the genital operations, the image she had come out with of his needing a *man*, that just made him sick.

He despised her, this woman who he did not, remotely, despise.

But as he was going out the door, and Anna was crying, at least she had tears, a slight swimming of them in faint red, and she came up with this: "You don't get that you were given a *gift*, not a burden. A gift to *see*, in and out, like from *all* the windows about a house. I have been working to *make* myself a gift. You got it by nature. We are as far from each other, so very far, as we are close."

"We could get together again, and try," he said it weakly because he didn't really mean what he said. . . While he also meant it: his meanings were as confused as his weird-born being.

"No," she said. "We can't get together again. We are too much one. While we are a million miles away. The other side of the globe. And that is so very sad." She sat up in her bed, perhaps to make her voice stronger, as strong now as were her large brown eyes, so wet, and her thrust forehead. "And yes, I have an answer for you now, Arthur, as to why I *do* it, what I do, lifting, sweating, lifting more, flexing my muscles in the mirror, all that—looking less pussyish, I guess you could say: I have become, or I am becoming, the *world*. Yes, I-am-*becoming*. A woman who walks through the world with a man's seen power—my brawn. When she wishes to. While you, Arthur, *you might have been* the world. All hemispheres. And you, you've *divested*. You are a *might-have-been*."

He said, "No," because he didn't understand her. He said No because he also thought that she was too smart for him. A brain. Like his "friend" Joseph, who had fixed them up.

Had she meant he ought to become a hermaphro-dite?—as he had the prerequisites, hadn't he feared that already enough. Or was her meaning only that he, somehow, ought to have been able to, at least, *get-it-up*?

Well, he'd only just had his surgeries. Endured them—unfinished as they were. She hadn't given him a true chance. Which he realized as he'd thought it, he hadn't given her one either. They, self-comforters in extremis, they were both making themselves nobler than they were—because they, the both of them, they did not feel noble and they did need self-comfort.

But, he felt about the both of them, they were not ignoble either. They were both pretty good goddamn people.

Maybe she was a woman going the man-muscle route, not because of her will and her intellect exactly, but because her DNA, her hormones, these were lodged in her brain cells as much as they were anywhere in her—and they had made her do it, all that Gold's Gym heavy-lifting. Which then, when you got right on down to it, the psycho-bio, it did make her exactly like him! *What she needs*, he considered—*and I need*—he trying to get himself to chuckle a bit within and thus to save his soul within and without—*what we both need is a psychoneurobioendocrinologist.* A good one.

Chicken-and-Egg City.

They both were just lost and swinging within the labyrinths of their processings of their truths.

Arthur wondered if his "opportunity" here was flat-out impossible to, much less reverse, revise.

I'll call her again. Some time.

Reassurance? Who can't but live without it?

V

After his final surgeries, his hysterectomy and his oopherectomy, whereby he had had removed his cervix, his ovaries and his fallopian tubes, and waiting again for his slow healing from all these laparoscopies and slicings (the surgeon had asked in smirk-jest "Would you like to keep these accoutrements as souvenirs?"— Arthur answering, "God, no!" then thinking, "Maybe yes," then after a moment of transient regret, returning to the No!), and his sutures being removed for once and for all, the end had thus become the beginning, now fully—and he returned to Carnegie Mellon University, and dramatics, his anticipated lifesaving acting and his beloved life-penetrating mime. . . . He often did think of Anna, of how—*somehow*—they might have made more of their togetherness than they had. Of how they might not have led themselves straight into this sad rupturing that seemed, from time and distance now, to have been a consequence more of the fear of kinship than of anything else. Maybe, if fate had anything good to it, if it existed, they might still come together, and even learn to love each other. After all, not so much learning would be necessary—distance again made him sure of this. Anna was such a sweet girl, such an honest, determined girl, she was so trustable. She had those bright brown benevolent eyes. She was insecure and she was kind, she was the sort of person that he wished himself to be—when he did not imagine himself to be that way already. . . But now he was back at Carnegie-Mellon, except that everyone was gone now—well not everyone, but the major figures as far as Arthur had been concerned: Ted Danson, the star student, he was off in Hollywood, with rumor having it that he would be the star of a new series set in a bar (*Cheers*, of course); and that super-wit Albert Einstein (who became Albert Brooks), he had made already a funny faux-documentary of a School for Comedy (vide the famous Danny Thomas "spit-take" of florid discombobulation), and so he too was on his way; and worst of all, most damaging of all, the great Cadeau Courir, mime of mimes, Arthur's centerpiece and idol—he had gone on a performance tour, to be one year long, all over Europe, he was just that magnificent and unmatchable with his pliant frame formed of rubber, of elastic, of air. So Arthur felt like a new student, alone, a man deserted; indeed, a man in a desert. And he was afraid, out of loneliness, the sheer absence of connection, of even latching-onto the essences of those people he might mime, which activity had been what had made him, or promised to, beyond those twisted fallible chains of the hormonic. It occurred to him that he was a foreign book that had succeed in achieving translation, but the book was a bad translation, and of a book of which no one had ever heard, so who cared if the translation was good or bad. He had become then, again, a close-companion of insignificance, of invisibility; there and not-there, he was no longer even mocked—and he wished for even a little mockery *("Hey you, mock me!")*—and he was afraid that he might well go insane.

Perhaps he always had been.

No, be yourself!

Who is that?

He especially thought such things when they showed at CMU on their Thursday evening film series the highly praised movie with that new-praised actress Hilary Swank, *Boys Don't Cry,* where the transman (Hillary Swank) is raped and murdered—Arthur had seen that fate coming from early-on in the movie, which was based on a true story, and the film did have him for a few weeks keeping careful watch on his back, especially when anyone looked even sidewise at him, which the-other-him knew wasn't even happening anymore. But that movie scenario had taken place way out in the rough-country, the lowlife country of rural Nebraska—surely there was no way anyone at Carnegie, or in Baltimore for that matter, would rape and shoot him, simple well-meant Arthur, depressed translation Arthur, shoot him in the head—and although Hillary Swank had been quite artistic and energetic in that boy-role she'd played, she was still a girl all perceivable, easy-perceivable up there on the Carnegie screen; and Arthur, he told himself and told himself, was *un*endowed now with any girlish slip-slightishnesses, any holdovers from his birth. He'd had a vagina, etc., and that was it—and that *wasn't* it anymore. And then he got wind of the fact that Chastity Bono, the "daughter" of Cher and Sonny Bono, was transman. And it was the abandoned-name Chastity that really got him—and the humor, even to Arthur, he had to admit, of Chastity's becoming (the ridiculable) *Chaz*—such a name indicative of trying-too-hard, a bowling-alley name. . . *I do not think of myself as either Hilary Swank or "Chaz" Bono. And so I am as horrible a bigot as all the people who have coldly made fun of me in the past... No way out! . . . But I'm free. . . If I want to be. . . If I can figure how to be.*

Now, the drama department was set to put on, of all plays, Shakespeare's *Comedy of Errors,* and lord knows why, Arthur was set to act in that early farce of identity confusions, supposed witches and madmen, lies and pleadings and beatings and "bewitchings". Was it so obvious to those in charge of casting that Arthur's life to this date had itself been one of identity-doubles mixups and so then perfect-amenable to grotesquery, to acting farce? Arthur himself, giving himself once-over after once-over, decided that he was indeed the choice logical for playing these two nutty twins, the Dromios, just as he was sure that the other students and the teachers (or coaches) saw in him the same duality. No matter how much he tried to walk about the small campus in the most male of manners, either to lope like a diffident ballplayer (or like a cocky "cunt-jockey"), or in the most dignified of Cadeau Courir manners, he could always perceive that, after all was said and done, there was, within and without, sometimes only slightly, *a difference*. His original being just held onto a place within him, it hung-in as if pressed and stamped. Plastered. Womanish, damnit—even if only slight—he just *knew* it—he could not throw that femalishness all the way off, not *all*; it was just like the situations he was inserted-into in that near-downright-amateur plaything of The Bard's plays, *The Comedy of Errors*, where Arthur as this Dromio, a twin, just as Arthur who was in real life a twin of himself-herself, had to cackle-out the line, *"I am an ass, I am a woman's man, and besides myself."*—and folks in the audience, students mostly, laughed: And Arthur figured, even while acting, even with his mind full-other with his Shakespeare lines, he figured that the audience had figured who he was, in real-life, who he had been and who he still quite maybe, partly, was[4]—so flop-sweat drenched his forehead (especially after he read the scrawled op-ed on his dorm-room door: "GENDER FLUIDITY EATS SHIT". . . But wait—*come on, don't give up, be fair—accept yourself!* He just was and was not what he was. Yes, life was hard and he was a twin! On a dime, at times anyway (just not exactly when he wished-to), Arthur could after all change from the dancey-bounce-stepping maneuvers of a boxer he admired on TV, Sugar Ray Leonard, to the elegant-straight-backed-relaxed English style of, say, the actor James Mason (old movies were "the thing" at the school, old movies were taught in coursework, this as they were written with far more and longer dialogues, even if those long-talk-interchanges might be artificial and stiff and over-Anglified, a bit like theatre performances, which had to be that way with monologues and dialogues in order to project, there being no movie close-ups—all so that what seemed in old movies inauthentic-talk today to the

---

[4] "a woman's man": Shakespeare had only meant it to signify that the fellow was married, not that he was a part of a woman.

average moviegoer was actually more authentic, deeper, more realistic, to the movie-*knower*), or Arthur might "become", without even so much as thinking about it and honing in on it, a muscularly-romantic mover-posturer like Gene Kelly (*he* was still a *mime*, really!— when you [he]) thought about it); or—and this was quite troubling and paradoxical, as it had not been the case when he had been in full possession of his female "accoutrements" and with zero male ones: *or*, he would drift into a borderline woman or girl, a toughesque such as Betty Hutton or Barbara Stanwyck (both as Annie Oakley, both two-hipped with studded holsters and six-shooters long and shiny). As if, unconsciously, now devoid of female-stuffings, his essence had to reclaim some of that, for his own inauthenticity to regain its full authentic.

I am a chameleon!

No, we all are chameleons!

No to that: I am THE Chameleon.

I don't like it.

I DO like it. My liking it or my not-liking it depends on who—I, me, half-of-me, all-of-me—at that time is doing the liking or not-liking.

One thing though for sure: I definitely seem to need it.

Dear God,

Please Help me. I am lost. I have had my surgeries and I am still a goner. But You have made me this way, and you are not cruel, that is impossible to believe. I know that I am insignificant when I think of the universe and it's great expanse, and in truth when I think of the universe and other universes beyond it I cannot believe that You exist. Yet I am calling out to You because my situation, my place in existence is so unplaced, I now have male genitals but I still feel within the female which I have had removed, and I don't know who to be, I don't even know if I *can* be anything, anything with a realness, an authenticity, a *belief* in its worth, in its effort— I don't know really if *I* am worth the effort, the effort of anyone, to love me, to be *with* me, the effort too for me to go on living as I am this Chameleon that You have deemed made—and You have made me for a reason, I have to believe it although I can't— even my beliefs are Chameleons. Please Help me, I am lost. How could what has happened to me have happened to me! I am so Lonely.

All people want to Belong! Please dear God! Please!

He'd become the child he had been, bent over his bed each night before climbing into it towards a hopeful deserved good boy-girl sleep. He who now did not believe in God—except for that part of him, that believing part, that resided, where?—in that deserved good boy-girl quarry, that stubborn fount as deep-down in him as the cells implicit in his conception. . . And he hated that prayer, call it what?—duplicity? But he needed it. No atheists in foxholes. So much so, his double-thought, that, the Vietnam War being still in "progress", and Arthur being so against it, America's unjust invasion, America's hated invasion, its bombings of Hanoi, he went and hiked the five miles from Carnegie Mellon on down to downtown Pittsburgh and volunteered to join-up with Uncle Sam—he might help somehow, Vietnamese people and American soldiers, *somehow*—he could identify with both sides, or rather

103

with the men of both sides, not all those stupid ideolo-
gies, there must be *something* he could do. Entertain, as
a mime, whatnot. . . But, to join up, he had to submit
his medical records; and once the Army got a load of
Arthur's dual identity (and there were photos, before
and after), even before the induction physical, where
he'd hoped his new artificial gonads would pass muster,
a superficial lineup one anyway, he was, out-of-hand,
rejected.

Dear God (his poor prayer went repeated).

VI

Except, the very core, the central point, the axis, of
chameleonism being change, of personality and of
personality's desires, personality's authenticity and its
presentation, it was dawning upon Arthur Becker that
this was only one section, one part of him and his
natural, authentic, urge toward acting-miming, that
wish to be an actor in role upon role, and to allow that
one portion of self to *be* the whole was therefore, in
essence, to be false, to be *in*authentic: Chameleonism
could lead away from The Chameleon—if chameleonism were the whole. Paradox but true. . . And, the next
thought, the consequent logic, led quite to a profession
that was, yes, similar, but was also wholly different.
And this was, believe it or not for such a loner as
Arthur Becker, politics. *Politics!?* The position-changes
to suit the "weather-changes", the protestations of
honesty and morality, the authentic wish to help, but the
authentic wish also for that help to be, in addition, to
Number One, oneself, the posing, the facial transmigra-
tions, the quick changes of clothing presentations, of

voice and intonation, the religiosity and its faking—oh God, oh all-of-it, nothing more pure, more pure-perfect for Arthur, far more unadulterated than acting, as it was change within change within non-change—you remained the selfsame politician all the while, all the time, nothing more bullseye for The Chameleon than "the noble profession of" POLITICS. . . Even actors' favorite roles were politicians.

But, come on, you sole, you inveterate keep-to-your-selfer, How!?

It took some time for Arthur, laying thinking on his dorm bed, weeks of this, to come up with it: Hey, I could make the sole-keep-to-myselfishness, an *attribute*, an attraction, an admirable, a drawing-card. The picture of The Best: The most Moral and Ethical. A sole become a Soul.

Still, easier said (or thought) than done: I still need a HOW?! Is a How within me?

Sure it is: I am a Chameleon's Chameleon. Isn't this what made of Cadeau Courir, with his one pose-motion subtly slipping-into another, and one with different meaning, far-off meaning, what made him such a mime magnificent! Isn't this why I loved him, why I hung on him. . . Isn't this what made of the phony-seem long talky-talk of old movies, in reality, well, talk Reality! To those who listened close.

And I listen close. I'll figure it. I'll practice, I'll rehearse.

Best then to leave Carnegie Mellon, so soon after he had returned there. Certainly no one on campus would miss him, but that was hardly the reason for his packing-up and leaving (no students even gave a double-take at his sweat-schlepping his two suitcases across campus to the bus stop where he would catch the Number 5 to the downtown Greyhound station, and thence back to Baltimore—obviously no students offered schlep-help.). The reason for his taking-off was that—could you believe it?—he had decided that, although he had been so far a loser, from that losing and suffering he had that Great Morality deep within him, and an Understanding of people, and Understanding *for* people, all by way of his incessant fragmentationing of himself—such aspects came almost immediately upon his meeting someone, anyone, and with his honed mime-prowess so internalized, so addictive, such truthful skills (*damnit, they were not mockery or any kind of fakery*) he could Help. But not being a native Pittsburgher, he did not know there the local ins-and-outs of the profession that he now considered might be right for him, might be The Best, for him: Politics, as implied earlier. No, he hadn't a clue as to the in-and-out machinations, and the players, and the allegiances, that played in Southwestern Pennsylvania, which with its Appalachian tenor, its surroundings of Yahoodom (although not in Pittsburgh proper), these seemed to be as far away as Idaho from Arthur's Baltimore home-town. So, Arthur returned to "Balamur" (the local whites' pronunciation, or "Beemoh"—the blacks. And for both, "The Most Northern of the Southern Towns, the Most Southern of the Northern."), where for starters he might tool himself up to run for the lowest of local offices, the Baltimore House of Delegates, or the City Council. . . And if he had the spirit for that aim, he might even telephone Anna Bass, who by now, when he thought of her, he still, yet, considered her his alter-ego.

To his father Mark's consternation, and his mother Elaine's, Arthur Becker moved back into the suburban Becker ranch house—but he did this at a very un-propitious time. Mark and Elaine Becker were in the excruciating process of becoming separated and then divorced. The two decades-long toll taken on them by Arthur's transism, in all its manifestations and its laments and its rationalizations, had been too much, it had worn them down, worry had reached to what Arthur, having read in English lit more Shakespeare than he could absorb correctly, called "the catacombs of their souls." Mark Becker, once a local hero, once an awesome figure whose very appearance could make eyes go aglitter in northwest Baltimore ("the golden ghetto of Jewry"), he was now afflicted by what people called "nerves": his fingers might shake and quiver in a board meeting, as if he were trying-out rapid chords on a guitar, he tended to look away when people looked to him, he didn't shave every day, even for his coming to the office, where he took afternoon naps necessitated by the after-effects of the sleeping pills he took after watching the 10 PM News. And Elaine Becker, that onetime admired goodlooker, that nowtime reality-battered looker, she had now to wear bright multi-colored scarves about her neck, which seemed to have collapsed and narrowed, showing its veins and withered ligaments above her also narrowed and thinned-out shoulders; and her once-blonde hair, so special for a Jewish girl (oh sure, all the girls had known it was "touched-up'), her great hair was thinning too. So, the Beckers, they were no longer the ideal enviable garru-lous couple who people wished to have crabcakes or lobster-chowder with at The Chesapeake or go skiing with up in Vermont, but rather the sorry modern version of van Gogh's *Potato Eaters* coupled with the sorry-skinny-warped lineaments of Modigliani's twosomes. Dinner at home had become a wake, often with ordered-out pizza. In earlier years they had consoled Arthur endlessly, and such strenuous supporting (which they hadn't even believed) had worn them out: They never even went to movies. They seldom slept together—it was as if they were underlining in their lack of sex the absence that they were sure was Arthur's inevitable life-sentence. Deep within the souls of both Mark and Elaine Becker resided the "truth" that Arthur's future was as misery-laden as was their own present. And this "vision", or fear, was only magnified when they saw their son stumbling along, even when he tried to "progress", to make himself "better".

Of course, none of this tyrannical gloom was lost on Arthur, and decent soul that he was he tried to help:

"I'm nowhere as bad as you think." He tried that one.

"I've got hopes and plans." He tried that one.

"I'm thinking about 'politics'."

Which was a laugh—had his parents now possessed the attributes and impoliteness required now for serious laughter.

"Dad, mom: You know, the fact that, in a way, I am two people—even with my operations—two people in my inner being, I guess, this helps me as much as it hurts. It may not be evident to you, and it wasn't even to me for so long a time, but I feel things differently, and from more angles, and more deeply than do your normal people—I'm not kidding. It's like I'm floating-in from the angles of both the sun and the moon. That's why I could go into politics, to help people, or even become a psychiatrist for that matter—well, a psychologist, or some kind of love coach." Arthur couldn't miss the dismal incredulity in their eyes: "And I'm not being naïve."

"We've made you this way," said a stern-faced Mark Becker. "Arthur, we're so sorry."

"It wasn't intentional," said Elaine.

"Now how in the world could it have been intentional?" answered Arthur, he now become the parent of the two of them, his indulgent and withering parents; he knowing full-well that he himself as a younger person, a lost child, had blamed them for producing him—and even, in his newfound wisdom, brought apparently by the need to help his parents, and by his having come to identify with the great-graceful Cadeau Courir, in his new wisdom, he knowing that blame is such a human thing, an immature thing, an aggressive fault-escaping atom in the genes, he knew too that at times in his life to come, he would blame them again, it was inevitable—but now he could certainly fight it.

"Please, mom and dad," pleaded Arthur, "don't divorce."

His parents regarded each other with the half-lidded eyes of folks who knew that what they were being asked to do was a thing long too late. That even if their son Arthur no longer blamed them for his being him, irony was that *they* now, having fought such blame, and knowing that there could not *be* such blame, now did their damned self-blaming.

"Dad, mom," said Arthur, "give yourselves another chance."

Elaine, constantly, habitually now, adjusting her

aged-neck-covering, that multi-colored scarf: "Arthur, do you mean for us to stay married with each other?—or to have another child?"

In perhaps his only humorous exhalation in months, Mark went low-key, "Oy."

And Arthur, in his naïveté (that was only a partial naïveté, but compromised by a partial hope), went, "A child. It's been done late in life. Why not?"

"You don't know why not?" said one parent, or said the other.

"I've read up," said Arthur. "It could happen."

"I know the science," said Mark. "I've read up too."

Elaine stared at her husband in the weirdest of affectionate-sarcastic wonderments.

Mark's listing head, his smirk had not one ounce of play in it.

Arthur noticed, and really for the first time, how bald his father was becoming, how his comb-over was finally revealing itself, as it was turning into a comb-forward as well, with the two types meeting-up. His "handsome" dad now resembled one of those liberal talking-heads who populated CNN and MSNBC. Thank goodness then for Mark's strong cheekbones, and that the better part of his head lay above those bones, as, say, Yul Brynner's had done. He was still a (sort of) handsome man. Arthur went with—

"But you two, you still do love each other."

His parents again bore those twin envelopes of half-lidded eyes.

Elaine: "Arthur, you're too young to know what 'love' is—and what it depends-upon, and how it can be sustained."

"And," said Mark, "how, while it might still exist, it

is just too complicated to exist as it was, or even. . ." His shrug said he was lost.

"Look, I know all that," said Arthur. "I really do. Being the twofold human being that I am."

His inclination then was to try physically to bring his parents together, to hold his arms about the two of them, as they did at summer camp Solstice for trans-sexuals, that refuge-redoubt that he had attended as a "boy" for more than a few years. That arm-encircle-ment of his parents, oh he knew it would come off childish if not accomplished in an adult manner—*and by adults*—so he didn't do it. And that night, no tears: somehow, Arthur believed, he would bring his parents together again. There was still time—he could not imagine these two apart. Life would not even be life that way. . . Except, he was adult by now to know that life was Life, and it would remain Life, *exactly* in that way. That was what made life Life.

And while Arthur's parents were impressed, bol-stered, by their son's new wisdom, or rather his attempt to fabricate it, and to enact it, or mime it, and then project it, they still had to separate, Mark moving out, and Arthur staying in wealthy nouveau riche Stevenson with his so older-looking onetime beauty mother.

Arthur kept thinking of calling Anna Bass, but he did not. If anything, having quit college he must have exhibited himself as more unworthy than he had been before, more a failure, more a quitter. That certainly would not sit well with the good young woman who suffered mockeries and askant broadside looks for her determinedly following through on her own personal ambitions about her own unusual physical appearance—about how she should be in the world, no matter how oddly-sexual it looked. Arthur would have felt a washout facing her. A weakling—and he had had enough of that. One thing, though: Arthur told his by now separated parents that, if they were ever asked, they were to tell whoever did the asking, such as reporters—*reporters!?*—or any unfamiliar people, that he was not their son, not by-natural anyway—rather that he was adopted. That he was not natural Jewish but, by birth, Italian. Craziness? Jewish self-hatred? Well: The reason for this request was simple and it sure seemed necessary. Like Rhode Island, like New Jersey, like most of New York's Queens and inner Long Island, Baltimore was run by Italians—it had a long tradition of "guinea" Mayors and Mafiosi. For a number of years Baltimore's head man had been Tommy D'Alesandro, and after him came his son, Tommy Junior—and on the other side of the law but just as powerful had been Mimi "The Barber" Lorenzo, the local Godfather (and he really was a barber)—and all were best buddies, gumbas. Tommy Junior's sister was also political, she was Nancy d'Alesandro, and Arthur had even met her once, and danced with her, when he had gone to a mixer years before at Nancy's local, and puritanical, college, The Notre Dame School for Girls—with his own sexual handicaps and dilemmas, he had hoped that meeting some plain nice girls, unthreatening non-doper non-promiscuous girls, would be the best thing for him. Would be, girl-wise, the only thing for him. In any case, Nancy was about to get married and move to San Francisco, to become Nancy Pelosi. Except, at present, she held the seat in the House of Delegates that Arthur coveted for his first, beginning, spot. And Nancy's position had never been contested. It was in all but writ an inheritance.

"From now on," Arthur told his father Mark, "I am to be known as Arturo. Arturo Becki."

"You're insane," Mark managed to spit-shpiel-out while swamped in wide-eyed (but subdued) laughter at this off-the-walls, and rather amateur, and rather child-ish, prankish, comicality of the name, and at his sensi-tive son's apparent sincerity in wishing to adopt it.

" 'Arturo Becki'," Mark repeated, deadpanned this time, as if he were Johnny Carson playing straight man for some eager bumptious comic.

"Arturo Becki," Arthur repeated, and now solemnly, gravely, even a bit angry-brandishing, but also as an underlining and grinding-in of the name for his father's memory.

"In time," said 'Arturo', "once I'm known I can go by 'Art'—same as Arthur."

"Look, Arthur," Mark said, "I can understand your not wanting any longer to be an actor. I'm with that, and wholeheartedly. But why not go into something substantial? I don't know—accounting. You take courses, then you take the CPA. The exam. It's a damn good income, and it's damn dynamic. Different com-panies, widely divergent, you go over their books. You analyze, you certify your approval, or your disapproval. You recommend. You make pretty damn good bucks. You wear a good suit, a pin striper so as to impress— how's that! You're not stuck in one office, you go all over the place: Dundalk, Lansdowne, Towson, Pimlico. Even way out over to Hagerstown." The first four were Baltimore regions, neighborhoods; the last was in Western Maryland, Appalachian no-man's land for a young man who still looked, at least, semi-girlish, and could give-off incongruous vibes.

'Arturo' did not dignify his father's advice with even the least of comments.

So Mark went on: "You can talk like an *Italian,* can you? You can strut your *walk* like they do? Arthur, you can't be an Italian unless you are an Italian—that sort of stuff is in their blood, just as in our Jewish blood there's. . . " Mark decided to not expound.

Miming-lover Arthur, miming-obsessor Arthur, he could of course do an Italian—or what he perceived as the baseline forensics of one. And as a neophyte with the D'Allesandro family, which was, as said, in "partnership" with the Balto-mafioso Mimi (the barber) Lorenzo, it was incumbent upon Arthur to begin his "political purity", his authenticity (and making apropos "guinea" friends"), by, sonofagun, learning *barbering* (e.g. at first: sweeping Italian locks [hair] off the checkerboard linoleum floors of that barber shop— Mimi Lorenzo's headquarters in Little Italy: which also happened to be a double front, for it served as camouflage for Mimi's back room World Sport bookie operation, which was a compound of computers and transmitters—in the techno-state of the mid-seventies: wherein Arthur, if he took the job, would have to learn in off-hours how to record and transmit the win-place-show-nags at Hialeah and Hollywood Park and Belmont Park and Pimlico, and even who triumphed in the grudge contests, thus big-bet money, between India and Pakistan at cricket; and, he knew, purity aside, lawlessness aside, his "health" would be jeopardized if he failed and fucked-up the World Sport operation—technology not being an Arthur Becker métier). Moreover, he suddenly realized something else. Arthur had identified Italianism, as opposed to Judaism, with manliness, unsquinchy unpompous unsententious manliness. It hadn't been only that he wanted to become a winning, noble, altruistic Baltimore politician, even as it meant defeating Nancy D'Alesandro; it meant that he, with his so far, face it, lame-like, lame-duck dick, that artificial thing that he was coming to despise (when he was not cherishing it as God's gift), that jerry built penis, damnit, he wanted it becoming the rightful, the justifiable-proven, attribute of a *man*—like an Italian's dick—along with (of course) helping people as a local "statesman"—okay, ombudsman. And, consequent upon these thoughts were—of course—those ineluctable ones of guilt: how could someone who still, really, truly, did know what or who he was (and who at times reveled in such a confounding being, when it was not torturing him), how could he represent people in general? *Any* people! Were his interests in accord with those of your average man? Were they antithetical? Were they either one? At times, sad to say—and the considering of running for office as a representative of the people, and therefore being, in a sense, more a person than an average person—this had him wondering not only if he were a man, and not only if he were two men, or a woman within a man and vice-versa, but if he were of too much a slip-sliding scale in the spectrum of *all* behaviors and identities to be *anything*. To be trusted? Might he not vote on one proposal in one way and on the very next day, in the opposite? Deciding upon the gender issue of entering the Men's or Women's bathroom was one thing—and he always did, when needed, enter the Men's—although nostalgia (if that is the right word) had him at times sensing a pulling, like gravity's magnet, energy's womb, towards the Women's. A queerish unthreatening comfort there—which, upon reflection, after leaving The Woman's (yes, honestly, he did sometimes enter it) was not unthreatening comfort at all—but skin-curdling self-contempt—and suicidal entertainings.

He dropped out of the race for the Baltimore House of Delegates and/or the City Council.

It was a decent idea, it really was: he truly wanted to help his fellow citizens. But it wasn't right. . . Maybe some day in the future—if he got nowhere in the meantime.

But cops, policemen, they were manliness personified—and there were Jewish cops in Baltimore, he knew this for a fact as he had been witness once to an officer in uniform praying (or at least faking it by appearing to *daven* while delving deeply into his *Siddhur*, the Jewish prayer book, this in his father Mark's synagogue, Chizuk Amuno [the inner city location, before it relocated to the nouveau riche suburb of Stevenson]), and Arthur had read that there were many Jewish cops in Brooklyn, just as there had been Jewish gas station attendants—when there had been gas station attendants. So Arthur would not be a phony-baloney effete outsider by being an officer of the law—*if he could get to make the grade and become one.* True there were not nearly so many Jew-police as there were Irish, they seemed born for that profession of law enforcement—lord knew why—just as Italians seemed born for bombastic politics and bombastic anti-politics, and law evasion; nor were there even as many Jews in officer uniform as schwartzes (*schwartzes*, could you *believe* it?—what ambiguities and self-torments those black men and women must have fought their own private internal crossroads through when they confronted their own people in their own neighborhoods, they probably had to act tougher to show their "creds" while at the same time feeling greater sympathy, soft sympathy). . . But anyway, yes, here was the answer, or here could be the answer: Arthur would become an officer-of-the-law. And Arthur didn't have to worry so much about his body, his physique, if up-top at chest level he was not quite the thickest-thickset, if his forearms didn't bulge as did, as had, those of Anna Bass, that sweet dearest of weightlifters, and female PoseDown champ—there were, after all, woman cops (and more than there were Jewish). Arthur might not yet to this date have achieved a full-fledged erection worthy of penile pride, but he just bet, damnit, that he could achieve a full-fledged erection of virtue and right, and thus pass muster to become a cop. That is, if not just emotionally and morally, but bodily, he prepared— the IQ stuff would certainly comprise no roadblock. So, Arthur Becker, having abandoned the ridiculous moniker Arturo Becki, took himself to the Downtown Dyna-Mature on Calvert Street, next door to *The Baltimore Sun* newspaper; it was locally known as having a membership of not one washboard stomach nor medieval-shield chestplate chest, as it was comprised in-the-main of weary hunchback journalists (who still smoked) and over-sixtiesers just trying to keep-up semblance-tone (other reason for joining the Dyna-Mature: he wished not to run-into the super-physiqued Anna Bass at Gold's Gym, not until he had developed his own more personal physique-pride), Arthur taking three months to do as best for his body as that inadequately-inherited crumbum core of his would allow.

He was accepted into the Police Academy (they always needed people, badly—and it was only a three month program, not so big on endurance), there where academically he shined—top of the class—and physically he squeezed-by, his greatest difficulty not any fellow recruit catcalls at his skinny-pole of a chest (that absence of critique did happily surprise him) and only one side-of-the-mouther at his still somewhat "pumpkin-ass"; but the killer was that motherfucker of a hamper-flounder obstacle which was provided by his being required to shinny-up and over a twelve-foot high concrete wall with the use of a rope (which was un-knotted: knot-grasping would have made the climb too easy), hard for him because he kept worrying about any skin burns in the offing for his new penis (all the recruits were in shorts, of course). Both the males and females seemed at ease with how their "privates"—as the police instructor named them with institutional neutrality—their "privates" would adapt quite naturally to climb-placement, "just as a chimp's would, or an orangutan's, you apes." And not unsimilar was the problem he struggled with when it came to the learning of how to "work a succumbation" of a suspect without use of an "espantoon" (what the fuck is that!?) or " your service weapon". This involved a kind of combination of Western grappling and body-slams along with Eastern "hooey" methods, Bruce Lee types of fancy stuff that not one student here could finesse—as mostly they didn't give a shit, and the instructor seemed not much to shine-on either. But engaged in being wrapped-about some other recruit in a practice session, legs-mixed, testicles just-about hanging in his face, again Arthur worried about the condition of his new penis and testicles, still unfullfledged—and about the other recruit's "privates", some of them female, which no other of his classmates seemed to be concerned about—not in this well-observed learning context. He lost every training fight (Luckily he never had to fight a female recruit: he feared losing, and then he imagined who else defeating him but sweet Anna.). Not surprising, then, that Arthur was first assigned to catching traffic violators—and on the outskirts of the city, where most of the scofflaws were not red light speed-throughs nor left-turn from right lane assholes downtown, nor multi-pedestrian threateners of the "shade-skin" urban dismal, but STOP sign unstoppers. Out in the colonial architectured heavens of Homewood and Roland Park, just north of Johns Hopkins University, a warren that was for the most part old wealth and old people—and Hopkins professors (the students lived in rowhouses south of the school)—Arthur stealth-parked his police car and patiently awaited these "criminals"—a number of whom seemed to declare cunningly contrived "truths" such as, "Officer, I *did* stop—I came to a *rolling* stop." Which, decently, but officially incompetently, Arthur did accept as arguments, as at least half of these STOP signs were unnecessary on these seldom traversed cross-streets which were barely more than horse-paths—and Arthur won, consistently, what they called at Police Headquarters down on Falls Road, The Weak Knee Prize, as he had turned in weekly the least auto-violation ticket copies. He was upbraided, he was warned, he was reprimanded and rebuked—but he

could not bring himself to issue much in the way of
tickets—hiding in his patrol car, summons-ready, he
felt too much like a spy, a piddling nitpicker creep—
and he was reassigned: To The Baltimore Department
of Public Welfare, where at times in the hallways—
those gaunt and stinkingly unkempt corridors of dead
linoleum—the occasional poor person, usually black,
usually one who had not received his weekly stipend
and food stamps, might harangue (but rarely attack) his
"worker". Arthur had only to stand "on-the-beat" in this
hall or that, merely show himself, strapped-on "espantoon" and black holstered gun. A peacekeeper against
the "mau-mauers of the flack-catchers"—who one
kindly, generous social worker took pity on and brought
for him a red plastic bucket chair for his assignment
hallway spot, which was on the recipient side of the
gray metal counter that protected said flack-catchers.
Where he tended to overhear what he considered the
Welfare recipient equivalent of the rich-neighborhood
vehicular "rolling stop" excuse: "Man, I *did* apply at the
taxi company (or the mineola [linoleum] place stockroom, or the Sanitation Department, or whatever), but
they weren't hiring (or "they were closed", or "they
said you got to give a *deposit*—what kinda job asks an
applier for a *deposit*!?—they wanted to talk to my *parole* guy."). . . And in these differently-hallowed halls a
truth came rushing into Arthur: He was coming to
realize here at the DSS (Welfare) that all the mockery
and contempt that he now observed (on both sides) was
no different from all the mockery and contempt that he
had endured in high school, and had he not been (somehow) decent and (relatively) cognizant of humans'
humanity he might well have turned-into one of those

benighted and psychotic kids who found their ways to AR-15 semi-automatics and proceeded to mow-down their innocent classmates.

Arthur was then stricken by another new idea, for another new job. A much better one than this one that he now "held down", this neutral umpiring of policing, which neutrality in his heart he felt was wrong—and wasn't even neutral anyway.

VII

He should have known all along, he chided himself, that being transgender, whether from boy to girl or girl to boy, and/or all the amalgams in-between, these would (and did) render him of such sensitivities and perspectives that there really was but one profession that would be perfect and ideal for him—how could he have taken so long to come upon it? Politics was out, forget it, as it pretty much required not so much sensitivity but its opposite, *in*sensitivity—a sine qua non, it looked like, addenda added-to by greed and fake-probity; and police work appeared, when you looked semideep, to be the same—although Arthur imagined from his limited experience that officers of the law tended to be more sensitive to an individual's pain, and less sensitized to their own narcissisms, than did even the best of politicians, they with their incessant big-name cravings. The saying went that politicians were merely ugly movie stars, and you could say that policemen (and women) were fantasizing soldiers, warriors, and certainly the latter was by far the better, the nobler. But, that all said, there really was but one profession that Arthur finally came to the conclusion was, as they say, right as rain. His being stationed at the Department of Public Welfare, that had brought him to a knowledge, a wisdom really, of his true destiny. He, a deprivee, was put on the earth to help the deprived—and hopefully even to undeprive them. His current experience with his parents had helped too, he having tried to mediate and to work to off-track their separation, which of course he knew that his "birthright" and his folks' trying to deal with that calumny had caused. And he vowed, he resolutely vowed, to not be the kind of magus-therapist that his one-time shrinker Doctor Jack Feder had been, him with that faker-famous-intellect-genius-name-dropper's hypno-phoniness that that man had relied-upon to experience himself as important. He would *listen*, Arthur would, he wouldn't pry, not so much; he wouldn't even adopt that arch-purist-caring mode of the man who first interviewed him and then became his superior, his supervisor (once he was actually able to land this new social worker job—or apprenticeship). This assigned new boss was Harold "Doctor" (PhD) Dwinski-Dwin, who Arthur just knew on instinct that all the "recip-iented-recidivist clients" made fun of—as much as did the social-workers of the recipient-recidivists . It had to be said though that Doctor Jack Feder, even with his megalo-mystery shrinker approach, his obvious wish to be worshipped as a movie-star or mayor or governor being greater than his wish to cure or to help, Doctor Feder had been Right—or at least not wrong: With his hokeyesque hypnosis hovering like a predatory-dyb-buk-raven in the background, even with its patent falsi-ty, Feder had managed to exorcise, hadn't he?—he had elevated Arthur's bifurcation, lofted it to a higher Seeing Ground. No, Arthur would not in the least be like that shaman Feder, but the man's advice to him, about him, being a sort-of "Woman-Man or Man-Woman for All Seasons", that "talent" might well help in his understanding of Welfare clients, and in finding ways to find and praise *their* talents—*didn't everyone have these!—talents!*—this was The American Anthem—and therein he would not be humiliating them as *he*, Arthur, had been humiliated for so long... But Social Work required grad school. Fuckass Years. Tedium. Living with his now singlish mother way out in that Super Burb of the nouveau riche Judaic, Stevenson. No?

Well, yes and no: At the University of Maryland Graduate School there would be social work placement, internship in effect, with pay, as one went through his (only) two years of training—if he were accepted: And with pay, even meager, even a subsistence stipend, he might *get himself a place*.

"You're transgender."

Doctor Harold Dwinski-Dwin, his aforementioned application interviewer, uttered the overwhelming world-walloping nuclear word so straightly matter-of-fact indifferent, as if observing 'You're a citizen', or 'You're tall', that even an imbecile could make-out that he was internally covering-up and internally stumbled-over by it. His short tannish arms were folded over his chest in the manner that most psychologists categorize as self-protective, but Dwinski-Dwin's chest-folded arms came-off bossy.

Arthur said, "Yes, trans, uh, trans, I am." Then, as if he had just raised his hand while his other was flat-out on the Bible and he was thus all set to give testimony on the stand before a crafty prosecutor, he considered for a moment. And reconsidered: "Well, I was, trans, uh, trans. I'm not now—not really, no." He was shaking his head—unconsciously. "Trans."

Actually, he was fully prepared for the awkward-ness—or he should have been. He'd already, only six months before, had to go through with this revealing, this emotional stripping, for the Police Department, whose official face-to-face interrogation would have been, one would have thought, more stand-up rigorous and threatening, almost mirroring an arrest. But the police officer had handled Arthur's "secret" so calmly, so offhandedly, so dully, that Arthur just about wanted to come round the interview desk and hug the guy— which would of course, considering Arthur's gender-state, had him rejected out-of-hand.

But the interviewer for Social Work: Arthur was pretty sure he had vaguely known this young man, relatively young (but seriously, intentionally, aging), in high school—hadn't he been a Senior when Arthur was just entering, a Freshman; he might have been, if memory served, on a sports team—an unimportant one for the "fairies', like cross-country, or golf; he might have even been in student office: Student Body Veep, or maybe even President. He was short, straight black hair, straight thick black eyebrows with no break be-tween them, and dark complexioned; Mexican looking one might have thought, but obviously Jewish—you could just tell that if you yourself were Jewish: the fly-swat arm-swing gestures supporting a well-modulated voice, the ironic smiles with his teeth not showing, the super-quick (yet still modulated) talkiness, the speedy

sidewise looks of, how could one call it?—confident
embarrassment: thus Harold Dwinski—now "Doctor"
(Jew-name evading and upper-class imitating) Dwinski-
Dwin.

Give me a break, thought Arthur. Sex-change,
understandable; name change, pathetic. Jewish self-
hatred. *I hate it—even though I'm guilty of it myself. . .*
And where were the inevitable braggadocio-love photographs of wife and children?—nothing like that on the
man's desk, which was a plain blond bulwark. The only
decorative element in this small office was a red
plastic-framed copy on the wall of a David Hockney: a
rolltop desk; a chair with a white dinner jacket draped
over its back; an open leather-bound notebook, no
human in evidence.

"How do you feel about yourself?" asked "Doctor"
(to Arthur) Dwinski-Dwin.

"Sometimes good, sometimes not so good," Arthur
answered honestly. Although even more honest would
have been not "not-so-good", but face it, shitty.

"You've also had a pretty varied background, of
college and employment. I could say, I think, it's transient."

Arthur nodded. "Yes, it's taken me a while to find
where I belong—but I just *know* it now, here, where I
belong."

"You *'know'* it? That's a pretty strong statement, all
things considered with you. So, how so do you
'know'?"

Arthur had been planning to put out twice as hard for
this Social Work trainee acceptance interview as he had
for the Police induction trainee interview, he was
determined to do that, but just now he found himself

looking past "Doctor" Dwinski-Dwin's Mexicanish features and out the window of his office. Across the street was the University Medical School in the University Hospital. And in that medical school was Anna Bass working by now on her internship. Arthur pictured her at the bedside of a patient, maybe taking a history, maybe actually doing something medical, whatever that might be. He imagined the patient looking at this woman with the paradox of absolute awe (and fear) at her muscularity and a quiescence and trust brought by her sweet warm empathic and quiet face. Could a woman be so gamin and be a doctor—or at least a successful one? Even with her build that was so powerful and counter-gamin? She was too confusing. . . Despite himself, Arthur kept up his imaginings of Anna as his own interview progressed.

"How is it so?" repeated "Doctor" Dwinski-Dwin. "How have you come to know, all of a sudden it seems, that social work is the rightful place for you? You know, Arthur, already you've had somewhat, more than somewhat, of a checkered past."

"I know."

"Glad you know."

Was this mockery?

It appeared that the interviewer did not remember Arthur from high school, or he was keeping slyly mum about it—politely mum. After all, how could anyone have forgotten this ambiguous boy-girl who had been the object of so much mumbled derision and mockery and locker room spying for the giveaway heard-of-but-unheard-of "way out" genitalia? Not that Dwinski-Dwin had been one of those cruel kids. Arthur could say that about him, and he appreciated this social worker, if not for his name-change, then for that past of decency.

"It's hard to explain how I've come to this—"

"Please try to explain how you feel. Please."

Arthur stared again out at the Medical School. It was a magnet. Ridiculously but rightfully ridiculously he felt the body-rush adrenaline of Love.

"As a social caseworker," said Dwinski-Dwin, "you would frequently ask your client how they feel. This is intrusive and it's like diving down and quarrying in a bleak whirlpool, but it's central. So Arthur, if you don't know your feelings, how can you expect any illiterate who knows nothing but busting heads and busting into people's houses and doing mucho drugs to sleep and mucho of other muchos to wake-up in an alleyway, how can you expect them to pull up short and delve into their "feelings"—for them such, well, horse-manure, is nothing but empty words." Dwinski-Dwin, little Mexicanish(ish)-Jew, went scowling as he closed his fists— he appeared to be just now acting-out the role of a crazed-mad recipient, or trying to. "And if *you* yourself, Arthur, as their 'worker', you can't your*self* delve-down into your *own* whirlpool, well. . ." He leaned back in his desk chair and took one deep breath, exhaling and nodding affirmatively, now as if he had just explained, and shrewdly, to a bunch of morons all the finer points of Diderot and the Enlightenment and their evolution up to and through our Constitution to this day here that we Americans so preciously "enjoyed".

Arthur stifled a laugh. Which seemed both childish and perceptively adult.

He explained that as a fledgling policeman assigned to patrolling the Department of Welfare he had seen so much more of misery than he could have imagined existed, and that, as a policeman he could do nothing but try to keep an order that, when you thought about it, was false and actually deserved for it to be authentic, the disorder that it had. As he spoke he thought of himself as well as of the complicated dear Anna Bass— who seemed to be listening to him. Disorder had so many faces.

"Are you sure," asked Dwinski-Dwin, "that in some way, Arthur, you want to be a social worker in order to, well, ameliorate your own . . . personal . . . disorder?" He maintained an unwavering brown-balloon stare on Arthur, as if he perceived the stew of emotions that endlessly heated in Arthur's soul. He did not look much sympathetic.

"I'm not sure," Arthur said, honestly. "but I am sure that I want to help. . . "

Dwinski-Dwin nodded as if to confirm his professionally-honed perceptions and critiques.

"And yes," Arthur added, "I want to find a . . . a place, for myself."

Dwinski-Dwin again went nodding, slowly, affirming his pro perspicuity. Despite his smarts, and with his shitheel nod, he was coming to appear the personification of a ripe asshole. He came out with—

" 'Social worker, social work thyself,'eh. "

Arthur looked befuddled. And he felt befuddled.

"It's an inside joke here," admitted Dwinski-Dwin. "And for being an inside joke, as we all know, it's no less true."

"Oh."

Silence. Anna Bass across the way. Anna drawing blood; Anna scrupulously examining a blood-test printout. Sweet-smart-sympathetic-hurt-strong-manly-self-built Anna Bass. Reflections on the windows of the Medical Building across the way. Reflections of the traffic outside, reflections of the dwindling-falling sun. Reflections blocking Arthur's sight.

"I just want to help," he said.

"Arthur, you've said that and you've said that."

Likely due to his Carnegie-Mellon training in the forensics of acting, Arthur was able to notice that when his interviewer spoke his lips, which were full violet lips, obscured his teeth—which made the man, who was in his mid-twenties, look like, or seem like, an old and toothless man. And with his teeth curtained he could appear less aggressive—more social workery? Had Dwinski-Dwin taught this protecting obscuring manner to himself, or was it, unintentionally, a product of social worker training? . . . But Arthur had to answer the man: He said—

"I feel that I could help, and that I *do*, I mean I understand, the people that you are working for to help, and that I do want to work for. I feel this"—he stared down at his chest, embarrassed, as if searching for himself. "I feel it instinctively."

" 'Instinctively', is it? Because you feel that you are they."

"Yes." Arthur couldn't help but smile at his own insipidity.

As did, for the very first time, Dwinski-Dwin.

"But don't you feel that a little objectivity is called for?"

Arthur hadn't thought of that. He was a man (or whatever he was) devoid, he feared, of anything in the neighborhood of such a thing as objectivity; he saw

131

pain and anguish and discomfort and the rest, and it was as if these unfair miseries doled-out by Nature willy-nilly reached out to him as a long lost son. He did wonder if the opposite were true, if he experienced the heaven-tuggings of joy—ever. Well, certainly this was seldom. Except perhaps when he had watched and felt through his own being the brilliant-sensitive motions of the great, the stupendous, Cadeau Courir—who was gone, *godamnit!*

"Yes," Arthur lied, "I do feel that objectivity is necessary." He badly wanted this damned job—or, rather, this profession.

Dwinski-Dwin smiled again, again managing to obscure his teeth. Those thick black eyebrows of his closed-in on each other to become one, a deadly weapon of perception.

"So-then, *can* you be objective, Arthur?—despite your GD."

"My what?"

"Gender Disorder."

Damn, he *knew*, did Dwinski-Dwin. And the phrase just sickened Arthur, but he closed his eyes, gritting, going along with it; he was also quickly ruminating, as if to see himself as the objective person Dwinski-Dwin required.

"Admit it, you can't, be so objective."

"Well . . . I admit it."

"You know, Arthur, you're an easy one for the changing of his feelings."

"I know."

"You'll have to work on that."

"I know."

"You do?"

"I mean, I will try."

"You know," said Dwinski-Dwin, "with you here, Arthur, I almost feel as if I'm being a social worker by, it looks like, offering you a spot *as* a social worker." He grinned broadly, as at a birthday or wedding celebration where he, somehow, didn't even know those honored. "Well, as a provisional one. A trainee."

Arthur was aware that this was a profession that needed people. That just about everybody today graduating from university wanted to go into hi-tech or reap the huge cold rewards that awaited the dry Masters degree winners from business schools. Apparently the interest rate and market fluctuations were as fascinating to them as the humanities might have been some fifty years before. He was aware that the population of social workers nowadays had been reduced to being white "do-gooders" or blacks without alternatives—asking recipients "How do you feel?" was pretty much their only recourse, i.e. black-on-black pacification. As a social worker, trying his damnedest to be a normal person, he would still be an anomaly. He wanted to ask this Dwinski-Dwin, this ex-fellow student with him in high school, if he liked his job.

"Of course," said Dwinski-Dwin, "you'll be receiving a placement as you train. So you'll be earning money."

"You mean I'm accepted?"

"You seem surprised."

"It's not that. It's . . . my . . ."

"You're surprised."

Arthur shut his eyes and nodded.

Dwinski-Dwin told Arthur that his placement would be in the Protective Services area of the Department of

Public Welfare, down on Greenmount Avenue: "I understand that you have experience there."

"Yes, as a cop. But not in Protective Services, and my experience, it was short-lived."

"Still, amazing. Arthur I can't see you as a cop. You're—oh well."

Arthur knew fully what the 'Oh well' meant.

"But, you know, that's perfect, your having been a law officer around here: Protective Services, you know, deals with men and women who have recently been released from prison."

Arthur knew that, of course, but he couldn't help from refraining what every social worker at Protective Services had thought: "Shouldn't that assignment be the, uh, province of the parole officers?"

"It is. It's your 'province' and it's theirs. You all communicate on the parolee's 'progress'. You decide who stays on the 'outside' and who gets a return vacation at—"

"Maryland State Penitentiary."

The most forbidding architectural "feat" in all of Baltimore. Located less than one half mile from The Washington Monument, and less distance than that from Welfare, the black, cracked-stone Gothic monstrosity, three square blocks in circumference located in northern center city, constructed in the Twenties, like-as-not by its ugly ominous haunting to deter the crime which it did not in the least deter. In the past, when Maryland had capital punishment, men had been hung in the yard there until they'd died. No women, for some reason—Maryland's having been a "genteel southern state"?

Arthur tried to not exhibit fear.

Then came that no-teeth pose of Dwinski-Dwin again. Neither challenge nor surprise nor belittlement nor confusion nor anything at all—just an all-concealing lip. Was this an idiosyncrasy of the man's or was it taught by cover-up example in The School of Social Work?

Outside, on Lombard Street, Arthur could have sworn he saw nice Anna Bass leaving the Medical School for the day. She was with a fellow. Arthur could hardly believe his eyes. The man was Joseph Lerner. Hunch-backed, broad-hipped so as to make of his anatomy a rumply triangle, hook-nosed, neck-dipped as if in thought or shame or neck-weakness, or all, Joseph Lerner—Arthur's best (and only) friend in the world. He couldn't believe it, but of course he could believe it—and he was hardly what one might call 'objective': his first reaction was that he wanted to *get* them, somehow—for this infidelity which, even Arthur knew, was not in the slightest infidelity, it was two pals (maybe, hopefully) just walking. Serious innocence. Serious doctorial innocence. But being male, with male aggressiveness, it being so newfound (and craving to be tried-out), and with the remnants of the female, with, well, female aggressiveness—which two were different, which two contained both aggression and duplicity—and passivity—but in different dimensions and proportions, and thus within his super-compound of rage, which should not have been rage at all, he was lost. After all, again the thought, those two might well just be friends, buddies, cohorts—mutual misfitters: and hadn't Joseph fixed-up (sort of) Arthur's meeting with Anna at The Checkmate—now almost one year ago—

no, more than that. . . Ought he run up to them?—
explain that he was in their neighborhood, across the
street, because he was now on the road, the acceptable
road, to being a Social Worker. No, he'd babble-away,
not-explaining but way-over overdone dissecting. He'd
be mannish, he'd be (he feared) womanish. He'd stare
too much at Anna, and she would see his strict focus as
enmity, screwball enmity—he'd have bet on this. And
even if he managed to divert his glare towards the
"betraying" Joseph, Anna would have seen through this
"ploy", she would have seen that Arthur's ignoring of
her was the most intense of sidewise scrutinies, and she
would have been angered by this patented childish
gesture—and Arthur would have been the one of the
three who came-away from the encounter the most hurt
by it—he a man who was about to become a placating,
soothing social worker. . . Instead of waylaying them he
followed them. . . The five torturous blocks to where he
prayed they were not heading. But that destination
loomed larger with each block: one turn on Paca Street,
one on Eutaw, to the five story converted tenement that
served now as one of the residences for University Med
School students and interns—and one in which Joseph
Lerner did not reside (his "rooms" were two blocks
south); and the one in which Arthur had experienced his
sorrowful penile stiffening failure with Anna Bass. The
two "betrayers" entered the converted tenement that
housed Anna's two rooms, and they disappeared.

VIII

The Department of Protective Services to which Arthur was assigned at the broken-down, jaundice-walled Welfare building was, logically off to the side: it had its own, equally decrepit, "wing" of Welfare. Just too many ex-convicts, "jailbirds", were committed—or assigned—to a compulsory "membership". It was mostly men, of any age—but the majority was young. And, of course, black. It almost seemed to Arthur, as he trained, that negritude was a requirement for "entry and belonging". And, uniquely, something else: As, as they say, "a pickpocket sees only pockets", could it have been that a transman sees only transmen?—for Arthur was, in Protective Services, coming to see—or believe that he saw—slews of gender variants, slinkers and aggressors. Such affinity of identity and sight had not been characteristic of Arthur before, indeed quite the opposite—he'd envied (and he'd sort-of hated) the "normalcy" of other men, *and the abnormalcy* (he seldom thought of transwomen, even when he thought of muscular Anna Bass, who might have put him in mind of such women although *she was not such a woman*), oh he tried to hide it, but Arthur just begrudged average men, they who had been brought into the world in their proper-set gender places, just like rich kids who had been dropped-down from heaven into privilege and money (as he had been himself)—Arthur had always seen, out of his own history of gender-deprivation, every male who he saw as perfectly privileged to be normal, and happy, plainly unperverse. But for some reason his sexual pickpocket syndrome seemed to have been brought out now by the endless stream of "societal misbegottens" who made their (oh so reluctant) ways into Protective Services, stumbling, prancing, tiptoe sneaking, barging with unstated threat, even sauntering with buckets of false-confidence as if they were doing Arthur and his social work colleagues a big favor by "visiting". Of course he knew that such a transman multitude was a statistical impossibility, and a coincidental improbability, but nevertheless there you were—or there Arthur was. Even knowing that these suspicions of his were the products of projection, and rather major projections at that, such did not stop him from spontaneous speed-projecting.

And, ridiculously, even amidst his sessions-training, he might slant the usual Social Work imprimaturs of "How do you feel about that?" or "Are you continuing to associate with the same crowd that you 'hung-out-and jived-with'?" (the social work text advised, to avoid rejection-stuffiness, the occasional insert of idiom, albeit mild), Arthur might augment The Usual with questions, meant to be deep-sympathetic, such as "Is there anyone you can talk to about your . . . problem?"

"What 'problem'?" they might answer, nostrils aflare at Arthur's perceived "D-L" (down low) pry-ass shit-snoopiness.

Thus Arthur might just level an empathic stare and a soft dropping of his head, to signify a tender 'I-am-with-you.' These men, after all, they had not had the economic good fortune that Arthur had had to afford The Surgeries. They had, in Arthur's brotherly (sister-ly?) mind and heart, (his deluded heart?) to live with it, "the lowest shit". To suffer. And no doubt (again, in Arthur's projecting mirror-mind) the untreated, un-solved, sexual conversions and reconversions and forced adaptations, plus the predatorial cruisings and "rough trade work" at the harbor hidey-holes, and thus all such infinite frustrations, these had been a great factor in these male delinquencies and crimes and rages that Arthur was being trained to treat—*treat!?*—and Arthur was almost immediately—from an instinctive jump-street rich-boy empathy (and fucked-sex sym-pathy)—training himself to improvise-treat upon, along-with and aside-from the run-of-the-mill, the "normal" established "accepted" ghetto-miseries and lack of education and bucks and lack of opportunities.

"It's so difficult, I know," Arthur might say, "when what you want to be, with women or with men, it just cannot be, you just want to live in the world as your true self, and you're prevented from that—and so, well, especially in the tough ghetto where you live, people can't consider every nuance, every wound of another person, they've got so many of their own scrapes and cuts, so they can be cruel, and so—."

"Whatinfuckdoodlin' y'all babblin'bout, jackass?!"

That was the usual approximate version of sullen-aggressive reply parried his stilted (well-meant) way. These tough men felt insulted.

But patient Arthur: "Well, if you don't want to talk about it, I understand. But, you know, you shouldn't hold it in; and you can trust me—I've suffered. You know, you really ought to talk about it."

So thus here had been the representative samplings of Arthur's usual offerings and responses. Never, never, *never*, did he go so far as to give-out-with, or even imply, his own transmanhood, with its historical jockeying confusions—which he was coming to feel should have been giving him a leg-up in social-work understanding, and, hopefully, ultimately if not at first, good plain help. Even more than with mime, he had learned the ins-and-outs-of human affinity and its absence or its loss. In fact, where he was finding himself now, was in the throes of the very opposite of mime. He was not copying, or interpreting, or rendering a surreality of human behavior, or mocking it with fun-hall warped mirror reflections; he was perceiving men in a deeper way, he was becoming an integral part of it all. This was a kind of anti-mime. This was the real deal.

There were complaints about him, and his supervisor Dwinski-Dwin had to call him in:

"I know you want to help, Arthur, but you've got some pretty tough characters affronted by you; they feel like you're mocking them, downing them, calling them, well, I'll use 'their' words: 'pussies'. And"—went Dwinski-Dwin, half-rising from his desk chair as if he were trying to act-out in disbelief his next words— "coons from Downtown Pluto. You're calling them, or implying to them, they're that, that queer measure, unthinkable off-specimens of our species."

"God," said Arthur, "that's not my intention. That's the last thing. I was trying to be on their level—in a good way."

"Arthur, your life's been pretty traumatic, I know that."

Dwinski-Dwin sat back down, slow-sinkingly; his lips went their-usual and draped social-prophylacticly over his teeth. "I know you want to be part of a team, I think so; but you're looking for brotherhood in all the wrong places, Arthur—the very wrongest of all places. I think this can only damage you."

He reached across his cheap city-requisitioned blond desk and took Arthur's hand, and squeezed it some, his large brown eyes ballooning so as to render his large brown Mexicanlike head seem small—the combination being how he must have expressed pathos—mixed pathos?—for his own "clients".

But that loaded word 'brotherhood' of Dwinski-Dwin's, it got Arthur seeing in his mind Joseph Lerner, his only confidante, the one buddy in all-the-world to whom he had told of his "problem", his dichotomy-of-being, and who had "betrayed" him with sweet strong Anna Bass. Why in the world should he expect any of the-losers-of-the world to confide in him, when look what he'd got for confiding in his (supposed) pal Joseph? Where in the world was trust?

"Hello, Arthur? Are you there?"

"Yes."

"You look unscrewed. Skewed. Not here."

"I'm sorry."

In the rather cramped office of Dwinski-Dwin, once again half-staring out the window past the bizarrely sympathetic-intrusive (and cloaked) features of little Dwinski-Dwin's swarthy face, Arthur saw the Medical School across the street, where Anna worked and chummied-herself with Joseph. Arthur sat up straight, rigid with intimidation and antipathies—the selfsame badges and stamps that his "badass clients" wore when facing him:

Boy, am I here!

"While you're working here," said Dwinski-Dwin, who was still holding Arthur's hand, "and especially while you're doing interviews with these men, you must forget who you are. Now, I realize that that's one tough order, considering who you are, Arthur, and who you've been in your life; but you really will have to try—I'm serious."

My mind, it definitely has gone cockeyed: me thinking right now that Dwinski-Dwin himself quite maybe is transman. His holding my hand, his slow-jumpy gestures, they're tentative-strong, his trying understanding, his—this is weird—his not firing me, or even really warning me. I suppose they just need social workers very bad.

"Do you feel that you can try?" asked Dwinski-Dwin.

"What?-Huh?" Arthur went.

"Where are you, Arthur?"

His supervisor had finally removed his hand from Arthur's, but too slowly, skin-slidingly, as if tendering a no-word message.

Arthur noted that—"message" was it?—but he had again gone rebounding, backing-back to imagining the "love-affair" that his "friend" Joseph Lerner was having with the one girl in his life that he so far felt that he understood or came close to understanding or even wanted to understand. All this despite the fight that they had had—over what else but *misunderstanding*: *Anna Bass-Anna Bass-Anna Bass-Anna Bass-Anna Bass-Anna Bass* . . .

Not even caring very much for this Dwinski-Dwin character, this lame-feeble "supervisor", this short, dark-complexioned syrup-acting Montezuma-Jew-cipher with his eyes now gone to a sweet-sardonic superiority, this in comparison to the long-gone elegant Cadeau Courir who could sail through life, oh the graceful Cadeau Courir who Arthur could not be, not by a longshot, Arthur not even caring if this Dwinski-Dwin embarrassment of a good noblesse-obligey Jewish man with his phony name elevation should be struck by a garbage truck leaving the DSW this evening, and dying, really, true—nonetheless Arthur (not the nicest guyish thingy in the world), he broke down before this ersatz stiff-of-a-man at his desk and began bawling, a tear actually formed and fell down over his cheek (he didn't wipe it away—that'd have been girl-worse). Like a drowner in one split-second (so they say) he traced-out his life and its aching wantings and its torturous mis-leadings and false-promisings, his fears of his own true hollowness which was at the bottom of his self—which was no self—and which he tried to cover-up by being "sensitive", or rather *acting* sensitive, and even by hating, too much hating, as if *any* hating was right in life—and how being now a social worker, or a *trainee* (he added quickly so as not to insult or presume and/or diminish this career choice, which he feared might be his last before he—oh this was too horrible to picture, to think, before he—what would it be? a bridge? pills?

a rope? he had no requisite savvy how in strict-Left-leaning Maryland he might buy a gun.), how being now a social-worker *trainee*, even if he was awkward by trainee standards, even though he had, so far, failed at *objectivity*, he could be, if left to develop, a *good* social worker, no, an *excellent* social worker—and all this while a good portion of his staring still streamed straight past the object of his confessions (most internal), and towards the Medical School of sweet Anna—until, not so objective himself, the stiff Mexicanesque Jew-hating Jew (as Arthur could not stop seeing him) Dwinski-Dwin, rose from his chair behind his desk (which occupied a good three-quarters of his office), came round to Arthur, who had been seated but quickly stood, as if in defense as well as politeness—for Dwinski-Dwin hugged Arthur—fucking *hugged* him. He held Arthur round the back and he patted—and then he came-out with: "You know, Arthur, it is said: Female-to-Males like you, they pass in the streets, while Male-to-Females, they pass only in the sheets."—thus said that hostile bastard. Hostile screwed-up straight-faking bastard. *Worse than me!* Except then Dwinski-Dwin, he went and he kissed Arthur on the lips. *Kissed!* Which, gesture or passion or intimate-understanding, or undoing of what he had just said was *not* received by Arthur with revulsion. . . which non-revulsion at this homosexual THING, this transgressive audacity, did, while non-revolting, revolt Arthur Becker with a sudden battering of his insides—Arthur who always these days felt that he had had far enough off-beat perverse symptomatology in his life and had junked it, for good—*but damnit he was a Man! And was this really homosexual on Dwinski-Dwin's part, or* *mine?—I did <u>not</u> send, I did not posture, I did not lure him! . . . Was I not administered enough testosterone? No, abundant testosterone bears no relationship to male-Gay or male non-Gay—everybody knows that. Have I then, even with all my female equipment taken-away, and me bidden a happy good bye for its not being Me, have I yet too much remainder of estrogen sticking to the walls of my DNA? like old paint—but they told me at the hospital that getting all that testosterone I got will provide an overpowerment of any stubborn-clinging estrogen, I won't be any what-they-call a genderqueer or androgynous, like, say Mick Jagger—at least like how he looks. . . Or? . . . Well, the 'or' was of course that Dwinski-Dwin was sheer homo, was a queer, gone filaying. But The Supervisor had seemed too blatant in his natural hug and kiss—as if he'd been displaying that A Man Does With A Woman What Is A Man's Prerogative and a Woman's Eliciting and Satis-faction Is A Woman's Prerogative and Her Way— Along With the Woman's Anti-Prerogative. . . And so what do I do now?*

No, he must be a Queer, that Queer, covering-up like I do with The Transgender Crap.

No, I've got to face it, he sees me as a girl—without his even knowing it.

I wonder if, like with me, this is troubling him.

Or if he is well-past that.

Which then I'd have to admire.

Or, worse, to him I'm just a Thing.

IX

At 5 PM (actually 5:08, as he did not wish to appear, ever, as a clock-watcher, as he was *not* a clock-watcher—especially in this new job at which he wished to succeed in his determined Helping endeavors) he went lurking outside University Medical School and Hospital, which was across the wide street, he side-stepping this-way-that patients with canes (the newer innovative ones with tripartite rubber bottoms for better balance), and he dodged round patients employing clunking shining walkers, and patients in wheelchairs being brought in and almost causing a wheelchair traf-fic jam (and he despising that he felt this unquashable rush of superiority to the ill and broken), and he self-consciously using as a concealment prop *The New York Review of Books,* which he'd just bought—*for eight dollars yet!*—at the corner kiosk (and he randomly opened it to an article, which it turned-out he could actually read and comprehend, forcing himself to (as he couldn't care squat about its contents), it being about how American football had evolved out of English rugby, which had evolved out of *English* football, i.e. soccer: *all this fucking sports-evolving, and here is Me, The Great Sex-Devolver.* He had never before read in *The New York Review,* but he did know that it was *the* pop-intellectual periodical, which was fortified in Arthur Becker's mind by the authenticating fact that it was produced in pulp newspaper form, it was not a shiny magazine like *The Atlantic* or *Harper's.* Likely it needn't be said here that Arthur was not a reader—he almost hated to read, it was so tedious, line upon line upon line, fact upon fact upon fact, or theory the same, it controverting the theory of the week previous, and as soon as you finished whatever you read you forgot it. At least Arthur did. His main goal in life now was not to be an intellectual, even a phony one, but simply, a man who Helped. A man who could behave as a Man. And this most assuredly meant, front and back, not just poverty and deprivation, everpresent as they were, but the Sexual—well, for him. After all Arthur was plagued by that crying need which superseded and substantiated to possibility all other needs—that being to have women see him as a Man. Experience him as a Man. And this was especially true, without his even thinking about it, because he had been—in effect—a woman. Or, okay, a girl. A woman by destiny. And destiny was *wrong.* Destiny ate shit. His (or his-her) destiny had been, finally, defeated by him, it had been denied. But he only felt that Great Denial at moments when he was feeling triumphant, or happy. And such moments were yet so awfully rare. Yet.

Anna Bass came out of the medical school, and again in the company of Arthur's friend and confidante Joseph Lerner. Both of them were decked-out, if you could call it that, in their surgical greens—this was comical and as it was dress for healing, it was perversely haughty *('I'm a doctor and you're not!'),* so it was intimidating, and it lent a sort of kinship, an intimacy to the couple—who Arthur hoped, still, was not no-way-in-hell a couple. At least Joseph's arm was not about Anna's shoulders, those powerful bulwarks you could call them, nor was the traitor's arm about her waist. But really the operation-functionality-looseness of the surgical greens went a decent way towards swallowing the swell of Anna's muscle, so that she looked considerably more girlish than Arthur remembered her. She and Joseph were laughing as they walked, it appeared that they maybe were repeating, reliving, some incident that had taken place that day in school at the hospital—and, ridiculously, with no hospital knowledge whatsoever aside from what he had seen on TV hospital shows, Arthur tried to imagine what it was that had got these two into their shared conniptions.

Hiding behind The New York Review of Books?— that's *a good coward one for me.* And then to hear: "So what's Chomsky have to say about Schlegel's being unfair to Hegel? What's . . .—oh forget it."

It was Joseph, his best (and still only, if friend) friend. And the mockery, had it happened in days before Joseph had cut him out with Anna it would not have fired Arthur ferociously, as it did now. He swelled-up, he steamed, he experienced these bumpings in his chest, in his pulse, as if his heart wanted to abandon his motorworks and jump out, but he still was able to observe that Anna herself was not in league with Joseph, she was not mocking Arthur. . . Yes, she was grinning, okay she was, but with that soft hesitant smile of shyness that Arthur had remembered, that sweet politeness that he had pictured on many nights as he lay in bed alone, but he saw too much of it as a smile of both sympathy and, well, pity—and therefore not a smile to be directed at a Man's earned manliness.

Anna's kindness of expression towards him, despite himself, just infuriated Arthur more.

Damn his good friend Joseph, who knew of his "problem" with manliness-being and was nonetheless rendering it worse.

And obviously it took no IQ of 170 to realize that both of these med students knew why Arthur was loitering outside their med school.

And had he not earlier experienced that "queer" confrontation with Dwinski-Dwin, that actual hug-and-*kissing*, and been struggling with what it meant and what he should have done in reaction, Arthur might well have hit Joseph, who was probably, with his scoliosis-hunchiness and his turkey-neck-gobble-geekiness, and hips wide as a small table's, the only Man who Arthur could have beaten-up. . . Of course, muscle-Anna could have beaten-up Joseph too.

And Arthur.

Was she attracted only to such men?

Attracted? Arthur imagined quirky-bodied Joseph "planking" sturdy-bodied Anna with a Joseph-hardon that his "friend" no doubt had had no problem achieving, and was sturdier than the rest of him.

Good Anna asked Arthur if he'd like to come with them.

"Where you going?"

By now though, rethinking his rethoughts, Arthur had forced himself, counter to himself, to consider

Joseph's friendship in a good way—*he had to*—and lock-on-it as something of seventeen years' duration, since Kindergarten, a tie that should not and could not be broken—unless Arthur wanted to live in life's lurking solitary confinement. And sure this re-regard required no small efforting. But face it, he and Anna had tried and fallen short and had even had bad words for each other—so Joseph had legitimate passport. Withal then, Arthur did not want to lose this one guy. Who else did he have? Dwinski-fuckin-Dwin?

Life without friends is life without anything—which is life without life, life without living! In a way you can't even have a Lover if you don't have a friend.

Anna said that they were on their way to Martick's, the jazz bar on Mulberry Street where med students and interns and residents often walked the six blocks to after their grinding work-study daytimes. Along the walk Joseph kept directing their conversation to the amygdala and experiments with learned and innate fear and PTSD, and although this amygdala stuff might well have been what was occupying them before Arthur joined them, he found Joseph's sticking to it, what Arthur could not possibly have a clue about, and Joseph's hanging onto it, and corralling it, impolite and crudely competitive. And maybe, Arthur wondered, if aside from being excluded by Joseph-and-the-amygdala he was being (intentionally) described as well. Arthur's opprobrium said Fucking bastard Joseph. . . Martick's was the last jazz bar alive in Baltimore; it was hardly fancy, just old chipped wobbly wooden chairs and un-intentionally usage-crenelated tables, no waiters or waitresses (you fought your way to the bar and brought drinks back to your table) and clouds of marijuana smoke amidst rushes of pseudo-hipster clatter (oldtime hipster, the real hipster, not its nowtime fashion opposite)—it has since been converted into a French restaurant. The same jazz group played every night but Mondays—piano, alto sax, and bass. The threesome took a table towards the rear where it was shaded in a benign and discreet (and inexpensive) light. Arthur loved jazz, it really was the only music that he cared for—he had been ridiculed and ragged-on, especially at Carnegie-Mellon, for his disinterest in Bob Dylan and The Stones, the latter of whom were a joke to anyone who looked at them and listened, and even the "hip-rhythm, hip lyric" types like Lou Reed, who seemed to be always trying too hard to show themselves as coolly disdainfully untrying. Folk music was completely beyond Arthur's ken. "Saints" like Woodie Guthrie annoyed him, although he was heartrent by that man's woeful death. But if the music was jazz, real jazz, not "soft jazz" like Kenny G, it was music; if it was other, it was noise, or ambient sound, or distraction, or bad taste. He could listen interminably to Dave Brubeck with the brilliant Paul Desmond on the most lyrical alto sax in existence, or to the romanticized cleverness of Bill Evans. Needless to say, the group at Martick's could in no way rival the brilliance of Brubeck's men or Evans, but this evening, when the threesome entered, they were playing Bill Evans's "Waltz for Debby", so Arthur was put in a lighter mood than had occupied him while they had been walking, and he became bold enough to look at Anna in a way that he felt was romantic and not stupid lovelorn—and he could see that she did not not like it. During this well-worked-on "look" of his he actually managed to trample on that feeling that was really always with him, within him, and in some varying quantity, often in some loaded iron weight, that he was partly a girl and could never climb the rungs of that damned identity ladder all the way out of costume to the one hundred story top of liberation and into thoroughgoing manliness-with-lurking-dick. He manipulated his shoulders up-and-back, as maybe an athlete would, and he looked his best dreamily throughout the Bill Evans song.

"Oh what a sap," said Joseph, patting Arthur's hand.

"No he's not a sap," said Anna. "He loves the music. I do too."

Joseph said, "I didn't mean the music."

He blatantly did a burlesque rolling of his eyes.

"Don't you feel it?" asked Arthur, though he well knew that Joseph was caricaturing him, not the players onstage.

"I don't feel it," Joseph said. "It's Schmaltz City."

And this guy is my best friend.

Arthur had the urge to hold Anna's hand, which rapped and bounced on the table, keeping rhythm. But he couldn't bring himself to do it. Joseph would no doubt have taken-in this gesture with amusement; and Anna's hand was no little bit larger than Arthur's: his placing his hand on hers might even have appeared as stage parody. Or worse—whatever worse was. Sin?

"Bill Evans died from drug overdosing," said Anna. "He was only in his forties.'

Arthur knew that, and he was impressed that Anna did. And that she knew the song being performed was Bill Evans's.

Joseph pretended to be indifferent. He looked about the club with that faraway countenance concocted to annoy people and to diminish them—as if his thoughts were of far more importance than their petty ones.

Arthur despised that look, and he was in the process of divining for some comment that might bring the superior-faced Joseph down to his level, or better, to beneath it, when he noticed a group of young black men seating themselves at the next table. One of these young men was Jamil Tandon—he was one of Arthur's clients. One of those sullen-threat kids in their early twenties who had been recently released from Maryland State Prison. Jamil was a bit over six feet tall with super-curly hair like heated licorice, his complexion was a kind of caramel, he wore no moustache as his lips were not black-guy "super-size", his hands—Arthur immediately took notice of this—they were larger than were Anna's large hands. Jamil had stolen a BMW 318i "corniche" from the sprawling Stevenson ranch house of Doctor Irving Raksin, who was the biggest endodontist and oral surgeon in Baltimore, and who was also the neighbor of Arthur's parents Mark and Elaine (just three long-stretch houses away). Doctor Raksin's two sons had both gone to Harvard—one was now a psychiatrist in Manhattan, the other a neurologist at UCSF in San Francisco. Both boys were probably, by this time, married, and floating on success's wings. Naturally, Arthur was very envious—even hatefully so. Which attitude was only added-to by what he had read in Jamil's record: that Doctor Raksin had had the option of dropping charges against mischievous Jamil, who had only wanted a joyride in a type of car that he would never be fortunate enough to own, but the combination endodontist-oral surgeon decided not to have the court go easy: he would teach the black kid a lesson. His "beamer" had been returned scratchless (nearly)—although apparently the car's radio station had been changed from Baltimore's one classical to one of Baltimore's many competitive hip-hoppers. Quite the insult and offense—and inconvenience. Although it had occurred to Arthur that the "lowclass" station change had quite possibly been effected not by Jamil but by one of the car-recovering police.

"Hey, Jamil," went Arthur. He refrained from uttering the white-man suck-up, 'My man'—which was whispering in his ears, begging to be transmitted.

Jamil nodded, eyes loaded beebees—the perfect hostile-sullen, the disdainful-impervious, which, one might say, he had been community-trained for.

"You know those cats?" said Joseph, sensing a perfect portal to a put-down.

" 'Cats,' " mocked Anna. "Oh Joseph, you're trying to be so hip. 'Cats' went out with Burroughs and Kerouac and maybe even Rudy Vallee and twenty-three skidoo."

"Who, what skidoo?" Joseph wisely laughed at his so unsubtle-subtle-"witty" self.

Arthur did not laugh at his competitor and "friend". He explained in a low voice that handsome Jamil was one of his "clients".

There was no way that Jamil could not lend a youthful antagonistic ear and figure out an approximation of what Arthur was saying.

"Hey" said Joseph, "he's one of yours, then maybe you oughta sit with him and his."

In sweet reproach Anna punched Joseph upside the shoulder.

Joseph made a hurt-act face and held and rubbed the

wound, the big-man belittling the little-girl in a, supposedly, lovesome way.

Arthur wanted to hit his "friend". This whole deal
was turning into a less than sophisticated poker game.

He called over to Jamil, "So (again, he fought-off
anything like 'my man') you like jazz?"

Jamil sullened back, "Nah, we're casin' the shit-
house, we're workin'-up a robbery. WhachoothinkI'm-
sittin' here for?"

Arthur faked a conspiratorial buddy-buddy laugh. He
enjoyed his client's temerity—or at least he told himself
that he did.

Joseph grinned at Arthur's taut cross-purposes, and
then he checked it. He could tease Arthur, yes, but
when it came to fully grinding his uncomfortable friend
into the ground—No, he could not do that. . . And he
was no little bit frightened by those black boys. Which
Arthur was too—outside of Social Services he was
vulnerable, a potential enemy, one of the historical ex-
ploiters—Arthur had been taught that in training class.
But he was no coward. He wasn't near as discomfited
as was Joseph. You couldn't but see the tension tighten
Joseph's face.

Arthur found himself wishing within himself that he
were like this threatening Jamil. He knew this was
crazy, so different from his having wished that he had
been like the graceful-kind Cadeau Courir. But wasn't
life crazy, like it's having stuck him hard with this
gender dysphoria that he really hadn't triumphed-over
just by the impersonal machinery of his physical surgeries and hormones. No, those medical manipulations
were too easy, as hard as they were, act and after-act.
More was needed—more of the mental, more of the

emotional. And here was this black boy, this beautiful black boy, this felon, who likely had no future but had at least with his up-front personage won the gender lottery and had got to give-out goodly doses of gender *euphoria*—oh Jamil could certainly, easily, get the girls—even if he had lost the American *socio-econ* lottery and could not get a decent brain-bank or a decent job and would probably wind-up again in prison or dead at a young age. You envied a young guy who you did not envy, him with his broad shoulders (broader than even weightlifter Anna's, and damned slim-sleeker too), his narrow hips, his long neat caramel arms, his strong hands; that envy of yours for all this which every man (who wanted it) might deserve, No?—if what we had here were a perfect world. So, thisall was the up-shot of the sick story-line of this damned gender dys-phoria that had come to the never-ending flaying of Mister Arthur, the son of a praised athlete (his dad Mark was built pretty much like Jamil), come to him for no good reason at all. . . And you knew that this black guy, who did not envy you damned well *did* envy *you*.

Life's balance, its queer equilibration: Hohohohoho!
Why did God operate by way of this bad shit?

"You're looking at those guys," observed Joseph, "as if they're in a fraternity that's rejected you." Joseph now was in the midst of concocting the ambiguity of a smirk that was also serious and sympathetic.

"Stop-it, Joseph," Anna said.

She reached across the table, which by now felt as if it were planted in a shroud of jazz darkness and did not exist; she reached as if she were going to console Arthur—and console him for what? she wasn't sure—

his very being?—but midway across she halted her
reach, and Arthur considered that her message was not
ambivalence but a message: I have reached halfway—
the rest, the remainder half, is up to you—I, well, *care*!
And why was it that Arthur did not complete the
contact? consolidate it (*I now pronounce us . . .*)—it
seemed because he was embarrassed-to in front of his
polaric "cohorts" of bad black client and long-life intimate (and recent-time mocker) Joseph. . . And anyway,
why should this touching of a woman be so difficult
before his black client? Good question.

And the answer, he was quite sure: for some instances, glancing at Jamil and his boys, envying them,
Arthur had experienced the sensation, it was vague and
really had to be ferreted-out and identified, and accepted, the sensation that he was wearing women's clothing—a skirt and blouse and underthings—and that
Jamil could plainly see this which was not there, and
which perception was certainly horrifying—beyond
that. Arthur was ascribing supernatural bigot powers to
this ghetto hoodlum, and he wondered how he would
deal with Jamil at their next scheduled meeting. It was
as if—and he'd had this fleeting feeling right there and
then in the jazz club where he was not more than two
darkened feet from Jamil—it was as if Jamil, in some
transubstantiated way, were the spirit, the ever-spying
spirit, of his jock and big-shot father, Mark Becker.
Perhaps that similarity, or affinity (which Arthur knew
was not real, was not real at all) was the implied
potency, the whole subliminal enemy that ever-haunted,
and that had been represented for Arthur by, at
Carnegie-Mellon, his fellow students Ted Danson and
Albert "Einstein" Brooks, and of course by the strongly

graceful Cadeau Courir who could glide like even a Pavlova while maintaining his manliness foursquare as a Baryshnikoff—even (*how?!—that was the secret!*) magnifying it. And add to that tough-enough amalgam Arthur's failed, cutoff efforts to at first be an "Italian" politician like overlord Thomas D'Alesandro, or, then, a gun-hipped cop. . . So yes, he was sure now that, if he had any future in life at all, any place of purpose and longevity and worthwhileness and authority, it was as what he had so recently become, a social worker.

The small Martick's trio was now playing another number that Arthur loved. It had been done beautifully, acted-out in song by Frank Sinatra so many years ago— but now this group was doing it, or trying to—they were off a bit, but it didn't matter—doing it with a bossa nova beat, with the piano player in baritone working hard at singing, or crooning. *Change Partners* was the song—

> Must you dance
> Evv'ry dance
> With the same
> Fortunate *Mannn*? . . .

and there was just *something* about that languid Brazilian rhythm, its halting confidence, its grounded nasality, even its near-monotone, it so seldom rising even beyond a fifth (in Drama at CMU Arthur had been required to take Basic Music, and he had learned all the seven modes—everything didn't have to be just rooted in the middle of the piano in C [quite the allegorical lesson for Arthur, had he then caught the allegory]; he himself loved that muted startout in E flat [or was it C minor?], which the players here at Martick's were attempting), there was Something here, inherent, that got Arthur to move away—as Cadeau Courir would have done, probably lightly in the air too—away he went from women's stuff, *to a woman*: He did not touch Anna's hand, but he'd begun, he'd ventured, this emboldened-deep vetting, this sort of goggling, into those shy eyes of Anna Bass, and he did not feel comic or overplaying, and he was sure that Anna saw that, he was sure that his fixing-himself on Anna had ridden-over his sexual failure with her and their terrible fight-of-identities that had been so painful in her claustro-phobic room at the University, or at least it had shown to her that he was bravely making an attempt, a *manly* attempt at connection (or even a womanly!) and that he hoped there was yet some possibility between them—even with her knowing the "truth" that he had begun life as a girl-in-form.

Anna caught Arthur's look, she held onto it for some moments, and then she turned it down by dropping her eyes towards the table.

Arthur wondered if Anna had at all been moved by the song. If she had any true jazz sensibilities. If she could feel the romance, as a *woman* should feel it, no? by the rhythmic-lyrical stops and hesitations in *"Change Partners"*, and then the deep baritonic rises and rushes. He could not help having his instinctive doubts, based upon Anna's manly muscularity—this thickness of hers seemed to militate against the Brazil-ian-black-Latin subtleties of the song, the dance within it—it just did. But this feeling, Arthur knew, was painted by his own dreamy prejudice. . . But why then did he feel as if he liked her so? So much.

X

"That girl you was with," said Jamil, "at the club."

"Yes?"

"She fuckin' looked like she was a *man,* you know that?"

Arthur couldn't believe that this "client" of his had actually come out and said that. Worse was that Jamil was actually glittering, almost religiously, saintly, his caramel birth-veneer of skin was a monk's cowl, it was well-suited to the streams of bright-fade autumn sun careening off this limb, then that, of the one oak tree outside Arthur's office window, that age-gnarled oak.

"She wasn't a man," Arthur said. "She is not a man. No way. She's a woman."

"You stone sure of that? Guess you ought to know."

Arthur wanted to reach over his desk, take his fist and, come-what-may, plough innuendoing-insulting Jamil straight into his miserable nigger mouth. Yes, that "nigger" description that laid-out flat in his mind, in his supposed unprejudiced mind, there it was arising. Arthur was no saint—and he knew it. He had even

161

forgotten the social work technique-mantra that would
have been applicable in this instance: He ought have
replied to Jamil something on the order of, 'What
makes you think she looked like a man?'—thus turning
Jamil's observation back onto itself, back onto Jamil, so
that Jamil the recipient, Jamil the felon, could seriously
consider who he was and why he felt he had to say such
a hurtful thing—especially to a man who was trying to
help him, not hurt him. But the sick part, the very sick
part of Arthur's thought and reaction was, and he knew
it, it was because he was attracted to this guy; and the
sickest part of that attraction was of course his envy of
this, face-it (for a normal man), slimebag, his covetous
emulation-thing for this unenviable unwanted uncovet-
ed unemulation-thing-shithead (for a normal man), his
just goddamn *wanting-to-be-like* the guy. All life was a
battle, for both Jamil and for Arthur. Battles same and
battles different—that were very much the same.
Struggle just was struggle. At a loss Arthur came out,
finally, with, "She was a *girl*, okay?—and I'm sure you
knew it, and I'm sure, just as *you* are sure, that you
know it—but felt that you had to *attack*, just as you
might in the streets, isn't that right!"

Not especially articulate or fluent, but on-the-spot—
especially for an angry-passive made-chaotic guy.
Arthur approved of what he had managed to get himself
to shpiel-out.

"Hey, okay okay okay." Jamil held up his hands in a
mime of his being arrested by a pistol-pointing cop.
Jamil added, "I didn'mean nuthin much by it." He was
smiling aggressively; and he seemed to be enjoying
himself and his provocation of his supposedly equani-
mous social worker.

"I think you did mean something by it."

"You sayin' I'm like hostile."

"You know the psychiatric words."

"Jail therapy." Jamil went knuckle-rubbing his black shirt chest in pride. "I was best student. And boy do I know the words."

"Yes I know you've been around the therapeutic block."

"Around it, in it, over it, and most certainly *under* it, my man. I know all the deals front edge. Boos'n'koos."

Arthur let the 'my man' take a therapeutic slide. Additionally, attempting some further nugget of cool, he did not ask what was meant by the ghetto-talk 'deals front edge' or the 'boos'n'koos'.

"Evabody's got their tastes," cracked Jamil, again smiling. "Cain't hold nuthin'gainst a man for his tastes. Like even for *that* man-girl-girl-man you got." Then the evil smile looped his lips again. "Total fucked-up as all our tastes may be."

"As you admit," said Arthur, holding on, "you are hostile."

"And I am proud to be ripe-set."

"Anybody in your shoes wouldn't be a 'man' if he weren't hostile. That it?"

"You got it, jim. We could close up shop now, and I could go on home. You want me to wear a T-shirt that's got a great big H stamped on it like an announce tattoo?: Hostile Man."

That suggestion was creative, it was clever—and Arthur was not of a mood to give the slightest credit to this slick creep who had insulted the woman who he decided, out of nowhere but jealousy—perhaps—that he loved. He also realized that he was being social-worked, by a "client" who was more trained and experienced than he at this professional mishigas, well it was a game, wasn't it. And, horror-of-horrors—at least it was so horrible to Arthur—he experienced, on his side of his desk, his thighs coming closed like a clamped sandwich, or rather like girls tend to do in skirts. He despised his natural doing that.

"You could 'go on home'," he said, repeating Jamil's declaration, and with his own hostility gone to uncapped swelling. "Except 'home' is not where you would go."

"You do got dat tune right."

"You'll wind-up back in prison, you know."

Jamil now ostentatiously, aggressively, gave Arthur the once-over, as if Arthur were applying for a job at a company CEO'd by Jamil. "You know, like that girl you and that other weak-shit shit was with, how she was so man-up, you got to know, just like *her* in the *other-op* way, *you* look *girl*-up—hope I ain't outta line." Smirk smirk. "But your shoulders, Mister Soshey-Worker, they ain't worth a shit. Your fingers are piddle-tippers, and you got a grace of a trace of the come-on *girl* lips, you know that?—you're paper mashay, you unnerstand what I'm sayin'?"

"What you're implying."

"No, '*sayin*'." Jamil did a towering brow raise, like they did overacting in old silent movies. "Oh yeah, '*implying*', college boy." Jamil enunciated that last word as if it were only used by Mister Chipsers and-the-like in thickest bifocals.

"I cain't work with no 'man' who looks to be like you."

Arthur's pathetic impulse—and he sure as hell knew

it was pathetic—was to say something of the order of 'give me a chance.'

I took all the girl-puberty inhibiting medications, but the docs did warn that you can only inhibit that "female-endogeny" just so much. And maybe I didn't take enough—as if anybody knows just what is enough!

I hate this goddamn Jamil. . . And I hate myself for the hating. This 'cat', he is bright, he is on-the-ball, except that it's one bad ball. He could become some-body, what with his creativity, his quick word-work smarts. But I'm so diddled and skunked by him that I've blown my chance of doing him his good, his deserved good, my working at improving him. As—what can I say!—I hate him.

Well, he hit me where it hurts, he's a honed-in missile, all ghetto IT, he's sheer racial Info Tech, a black bigot. I shouldn't use that pain of mine as excuse for letdown, as it's why I just started-in this new social-help field, but how many people in the world have a weakness like mine, such an Achilles heel.

Stop feeling sorry for yourself.

I can't.

Failure again, again, god-damn-me.

Stop feeling sorry for yourself!

Jamil just got himself up and, blackster-loping, all turbulent quintessence, he left the room, without Arthur announcing one word of alert or threat or dismissal. Jamil must have observed that Arthur's head was risen-up-back in its turmoil of thoughts and Jamil had seen therefore there was no reason to be in his "worker's" troubled weak-ass, empty air-ass, presence.

But this was an insult! another one, *too much!*—your client, this jailbird loser, he regarding you as even more of a loser than *he* was, and he then feeling the entitlement to simply get up and leave the office without permission—Arthur couldn't take this, even in his beaten state he couldn't. He ran out into the hallway, he saw Jamil hightailing-it, and he just about exploded: *"Get back here!*—if you know what's good for you."

Jamil turned, this Becker-man pussy more man than he'd let on. Jamil's eyes were shocked to a starker blackness than was usual for him—and they'd shrunk-down small, impotent beebees or sharpened ones. He was frozen in place. Other workers and other "clients" were watching, which put him in a bind: He could gain respect, and even a kind of perverted heroism, by disregarding Arthur's order and continuing on his way, going out the front door onto Greenmount Avenue, and "freedom". But what freedom would that be? The functional procedures of the DSS, of Welfare, would have him sought-out and arrested—and he knew what would follow, jail cell, court, bail inflated to the impossible, ugly crud-walled prison. . . He walked back to an Arthur who felt proud of himself for having done at least Something, powerful, potent. And Right.

"Sit," he said to a re-entering Jamil.

Jamil sat, even more sullen than when he had first entered the claustrophobic closet of a social-work room.

Arthur rolled up the sleeve of his right arm—he'd worn a button-down Oxford shirt—he loved these "classy" clingers even if they were the stock insignia of privileged stock market types (like his father). Arthur placed his elbow on his desk and raised his forearm. "You see me as a pussy," he said. "Is that it?"

Jamil said nothing.

"We're going to wrist-wrestle, you got any

objections?"

"Uh-uh, if you want it."

"I want it."

"Prove y'all can roll with the rollers?"

Jamil was grinning in a tide of bemusement. He had ghetto strength. He never worked-out, he didn't need to. He could slam this wimp-worker's arm and hand backwards down to the desk-top in nothing flat—he knew it—he could break the dickhead's flimsy arm. He wore a painted-up two-strap jersey, what they called a wife-beater, as it was the conventional-habitual shirt supposed-worn by poor wife-beaters who sat out on their fire-escapes for recreation (when they weren't beating their wives for recreation), white men these originators, in Brooklyn—the land of the shirt's origins. Jamil's shirt was tattooed with messages and drawings that were colorful and inscrutable. He matched Arthur's hand and arm in placement on Arthur's desk, and their hands grasped—it occurred to Arthur that this attachment of fingers and palms might resemble one of the universal ghetto-guy greetings. . . Arthur had made the wrist-wrestle challenge on impulse, he had a few times wrist-wrestled his onetime athlete dad and gone one-for-three, though he was sure that his one win had been a gimme from his caring father Mark; so he wasn't especially confident, he had worked-out in gyms and at home ever since beginning his hormone treatments— these, he'd hoped, to whisk him away from his original female "fluffiness"—but such presses and curls and pushups could only do so much with a nature-intended female body coated with its extra layer of female fat, unless—it did indeed occur to Arthur—you pictured how much it had done for Anna Bass, so probably she

had some excess of male DNA which she hadn't
wished to cop to?—she being maintained of pride,
absolute sticktoitive pride, in her femaleness, and
rightly so, she being so sweet and, well, female, in her
generous eyes and swollen lips and just generally in
how she was within herself—and so comfortably
within. . .

It was like a mime, that was Arthur's thought,
simple wrists like ghostly puppets, a minimalist texture,
what with the two men's grimaces and grunts as they
pressed against each other's hands (a few hand-farts
exuded, a kind of disgusting brotherhood), those hands
and their supporting-army forearms contending as if all-
the-world were in their dependence, their eyes not on
each other's eyes and not either on their hands and arms
but closed tight within their own essences, their
important crucial (seeming) senses of themselves. . .
Jamil, being lackadaisical considering his pussy of an
opponent—*just like a white nothin'burger tryin' to test
himself against a superior type of man (after-all who's
the biggest bulk of ballplayers in roundball [basketball]
and football)*—Jamil didn't start out with his full
strength, and Arthur did—and Arthur managed to pull
Jamil's "weaponry" toward his own side, maybe three-
four inches, Arthur swelling with joy within and seeing
maybe even victory and serious Respect, *manly* respect,
not social-worker jive respect, which maybe he could
work with with this too too arrogant Jamil—and Jamil,
seeing what was happening, what unbelievable
WRONG, he called-up his fullness—and still he could
not bring Arthur's wrist and forearm down to his side.
What he did manage though was, while Arthur held
steady, Arthur wouldn't have his extremity budged

towards a victor-Jamil, Jamil's stronger strength brought *all-of-Arthur,* him with his arm steady as if sculpted-in-place, as if rooted in his *manliness,* which brought Arthur in his rolling forward desk chair to the desk-edge, to Jamil. It was not unlike the Statue of Liberty yet upholding her Torch while some great ship-and-tugboats moved it from its moorings. So Arthur had won by not-losing, but had lost, in a way, by his wholeness-of-Arthur being rolled towards Jamil. E.g., losing.

Except, more than winning, Jamil had wanted to slam Arthur's arm down to that desktop on his side of it, he'd wanted to make a noise (which other social workers would hear and rush in and see), and Jamil couldn't do it, because Arthur, while (he excused himself to himself) was yet girl-weak in his female remnants, he yet had an arm and a wrist that were his first-macho heart and would not budge. So, Jamil did not feel as if he had won, not the wrist-wrestling contest.

"Y'all be some strong man," Jamil said. "Nobody'd'a-guessed."

Childishly, Arthur felt as if he had validated himself, and with one of the most important people with whom he'd ought to have validated himself.

"Your next appointment's next Thursday," Arthur said. "You can go on 'home' now."

Jamil did a vaudevillian's imaginary tip-of-the-top hat to his worker Arthur, and took off.

But Arthur's trainer and supervisor Harold Dwinski-Dwin had happened to have walked by Arthur's open office door when he was arm-wrestling Jamil Tandon, and he'd been flabberghasted and scandalized by what he regarded as this insipid roughhouse boyishness taking the place of perceptive psychological social working—and, although he did not admit it to himself, he experienced sharpish jolts of jealousy. And anger. . . So, at the end of the workday the little syrup-haired Mexican-looking Jewish fellow entered Arthur's office, as if he owned it, and sat, and crossed his arms over his chest bosslike while crossing his legs, almost girl-like. With his eyes narrowed for interrogation, and with a pitter-pat exactitude, he bluntly asked—

"What in the world did you think you were doing with that boy?"

Not knowing that Dwinski-Dwin had observed the determined strength bout, and in just about its entirety, Arthur calmly, and honestly, answered, "Therapy."

"*Therapy!?*" The entire first floor of the Protective Services Department could have heard the squeal. "That's not 'therapy' that you've learned *here*. Were you attempting to, uh, buckle-*up* to that boy? To make yourself his *buddy*?" Dwinski-Dwin enunciated 'buddy' as if it were maybe 'lover', or 'slave', and Arthur of course recollected his supervisor's having not so long ago touched onto something in himself and reached out and hugged and kissed him.

Is Dwinski-Dwin jealous? Or is he just following the company line?—which certainly requires variation at times, improvisation due to circumstance, due to who the people are who are involved. Dwinski-Dwin must know all that—he's made Supervisor for Chrissakes. He can't be such a puritanical stickler. That can't be what's required.

"I was working," Arthur said, "on making good contact, a kind of intimacy—I guess. That Jamil, he is one tough customer, he's so rebellious and a wise-guy, so I—"

"So you dropped-down to his own level. You descended. This is about the worst maneuver you can fall prey to, it lowers you in your client's eyes, even lower than he might have regarded you in the first place."

Dwinski-Dwin was now leaning over Arthur's desk, chin on fists, his elbows in support. And what with his Sephardic ochre skin, his so dark hair, he couldn't help but remind Arthur of black Jamil. Except of course that Dwinski-Dwin was only about five-six and Jamil was Arthur's height of six feet, and exceedingly handsome.

"With all due respect," Arthur said, "I didn't think I was, 'descending'. If anything, I believed I was—"

"You were *lowering* yourself—believe me."

"But shouldn't we be helping these boys develop a sense of equality?"

"Sure, once it's earned, yes. And it's earned by these 'boys' talking, learning to talk, about themselves, with some sense of self-knowledge and some sense of an improvement need. They need to unclutter and stop hiding and then *divulge* themselves, their weaknesses, their fears—and not just their hatreds, which is easy, too easy, that's their instinct."

Arthur closed his eyes, picturing that strenuous wrist-wrestling scene. That tough nut Jamil had certainly not seen Arthur as lowering himself. If anything he had come to see Arthur as heightening. If anything both 'boys' were raising their estimates of the other, despite their not wishing to.

"Please, Arthur," said Dwinski-Dwin, with the false-calm and half-lidded eyes of a boss delivering an order that was constrained and incontrovertible, "do *not* do what you did again. Not with that Jamil nor with any other of our clients."

Arthur said "Okay."—but he did try to inject at least a minor downsloped chord of reluctance and resentment and even rebellion. He had to, for his own self-respect. But he did say, "Okay," again.

Anyway, he knew that his moral victory in wrist-wrestle loss would get around. All the "jailbirds" on probation would learn of it, and they would regard him with more respect, he bet, than they did the lame-straight little by-the-book Dwinski-Dwin—and maybe more than all the other social workers around this dilap-idated DSS Welfare factory of despair. They certainly had zero regard for all their "fellow", "brother" black social workers—who had obviously still been rejected by the white managerial world of advertising or broker-ing or any bigtime entrepreneurial matters, even with a lithograph-scripted degree-upon-the-wall in Latin, that crud-degree likely issued by the black Baltimore Morgan State, or Howard U in D.C.

To Arthur's Okay, Dwinski-Dwin nodded, in a kind of stern approval that really said You'd-better-watch-out, and then he said, "There is something else."

What's he, putting me already on probation?

"I don't wish for you to be getting the wrong impression of what went on the other day between us."

Well here it comes. And anyway it wasn't 'between us', that weird hug and lip thing. It was all him—Mister Supervisor Dwinski-Dwin. All Him.

"I'm not gay," swore Dwinski-Dwin.

"Okay," Arthur said, extinguishing any impulse of expression.

"It's you, you know. You do know."

Arthur just shook his head No. Any vocal assertion of his non-gayness, he feared, would constitute, one, an assertion of his gayness, and two, an assertion of his boss's homosexuality.

"It's how you present," said Dwinski-Dwin. "I did not kiss a 'man' when I kissed you."

Thanks a lot—Arthur's ironic thought. *Thanks a fucking lot.* And this gay-accusation, coupled with Dwinski-Dwin's criticism of Arthur's manly "technique" with Jamil, unorthodox though it was, such had him unable to contain himself: He answered his "boss" with, "Well, I can tell you, when you kissed me (*and it was You who kissed Me, not the other way round*), you did not kiss a *woman.*"

"Well," said Dwinski-Dwin, rather obliquely, rather excusing nothing, rather maintaining his Arthur-appraisal in a way that was pathetic-petulant, "You do know, *Marta*, that *women* do make the best of social workers. You ought to make good productive use of your deepest instincts."

The bastard, he called me by my original birth name. I know that in my application he'd been fully apprised of my sex-change, but I didn't know that he had all my records, going back in ancient history even to my birth itself. . . And, knowing all this, he was attracted to me? Has he become unhinged by my noncomformity? What's wrong with him?

And with such thought, Arthur wasn't not aware that he was pilloring this little chubby Sephardic Jew in much the same way that he was ridiculed and stigmatized for so much of his own life.

And then that similarity did come to him, and he wondered if Dwinski-Dwin were, in the least, inclined to kiss Arthur now, once again, assuming he could get his fat little ass round Arthur's crappy little desk in time. It seemed unlikely, that was for sure, but then again the man's antipathy and scolding could have meant either that he was or he wasn't drawn to Arthur now—or that he was as confused as Arthur had been for most of his life. People do behave in such perplexing ways, so oppositional and counter-oppositional. For example, as Dwinski-Dwin left Arthur's office he turned back for an instant and said: "Arthur, have you considered FTM International?"

"Yes," said Arthur, "I've heard of it."

It was a support group for transmen.

But such a public pleading-whining-revealing-uniting-gathering as FTM was, although it may have done serious good as did AA for alcoholics, it was not the sort of thing for private-hermit-loving Arthur Becker, internal thinking, internal obsessing, God-ambivalent—and certainly hating—Arthur Becker. And the fact that it was recommended by the instinctively smarm-ridden and duplicitous Dwinski-Dwin made it totally off-limits, no matter Arthur's pain—even when he was overwhelmingly afflicted with his pain.

XI

After work, which included four other clients, with whom Arthur had felt that his "interactions" were well-done, confidently accomplished, scrupulously accomplished (due to his having wrist-wrestled Jamil so strengthfully—and the story of that legendary contest having gotten round), but after as well his strange interaction with his supervisor Dwinski-Dwin, Arthur went and straightaway took himself to the apartment of Anna Bass. If Joseph Lerner was there they'd have it out. Why in the world did Joseph, who was normal—not like Arthur and not like Anna (who was, true, not as "abnormal" as was Arthur)—why did normal (although bodily handicapped and distortedly slumped, but still a legitimate *birthman*) why did he, Joseph, want to be with Anna, especially as he had been the one who had recommended Anna to Arthur? Joseph had been his confidante and pal, his only friend—what was the story here? Competition? And if so, what a measly-sad competition. Was there no man to be trusted enough to be trusted?—*what a world of ugly rivalry!*

Arthur knocked on Anna's door, trying to rehearse what he might say to Joseph if his "friend" were there—use reason? emote with an emotion that was usually beyond him? attack as if almost crazed, which chaotic behavior was usually beyond him as well?—but no, do what you'll do in the passive-aggressive mis-leading-lead-soft-style of the smoothest social work—which, of course, face it, none of the cagey black parol-ees assigned to their camouflaging workers trusted? . . . Be everything, be all of these behaviors, just as he was, in his form (and maybe still yet in his psyche, if Dwinski-Dwin's behavior were to be put stock in [and excused?]), all things.

Joseph wasn't there.

They spoke, Anna sitting on her bed, but straight-up at the pillows and the bedstead; Arthur sitting on the bed way down at its foot—in this small med-student flat. From this prospect he noticed out the window that in the now twilight the Bromo Seltzer tower down the way had gone to lighting up in slanting lines of blue, which seemed to make Anna's room both cooler and warmer; it had been constructed in the image of the Palazzo del Vecchio in Florence. It was a Baltimore landmark, even a Baltimore pride; but it was also a Baltimore absurdity. Had the tower been made for housing something artistic, like a museum, or for even just a plain old office building it might have made some sense. As it was it was too much like Washington's Baltimore penis, on top of the fact that, instead of glorifying Papal religion it advertised curing stomach pain. . . On the bed now, Arthur at first apologized for his failure at sex days before—that image of the marsh-mallow-stuffing was so horrible and so comic—but then he said, boldly (surprising himself) that Anna's sweetness and consideration at Martick's, the jazz club, had heartened him and it reminded him that she, Anna, had a heart and still liked him, for what he was. He did not wish to add anything on the order of "Well, can't we be friends?" for that, he knew, was a sentence of flat love-death. And he did love this strange good woman, he did—and as past-reason as it was—he sensed within her a living love for him.

"Do you, are you," he asked, "with Joseph?"

"Joseph," she shrugged, as if in excuse (oh those powerful muscle-shoulders rising), "we see each other every day."

"I know."

"Closeness develops."

"Sure, but. . . "

Anna couldn't restrain her grinning at Arthur's 'but'. Her kindly grin was welcome but it also hurt.

Arthur could barely restrain from forswearing *I-love-you*.

He felt his fingers tightening. He was sure that Anna saw this. Well, she was a medical professional: she was trained to observe. . . Joseph had told Arthur that patients lied, all-the-time, to avoid operations that they needed, or medications, or just to show that they were stronger than the weak person they had been who had themselves first brought themselves to the doctor. The doctor had to observe. All the time.

Arthur washed his fingers with his dry hands.

A nutty notion struck Arthur—a kind of laugh, an ice-breaker: He might challenge this sweet powerful woman who had won Female PoseDowns, challenge her to a wrist wrestling contest. He being strong from his workouts intended at his not-being-a-woman. Should he win the wrist-wrestle though, did he win Anna?—or did he lose Anna forever, considering the pride that she must have felt for her strength beyond her sex but built-upon her sex. What sort of man did she want, did she really want?—for she did seem to want a man. When you considered that she hung-out so much with handicapped-slumpy scoliosised Joseph (and made love?—to a scoliosised penis?) you had to come to some kind of conclusion that she did not want an Arnold Schwarzenegger. But, when you considered her anger at Arthur's struggling failure in bed with her—oh that marshmallow-stuffing horribleness! that indignity beyond words!—and her "suggestion" that Arthur the transman find himself a nice transwoman ("Which *I* am not!")—you had to accept that she wanted no deep-closeness with any Arthurs either—*what had she been thinking!?*. . . But then, at Jazz Martick's, she had been so sensitive, so nice, so—to Arthur's way of thinking-feeling-hoping—she had been so drawing-of-him-in. People were within one person just so many people. Probably too many. They didn't just divest what they had first made investments in. . . Well, sometimes. . . Well, hopefully—or not? He was the perfect example of that, that desired confusion.

"Let's not try to make love," she said.

That startled him, it threw him off—but the absolute truth was that he experienced relief. He could almost have breathed-out visibly, audibly. In the whirled-confusion of his mind, he realized, that his romantic feelings were in the weird-child-heaven of wanting to have this woman, this wonderful woman, while not, in sex (necessarily) having her at all, while this not-having might still manage to have him have her, and have her beyond the "having" of betraying Joseph, or anyone—including himself. At least all this nutsy stuff for the time being. He recollected her sort of "lecture" to him on evolution at The Checkmate, that old-ladies' café in the shadow of the extending, growing-seeming, cement "penis" of George Washington, the cafe that had once been the "hippest" place in town and had devolved while believing that it had improved. Anna had spoken about how humans had evolved from rats to we creatures who had now rocketed their way to the moon. And how that evolving had justified, had demonstrated, had made undeniable, the in-between existences of both she and he, as if they too were instruments, not of human faultiness or mistake but roundabout progress. Something eventual.

Who can wait for Eventual?

"Can we touch?" he asked, and then turned away—there was the blue-lit Bromo Seltzer tower. He realized that he might just now have preferred an undreamy rational disc of morning sun served with coffee.

"Touch," she said. "Well, we had better."

She was smiling as if at once teasing and consoling.

"I love to touch," she said.

"Me too. . . I love it. . . . So I can come up to you on the bed?"

"Unless your arms are as long as George Washington's dear hooked penis."

"You know, I was just thinking of it."

They laughed, without forcing it. Well, not so much. Anna's laugh was a kind of burbling giggle—and she actually, for an instance, covered her mouth, as some young girls will tend to do, as if their laughter were a violation in a Puritan colony at Plymouth and they'd have to wear on their black frocks a giant L.

With aimed-fixed meaning in her brown eyes Anna now said, "Arthur, let's just take it slow."

He was happy that she was even capable of conceiving of their 'it' as a potential It to be taking. This It had the promising taste of an elixir.

He touched her arm, with just the index finger of his right hand. He was drawn to her bicep, out of attraction but also out of envy—and he knew this. When he touched lightly enough he did not feel the muscularity developed there. Again, he questioned why she, a female, had done this developing. But of course he said nothing, although he knew that she saw his questionings in her eyes. The light down of her arm seemed paradox, it put him in mind of a sweet caressing kitten capable of clawing its housemate puppy-dog—or its owner. He traced his finger along her down. . . While he entertained, or pleasured, himself at this down-tracing, she did the same to him. It was not parody, he was sure, not, in any way, a mime. He was sure that to her it simply felt the right thing now to do. He was also sure that she experienced quite the opposite of what he had. Although strong, his skimpy arm was hairy, you could hardly make-out veins and muscles, though he did have some, hidden down within somewhere. Paradox was anti-paradox—little of down and little of muscling.

"You are not rawboned," she said.

"No."

"Some men are so rawboned."

"You don't want yourself to be like those men?"

"No, for godsakes, no."

He stifled the question of What do you want to be

like? He was sure he had asked it here in this room before. It would come, only, to disturbancing, and then more of that, and they'd be irretrievable. He touched her sturdy neck. Three fingers this time; her neck felt surprisingly soft and yielding, all along beneath her jaw.

"You're touching my thyroid. Maybe what you really want is to be a doctor."

"No way. I'll leave that to you and Joseph, that—"

He'd censored 'betraying', and sensing that censor was an activity fully within her smile.

She touched his neck, continuing her smile which recognized and made known (for his confidence-building) that she was following his lead in touching. . . But then her expression turned to an eye-levelling concern she couldn't halt.

"Have you ever fallen down?"

"Huh?"

"I mean, like in the streets, felt like your armature was giving-way, melting, and you had to go down—maybe for only some few seconds; not passing-out or anything."

"Well, yes."

And he had, gone down: once in his bathroom at his parents' house, and he'd tried to make it to his bed, no more than fifteen feet away—and he couldn't: he'd had to drop down midway onto the bedroom carpet.

"It feels," she said, "like you might have Hashi-moto's."

She was sorry she'd brought it up, this diagnosis might put the kybosh on their progress here, but a new internist is a new internist.

To be funny, to exhibit a lack of worry, he toyed

Jap-style, syllable-chopping, with that so Nipponish name: *Hashi-mo-toh.*

She laughed, she liked his humor. But then she the sudden physician said: "You know, only twenty percent of Hashimotos are men. The other eighty are women. It's low thyroid. Have you ever seen people with those awful-looking goiters?—they have Hashimoto's, untreated. You ought to get yourself tested."

Damn, there I go again. I'm going to kill everything. She could have kicked herself.

"Eighty percent to twenty, eh. So"—his discouraged voice—"I'm still a woman."

"Arthur, stop it. That sorrowfulness for yourself, its, well, it's not the most attractive."

It's my fault, she thought: *I'm the one who had to go and bring this stuff up.*

"I've been told by an orthopedist," he said, "that I have the beginnings of osteoporosis too, in my hips. He had one of those X-ray-like machines. That's a woman's thing too, more like."

"The beginnings? Osteo*pen*osis."

"Huh? Anyway, it's more a woman's thing."

She simply shugged her shoulders, as she might have at a patient who worried too much. She was so hellfully sorry that he'd brought all this up. Why did she have to!

He asked, "How do they test for Hashimotos?"

She wanted now to just shove a sharp shim into what she'd just started, but, maybe out of her own fear of their quite possibly befuddled bed-endup, she'd gone and stuck herself good with this medical detour. So: "Blood," she said, "that's the test. It's simple. Then you take L-thyroxin and it's all fine. And you might start building up with vitamin D while you're at it—for the bones."

"I'll get right on all that," he joked, he wanting as well to put an end to this physician bullhockey-diversion.

Then, to get her ass off all this intervention-crap she broadened her fullish face, as if her teeth were gates expanding. The super-smile: The doctorial dismissal-joke smile. And

she sat up and leaned forward, her powerful slats extending and obscuring her quite nice breasts. Oh these two boggled-doubter-people crisscrossing all over the place. . . And Arthur found himself looking away from this woman who was, still to his mind, half man herself, although not in a way biological—*as was himself.* He stared out the window, again at the Bromo Seltzer building—there wasn't much else to look at in this redoubt of southwest Baltimore. The Bromo, as it was called locally, was by now drenched in darkness, beyond the shade of dusk. Such a non-belonging building, a Renaissance monument dedicated in modern times to indigestion.

It was obvious that just now Arthur could not continue his tracing of his hand, of his fingers, of his being, over the being of this Anna. Their hands had been upon each other's necks and by now they had lifted-off in med-talk-flight away, to their sides. The loss was Arthur's fault, he knew it. The loss was Anna's fault—she knew it.

Faults' salvation and regrets cushioned a knocking at Anna's door, which had been going-on for some time, intermittently. And now, finally, Anna did respond to it by getting up (she used merely her forearms' potency to raise herself as a gymnast might), walking to her apartment door and opening it, and inviting, "Come on in."

It seemed that Anna's apartment building was full-up with many med students and interns. This one was a young woman, like Anna, but unlike her in every way aside from their both being at the med school. Her name was Lisa, and she seemed at least a half-decade older than would have been the age of the usual med student or intern; maybe she was a resident; maybe she was even thirty. Neither girl this day announced Lisa's surname. She had come to ask Anna if she wanted to go to a new hit movie, a smart one about "the dubious and malicious control of people's minds by the media"; it was called *Network*, it starred William Holden and Peter Finch and Faye Dunaway—but Anna had shaken her head No.

"But don't leave," she said, "don't take off yet."

Arthur wasn't sure if this invitation for this Lisa to stay meant that Anna had had enough of him for this evening, she was full-up just now with his endless life-complainings and worries, his general negativism that seemed to carry him on drafts of sour air like some kind of desolate carpet, and this just as they might have been getting somewhere too, with their tentative touchings and their tracings. Lisa sat at Anna's rolltop desk chair. As Lisa walked to the desk chair, Arthur did what men do: the usual routine guy once-over. Lisa was blonde, her hair was long and straight; she was taller than Anna, about five-seven or eight, her form was about as ideal as a woman could get, her breasts were proportionally perfect, her legs quite long, hefting her rear in the lightest way (these carried her on a feral glide-gait that dictated assuredness and leadership), her hips were high, her shoulders wide but not muscle-bulky as were Anna's—they were more like a thin resonant coat-hanger; her eyes were a pale gray-blue, and if a woman could combine both saucy challenge and tiresome indifference in those eyes, Lisa had that talent; in short her face was undeniably beautiful, and in an angular way, as we Americans tend to associate with "sophisti-cated" Europeans—but she had no accent, not even a British one. Her cheekbones were "to die for", as their prominence expressed a sharp intelligence and even a cruelty that seemed wise; her lips, however, were too thin. Mean lips. Critical lips. Selfish lips. And those eyes of hers, they slanted upward and outward—which was abnormal, no? even as diabolical as they were erotic. Might she have had a face-lift even at her relatively young age? She continuously ran her right hand through her long blonde hair, as if to show it off, or to remind herself that it was still there. And she wore a dress, apricot, beneath a lemon sweater. Who dressed-up around this cheapo apartment building?—well, she had been readying to go out to that high-rated movie, had she not? . . . Funny, Anna the muscle-girl projected softness personified; Lisa the lithe showed-out as model-hard. *She eats nails*—that description came driving into Arthur's head, yet she sure managed to shanghai the attention that Arthur to this moment had attached to Anna. Perhaps also because she had been staring at him with a questioning, and a disapproving (seeming) harshness—and what also seemed an eerie self-possession—it implied a torridness, it advertised it, well to Arthur, naïve Arthur, it did: she came off as subtle-savage.

"No offense," she said to Arthur, "but"—and

damned if she didn't come right out with it—"are you a drag queen or a dyke, I grant you without the bull part, or are you, a transman?"

And she was intensely, provocatively, eyeing him as if to say *Well, this will be the first time I've conquered some fellow as precariously off-the-rails as a transman.*

This was absolutely the first time in Arthur's troubled-evasive life when a person had so directly, so straightforwardly without a hint of apology for intrusion and insult—called Arthur what he was. And he could feel Anna's stiffening, in the nakedness of discovery.

"I'm transman," said Arthur. What choice did he have?

Lisa grinned, her narrowed cruel-tight lips stringing-out with a sort of malicious pride in her perception and in her fearlessness of propriety, her flat-out physician boldness devoid of physician solicitude and tact and care. Her blue-gray eyes had narrowed as well, as if a ghost were squeezing them. She said, "You're not joking, are you?"

Arthur said, simply, No.

Lisa said, "I haven't seen you around Med School."

"I'm a social worker."

"That I should have guessed."

Jarred by this so sudden, unexpected, interchange, perhaps waiting for what would come next, Anna remained quiet.

"You two can't be *lovers*, can you?"

Was there no end to this Lisa-woman's insensitivity? No one could be this way. What was wrong with her? Obviously her own felt inadequacies—which were not now in evidence.

"But then again," said Lisa, "Anna, you are a bit out-of-the-ordinary yourself."

Anna forced a laugh, which came out more like a quick-breathing exercise one does before attempting some heavy lifting.

And Arthur, to his surprise and, he felt, to his disgrace and his disappointment, was experiencing this devout attraction to this beguiling but horrendous woman. He wanted to be on top of her. He was sure that his artificial jerry-built penis could have got all arteries going and achieved an erection, as the doctors had promised that it eventually not just might—if he were lucky—but would, no luck involved; he'd have got himself a flagrant hardness aimed at this no-holds-barred female hardness—damnit he'd have *split* her— and she'd have done splitting-things to him. . . For this reason of this damned Lisa's allure, and to be decent to Anna—who he still felt that he could love—Arthur did his best to not betray one iota of attraction.

At that Lisa knew he failed.

As did Anna.

They spoke for a time about this movie, *Network*, which all of them knew about, as the critics, even those of the once-great *Baltimore Sun*, had been praising for its emotional dissection of the great false power of the media—Arthur then recognizing that the female star, Faye Dunaway, was to his stricken mind the deadpan image of this unconscionable woman sitting before him, this cold Lisa, whose crossed legs and thighs he could not prevent himself from staring at whenever he felt he might risk the venture. . . After Lisa took off, Anna informed him what Lisa's last name was: Lattin. She was Lisa Lattin. She was in training to be a psychiatrist.

"You were attracted," Anna said.

"I was not. I was repulsed."

"Don't lie, Arthur. Don't cover-up. A dumb sloth could have seen your being riveted."

He felt his jaw tremble, and he hoped that the tremble was too microscopic to be visible—even to an observant internist. "That's ridiculous. I was just being polite."

"Polite, as in sniffing up her rear end, had she so requested."

"Anna!"

"I'm sorry. I just—"

"She is not the type of woman I like, okay?"

"And who's talking here about 'like'?" Anna did not return to the bed, leaving Arthur there alone. She went to her sink. Arthur saddened by the klunky difference between her way of walking and that Lisa's. Nervously, noisefully, distractedly, and constantly turning back to Arthur, she began washing dishes. "And do you suppose that she was, in any way, drawn to *you*?"

"No. Of course not. That bitch, she was *mocking* me. The only good thing about her was that she was direct about it—which I do appreciate."

"No you don't. . . Oh I mean you do appreciate it, but you *hate* it—which makes you appreciate it more."

That exciting image of Lisa Lattin remained an imprint in Arthur's mind. If truth be told he would have liked very much to have gone to see *Network* with Lisa Lattin. He imagined his hand traveling along her thigh and up her dress, as she sat there in the Hippodrome Theatre so erotically, so cooly, indifferent. Hell, he'd have shown her what a transman could do, *this* Arthur transman would have, as much as *any* man—damnit *more* than any man. . . But: He wanted as well to be here, to stay, with sweet kind (and maybe hurt now, obviously hurt now) Anna. He wanted to resume their closeness, their sense of rare identity (he was sure that there was that, even if hidden) broken-apart by that sensual-smart-mean superior-acting Lisa.

Broken-apart? Come now. Hardly. He was not so naïve a child of twenty-two to not realize that his cosmic arousal by Lisa Lattin had not worked its transfer onto Anna. No, he would not close his eyes and imagine that one woman was the other, but he yet would be driven by Lisa's sex-generating to take the plunge—and with The Woman he truly should have been with anyway.

So, be aggressive, the word came to him as if preached by the bare-audible whisper of the social worker in his soul, the urging but prudent sex social worker. He rose from Anna's bed, and quickly, to show his confidence (which did not exist, which was but simulated Cadeau mime) he came to her and from behind he wrapped her about her middle, feeling, and he was unhappy now to feel it, her temper-tautness of stomach, her expansion about the ribcage as if she were a crate protecting oranges within or eggs; and her rear end did not, as he had hoped it might, bulge and arch backwards so as to, as he knew women did quite naturally, quite sexually, arouse his penis and its desires. . .

All is lost with Anna.

But no, untrue. Not being your average woman with your average-woman modes and methods, Anna just simply stood at the sink, at her dishes—her sexual way, or her plain unromantic-romantic way, was not to press ass-backwards into his genitals but to unobtrusively hold still, not to cause something to happen, but to, perhaps, await for something's happening, if it could happen. . . And he was moved, sentimentally: No, not as would have been the result of the confident taunting to goosebump that would certainly have been Lisa's causation, her subtle-unsubtle way, but he was moved too by what seemed the steady-stillness within Anna—a wife might have held herself so for a beloved husband after months of marriage, after loving *years*. Anyway, that was how Arthur was seeing it, inexperienced Arthur—because he desperately wanted to. Especially as "horrible"-enticing Lisa Lattin was the hell *out-of-there*.

He reached round and he held-to Anna's breasts.

Her head rocked back, straight into the bridge of his nose. It was as if she had been punched. She did not remove his hands from her breasts.

Is she liking it?

How conceivably can I know?

What now?

She turned round to him and she said flatly: "I can't for the life of me see how any man would like her, Lisa."

Arthur: "Do you like her?"

"That's different."

Arthur left that one alone.

He said: "I can't either, see how any man could like her."

Anna said: "I mean, I can and I can't see how guys *want* her." She turned round to face Arthur. "So you didn't like her?"

"Not especially, no."

" 'Especially'?" Anna maintained her facing him, and without the slightest motion, sexual or otherwise: "You're not just saying that." She searched his eyes, widening her own fully. "Many guys want her, and I just don't understand it. They're darned fools, a lot of them pretty brainy types—some went to Harvard under-grad—and she knows she's got them. . . 'Especially'."

Arthur tried to come up with something smart: "It's her weird mean streak, she takes it to seductive. Who knows what's happened in her life that—" his own life came slapping him in the face. He heard the sneering echoes of "mutant" from high-school.

"Anna said: "It's hardly a streak, what she's loaded with. And oh anyway she loves her streak. She couldn't give it up if she wanted to. It's weird."

"But *you* seem to like her."

"I said that's different. I'm a girl, remember."

"I remember."

Anna smiled, hesitant, insecurely—which had Arthur recollecting Lisa's potent smile.

And it definitely seemed that Anna was lying: she did *not* like Lisa.

"And anyway: she's stolen no one from me. And, by the way, she's about the smartest student in med school, except for Joseph, who she taunts, for the fun of it. She could make him crawl behind her. Of course, she's older. She was a nurse for some years, maybe five."

Again came that all-encompassing searching look that Arthur threw in upon himself, as if his learning of Lisa's brilliance would entice him to admitting more feeling about the woman. More of that music that he had felt coursing through him, leaps within a symphony, and within the up-charge of just one note. Arthur said, and surprising himself—but he had to say it just now: "Anna, I want you. Not Lisa."

He felt as if he were at Carnegie-Mellon, acting, but experiencing the acting as truth.

"We have that problem," Anna said.

For an instant, even though he had been thinking about the same thing, he didn't know what Anna'd meant about 'that problem'.

But he got it.

She lowered her muscular arms and held softly to both sides of his neck and kissed him. It was a generous kiss. Not sensual, but it did have this quality, not symphonic but solemn, and not sex-intimate. So by the sink they stood.

By the sink: the domesticity of it, this was pleasing, they two even bounced a bit against the sink's rounded porcelain edge while standing—and this was promising, this homeyness, this was Nice. But there was also a slight taste spreading in Arthur's mouth, and down his neck, a taste of two maids kitchening—and there was no way, none on Earth, to go back to Anna's bed. The bed was gone. . . For now?

XII

Dwinski-Dwin was envious of Arthur, Arthur decided. For one thing, "client" Jamil Tandon had convinced his friends, deadly mockers and maligners and threateners, that Arthur Becker ought neither be maligned nor mocked nor threatened—while Dwinski-Dwin ought be. Why? It wasn't only the high regard that Jamil had for weak-looking Arthur's gritty determination at arm-wrestling; it was also that Arthur had managed to acquire for the wiseass but (now) decent-friendly black felon a job. Jamil would be working for Vander-Diggins, the public relations and investment firm now headed-up completely by Arthur's father Mark Becker. Vander-Diggins had now acquired the largest share of the largest supermarket in the Del-Mar-Va area, Lauterbach's, and so it desperately needed more employees. Arthur convinced his father that Jamil, while a bit of a joker and roughneck, had an ethical side, a moral side, a brotherhoodish side—he could be trusted if you let him know that *you* felt that he could be trusted. (Did Arthur really believe this?—what does "really" mean?). In any case, Jamil would start-out in the stockroom, carrying-off for replacing and refurbishing the depleted inventories of products, with the promise that he might be able to gain a promotion to one of the check-out lines, where he could joke with customers as they paid—and, who knows, if that job worked out, with Jamil's personality, he might make it to, where? upstairs, where "plans were made", whatever that meant, and where—Jamil didn't like this part so much—you spied on the aisles beneath through one-way windows, for shoplifters, thieves, even picayeurs of cantaloupe and cheese and olive samples from the open display tray. The particular Lauterbach's to which Jamil was assigned was, you-guessed-it, in the ghetto, the eastern ghetto—on the corner of Broadway and Lombard, down about one half mile from Johns Hopkins Hospital, where Arthur had endured his many surgeries of sex change. . . and while Jamil fulfilled his duties Arthur's chest expanded with his success at the young man's placement and his possible brightening future: Twice he visited the Lauterbach's where Jamil labored, and he watched his "prodigy" stack and unload cartons, receiving in return the fraternal fist-bump invented and developed by blacks. Boosted-up by that fist-bump (which, had Arthur had any dollop of "hip" sophistication, he would have felt as a diffident pop of hostile nonchalance) Arthur now tended to walk about the halls of the DSS (Welfare) with a bit overmuch oomph and energy, as if he owned the place, as if he were the best social-worker who had ever lived, as if this reforming of felons was his definite calling, a piece-of-cake—more was you bet in-the-works. When he ran into his supervisor Dwinski-Dwin, he met that squat man eye-to-eye, an equal, just as he did in their weekly training meetings. After all, Arthur had felt that Dwinski-Dwin required something on the order of refutation. For his own, Dwinski-Dwin put on his patient look, his social-worker mask, and he maintained it, with wise waiting.

In less than two weeks, Jamil was fired from Lauterbach's.

He'd been siphoning-off "product" out the back doors to his boys: drugs (over-the-counter stuff like Tylenol and Advil); liquor (especially Jack Daniels); meats (prime free range beef and lamb); and Gillette razors and razor blades (which, due to their smallness and super-expense were not even kept in the aisles—a customer had to notify the checkout person, who would run back to the stockroom to retrieve a package—which was how Jamil was caught slipping the "valuables" to his boys.).

Jamil went to jail, a different stockroom from Lauterbach's—he certainly had no accessibility to bail.

"Well, your heart was in the right place," said Dwinski-Dwin to Arthur in his office. He no longer looked, in the least, envious.

"I could have sworn," said Arthur, "that I could have trusted Jamil. I really wanted to."

"I know you did, Artie," said Dwinski-Dwin. "I appreciate your trying to break single-handed the infamous Baltimore-black-boy school-to-prison pipeline, but these guys, they are sharp. They know how to 'play' trusting people, they live for it." He scrutinized Arthur with an expression that was, in its triumph, acting so empathetic that it came off even more triumphant. "You know, Artie, when you started-out here, because of your, well, handicap, I was thinking of assigning you towards being a worker for the parolee women."

"I wouldn't have liked that."

"You'd have felt belittled, as a man."

"Yes. And I'd've quit."

"I know. Ironic you have such a low opinion of women, you know."

Arthur took that in. It was ironic. And it was shaming, considering all that he had been through as a woman—or as a part-woman. And all that he had avoided as a part-woman. And all that he'd had to report on his social-work application.

"And," said Dwinski-Dwin, "as you can see I didn't assign you in that direction."

"Thank you." Arthur meant the thank-you, but it also contained more than an expressionless tinge of the sarcastic.

"Arthur, you will be staying with the men, but, as you can now see with that Jamil hustler, you just have a lot to learn."

"Apparently."

"Strange to say but you have too much confidence in yourself, and at the same time you have too little confidence in yourself. I guess it's your—I hate to keep harping and carping on it—your . . . handicap. You've got to get tough. I hate to lay this cliché on you, but, you know, you've got to be-a-man."

"Apparently."

When Arthur had responded with that double-'apparently' of his he'd been hurt, hurt good, and he'd gone thinking, cover-up thinking, escape thinking, not only of social work and of Jamil Tandon's betrayal, but of Anna and this new Lisa woman and his sex-love ricochet in-between. And then he went to escaping from escape into more escape: He was thinking, indeed back to thinking, of his early thoughts that he'd thought he'd triumphed-over, leaped-over, that, having been born of one sex physically and the other emotionally, the emotion-part hadn't just obliterated the physical, not as simply as his surgery had; no, he was like a feather in the wind, he still was—and that maybe there were not even just two sexes, or genders, but that there was, like most things in life, an entire range, and he was, as that feather, blowing all across them all. It must have been *his* fault, then, when his supervisor Dwinski-Dwin had hugged and kissed him on that day weeks before, and the man, although he was an imp-frail type, almost as frail as was Arthur, he was not gay—he was just reacting to the all-gender moving duck in a shooting gallery that was Arthur Becker? *I had loved mime*, Arthur thought, *because mime is what I am. I mime this-way-that, even unconsciously, without making a swoosh of noise. I am the full spectrum. I am dangerous.* Superciliously, and masochistic, and yet egotistic, gloriously egotistic, he pictured himself gathering all of the Welfare Department and its "clients" into their small Welfare auditorium for a show that he might put on, a show-of-self's self's selves. A pre-Copernican wish, this was (and damned if he didn't know it!) to be Little Earth believing it was Big Earth, bigger than stars and sun—and he realized that this craved delusion to be revealed to all, this called-for a miming, a major-miming, as Cadeau Courir had done at Carnegie-Mellon U. He would illustrate by deliberate slow grace-motion and by quick-changes of outfits, that he, or his unthought instincts, they understood all beings, or that, given time, as what seemed his (supposedly) drained estrogen refilled, as it rose in fight-back to face-off against (and *with!*) his cranked-up-but-sham pool of testosterone (and where the hell did that (good-bad) shit come from? that jive artifice hormone injected into him?—from a horse? a pig? a bonobo?, as those bonobo-fuckers fucked all the time—he could, he could show his sphere of understanding, he would have, this came to him, *trans-orbit*. He'd be man and he'd be woman—and these two were just the poles of it all, the whole deal. He would strut in slow motion, he would utilize his hips to fullest extent, he would do manly grieve-glowers and struts like "King" Lebron James and he would do feminine come-hithers, and he'd show how they had evolved out of, well, whatever mix they had evolved out-of, that evolver or evolvee being him, him-her, being the product of lord-knows-what, even beyond his parents' fucking. And, by observing his observers, he would learn, and then show he knew, the essentials of *all folks*. He was thinking in hurt absurdities. A show-off who should not show-off. . . Of course he could never do any of all this, this crap.

Seeing that he had trapped uppity Arthur into an apologetic caging, an insecure and questioning (and perhaps insane) box-in, but not trying to triumph over him any more than was necessary, Dwinski-Dwin tamped-down on the schadenfreude and got (or looked) serene: the little brownish Sephard came round his desk, passed the walled David Hockney print, and once more he hugged Arthur, and once more, with his full lips, he kissed him—although this time the kiss was not on the lips but on the cheek. Was this desire, or support and comfort, or mockery? . . . Arthur certainly wanted to come-out-with a firm loud, *'Stop doing that!'*—but not knowing his supervisor in any depthful way, and considering his failure with Jamil (who, face-it, *he* had wanted to kiss), he demurred, he let it happen. . . And then, damnit, he felt like a girl. Or like he felt a girl must feel. . . And the uneven seesaw split of it had him quivering. . . And does one inspect one's quiver?—can one? Is quiver, on balance, good or bad?

Ah, mockery—that "brilliant-driven" falsity of "human" sense. A life lived within its chasings and then its cruel embraces and then its imminent clobbering suggestions and of course its always lingering threats—who in his right mind (or in his wrong mind) can escape what instincts one may have inherited for self-abnegation? What latencies in the genes. . . With his new job, Arthur had been able to rent his own apartment. At first he'd considered taking a place down near those flats that most med students and residents occupied—reasons obvious. But wiser reason had won-out and he had gone for an efficiency near Mount Vernon Place, near the Washington Monument. And in that small two-roomer of his, in full privacy, in order to observe himself as fully himself, which activity he had rejected as a child and as a boy and as a younger man, and which activity he was coming to now see as saintly, as saintly as his hero (or heroine?) Cadeau Courir had demonstrated, he went about acquiring and then donning an outfit that he, with no woman's aid, only the assistance of television shows and magazine ads, had picked-out. As it happened that his flat near Mount Vernon Place was on Charles Street, and that Charles

Street was the locale of so many women's clothing stores he had but a short afternoon's walk to fulfill his feminine apparel needs and his female curiosity. Blatantly, unambarrasedly, he entered dressing closets of ladies wear shops; he purchased lacy underclothes, two blouses (one transparent), a midiskirt (a miniskirt was yet asking too much of himself), a green velvet top that reached halfway down his thighs to meet his new stretch pants, a bright red waist-belt, and green pumps with heels of only one inch height—just about all he could handle without (unfeminine) bumbly-wobbling (he was after all six feet tall). As the western world had become more and more sophisticated, with unchagrined cross-dressers on the increase, and as Arthur, despite the weight-work that he had suffered to do when younger, was still constructed in the skeletal basics of a female build, sales-women seemed to be not shocked in the least—indeed they seemed only too happy in their falsities of sense to help out with suggestions and criticisms and rejections and, ultimately, approbations. And would they have approved of the spectacle that Arthur next presented only to himself and his drab rectangular mirror in his furnished flat?—as he cross-dressed (no, this was *not* cross-dressing!), as he practiced the dignity and poise of women's walking, which elegance he did try to deflagrantize and mute (because of the enemy-countering testosterone called-up like a platoon of the auto-immune at this moment of sex-combat), as he practiced the grace that men did not have and never would have (except for the athletic grace of certain quarterbacks and basketball forwards and lacrosse players on attack as his dad Mark had been—and Fred Astaire, sure, sure—and that he, Arthur, could never have approached before), as he studied the seeming *understanding* and the appearing *sympathy* that returned to him from that mirror reflecting him now in his couturieresque raiment and his long-lost estrogen ascending to its original place as if his new clothing was woven of venerating estrogen; and oh there was, confronting him, this voluptuous attentiveness, this ladylike *confidence*, the see-through spiritism that women had—and that he knew was called in the "professions" transvestic fetishism, or better yet, the frightening autogynephilia—he knew this from the psychological pamphlets he had read years ago before even having had his surgery, *and* from the sensation of his penis now angling *upwards*—what was this? The ultimate in narcissism or the crowning lance of pan-sexism *or* the superabundance of self-subversion masquerading, *miming*, grandiosity!?. . . So, thus enigmatically attired, and equipped with his mime-talents, he walked the imaginary runway as a model, ascribing and approving and rejecting, siphoning what was Right and fit him and what was Wrong, so Wrong, and did *not* fit him—for even while staring at himself in this female getup, and respecting himself within for having the balls to wear it (hahaha), he was, he remained, unhappy enclosed in that tug-o'-war that now became his psyche—and that so long ago he had escaped.

Does it never escape?—even when you have had your vagina excised, and your cervix, and your womb.

One solution then: Go out. Test. Take a sample of reactions he might kindle, an unscientific survey but better than nothing. And he did live only one block from The Checkmate, that now dowdy homestead where he had first met Anna Bass. So there, in heels and girl-getup, he went, and sat at a table, drinking, slowly, cappuccino after cappuccino (he'd ordered with such an inflected squeaky-faked female voice that the waitress could not but turn-away so as not to smirk), he sat cross-legged, in that newly-acquired outfit, and looking about with the sneakiest of peripheral suspicions—expecting to be called by the old-lady frequenters "you crass vulgarian". And fortunately this day there were men there, at The Checkmate. Most sat reading their *New York Times* or their *Wall Street Journal,* or with their open laptops (and their earplugs) they were tamping away on their own books—but sure they did look at Arthur. But, and this did not surprise Arthur, no one came over to his table and made a play for him or against him. No one seemed eager even to talk with him (or "her"). No one seemed to care one whit about his/her newfound and dressed-up *sympathy* and *understanding* and female *confidence.* In his flat hallway mirror he hadn't looked, to himself anyway, so unattractive—but that was *to himself.* And his reaction now—it was not disappointment. It was, he realized, validation. While he had incorporated femaleness, face it, *he was a man.* Sothen: *be* one. *Act* like one. Congratulate yourself for having gone whole hog with the female-dressup, external and internal—how many men would have such guts? just about none—even though all men had estrogen laying back within them trying to make them better as human beings. Just be a better human being. Don't take your failure with Jamil as your failure with all things and all clients. And don't lay all the blame for Dwinski-Dwin's weird kissing of you on yourself. *You* didn't *try* to make him do it. Dwinski-Dwin had plenty of estrogen himself, you could just about see it floating round and softening his brownish Jewboy skin—and being a social-worker, and a social-work supervisor, that had probably brought it out all the more. And, when you got right-on-down-to-it, had any man, any garish septuagenarian in The Checkmate, come on to him, what in the world would he, Arthur, have done? Women had their ways of rejection, untold myriads of slights, such buds grew in their bloodstream—and that was power as much as any power was power. Arthur would have rejected the "masher", but how would he have done it?—that might have been some funny sex-discombobulated scene. Would he have slapped the *alter-cocker* "ladykiller"? There might even have been a fight—and maybe with him, as lady, kicking the everloving shit out of that brokendown pickup guy.

When Arthur left The Checkmate, he walked clumsily as a woman, moreso than he had on approaching the place—his instinct seemed now to be to man-up. But that sort of male trouncy-walking in his short skirt and blouse and all, as vaudeville comedians sometimes did, it would have made-for a mockery, just another one. So, while the sampling-test was done and he had already decided, once again, to *be-a-man*, to be confident in a man-way, to be defiantly himself (defiant *against* himself?), he walked back to his apartment with female hips aflagging and shoulders straight-up elegant, not at all in that hunched-up-and-over way in which most males (at least American ones) tended to carry themselves. (And sure, *now*, he got stares). And once safe within his tiny pathetic efficiency—which he hated—he just about tore off the ladies' ware as if he had been imprisoned within that costume, and if it's possible to feel both foolish and brave at once, this was how Arthur felt. . . Except, one thing: once he got his frilly panties off (and sniffed the crotch as if he were not sniffing his own stinky crotch but that of, well, that super-sexy Lisa Lattin), he now saw the full erection that he had felt as he had been walking home, and the stiffness was so importunate that it rose even above horizontal level, as if aiming heaven-high. And he was not sure at all what that ambiguous confusing hard-on meant. . . It was not even possible for him to now jerk-off, as he did not know over whom he was jerking.

XIII

Evening: He thought Do It, Don't do It, Do It, and then he went and took himself to Anna's apartment: Mister New Man. He more than half-hoped that she would not be at home, maybe she'd be at the jazz club—Martick's. But where else would a determined emotionally complicated (and insecure) internist be in the later evening of a weekday but studying-up on human complications: on the lobes of brains—which came first? the chicken-limbic or the frontal egg? the connections and disconnections and mysteries of the pituitary's reliance on the unreliable tetchy-twitchy amygdala due to feisty dopamine, she memorizing where the duodenum met the jejunum and then the ilium, and then that small intestine left off in favor of the colon, the large intestine, and why such had to happen in order for shit, a good solid shit, to be amalgamated (all that expert-postulation he had sped-read-up-on while trying to figure out the origins of his own damned unfair problems: mere allusion to the hippocampus still got Arthur giggling, as if he were reading an Ogden Nash poem on the hippopotamus[5]), Anna also boning-up on meds, she categorizing side-effects—and thinking of portents, good and ominous, for this patient, that one? . . . Hell, it was after ten PM, ought he interrupt? . . . You bet.

"I love you," he breathed-out, as he had not expected he would, just as she opened her door a crack, and then, surely because he had been so bold, she opened the door fully, and he entered (a step), and her eyes betrayed that impenetrability and yet openness of hers, that fragility of enigma, as if they two had been through a war and were just meeting alive as survivors, as remnants, and were the only soldiers rightful for each other; her eyes betrayed an echo of what he'd brought himself to say—her large brown eyes told him understanding— because he felt that they told him that; and to him they said, because he wanted them to say this, 'I have been waiting for you'—although he doubted even a fragment of rationality in that, she had not calculated such showing in her eyes. She was in a T-shirt and panties, cotton male-type ones, plain ones, and to tell the truth it smelled, a little bit, within her small closeted and study-sweated internist room, and *she* smelled, you couldn't avoid the whiff of it—but which did not arrest their embracing of each other, and their long kiss which had been so long deterred, and in so, tendered, by Reality, and his feeling of her strength, which was not, as in his case, the smaller strength of the sex that he was born with, that female sex strength that he had just tested-out at The Checkmate; but hers was the sex that was the opposite of her born strength, her was the chosen strength of Man. All this in his mind as they went

---

[5] Of which there were none: Arthur confused hippo with rhino.

kissing. Well, opposites attract, but opposites, in their oppositionalism, can be similars—if one thinks of it and wants it and accepts it, in full recognition, and respects it, or learns to, and then even praises it, teaching oneself what in life is most important, what in a mate is most important—and what the hell is that!? And, following all that, it was their personalities—they so fit, did they not. . . And, most of all, it occurred to him, that had there been a witness to them, had they been on a stage, what they were enacting was—sometimes like everything was—a Mime. A truthful Mime. And thus, sonofagun, one that has lost its mimefulness—that artificiality one sees projected in an oldtime silent film and falls asleep on. All this while still at Anna's door. It was like, to him, Arthur, the honesty, the authenticity of Colette—he visualized those aspects without trying to—she who his French teacher at Carnegie-Mellon had acclaimed and hailed and glorified as the sheerest teacher of love's poetry and love's accommodation and love's touch and love's loss. Which, then, he had not understood—so schmaltzy-Frenchish-wordish Colette had been.

He entered, not breaking their embrace they lay themselves on the small bed, and they feared, they seemed to fear, too much of the question-staring at one another. This would have been as trite as declaring, 'I have been waiting for you my whole life'. There Anna was, in her T-shirt, even within its long looseness Arthur could perceive her sturdy bulgings, the mountainous earnings that had come from her sacrifice-intensities at Gold's Gym—while just two hours earlier he had been a tryout model on the old-folks' "runway" of Charles Street, all muscles shed (what he had of them) for the other-muscle of lady-dress sensuality (if he could locate it within and then accept it?), he in skirt and blouse and lunatic strut just beneath the rounded obelisk of George Washington—and he *did not* wonder, now, as he *had* wondered before, and which wondering had deterred him, how she, strange Anna, she would look in a female outfit, skirt and blouse and pumps-type-strut. And he could see in her eyes, he was sure he could, that she did not wonder, as she might once have, how he, with his unsinewed ams and shoulders, his unlocatable tendons, and his skinny thighs and all, how *he* would present his "manliness", his *alter*-manliness, at Gold's.

They were clumsy.

For some reason, obvious but not, he wished for her to be on top—but then he rejected that idea, that notion. With most women he would have liked for them to be on top—as he fantasized with them, he just did, *au natural* (for him)—for this allowed fullest view of their beauties, their breasts and slender necks and risen-up narrow jaws (you saw the skeletons of their faces); and their expressions, the ecstatic distance involved in their relished intimacy, this their aloneness, which he, of course, always felt—so he'd figured that they'd felt that too. . . No, he wished for Anna to be beneath him; not that she would be supine-and-waiting in self-abnegation and imploring, the beginning traditional-instinct way believed-in for us male-humans, but that this, instead of yielding, would have her supporting him, his light weight, his reliance on her prop-and-bracing—and in truth he'd feared what might be her clumsiness had she been on top, her balanceless falling left way, right. But otherwise: on top, despite himself, forcing himself, *he* would be the boss, *he* would have to be, *he* would be the director, the leader, the plunger and the hunter-man splitter, the one who inaugurated their kisses while they loved, the one who might rise at intervals to look down, and to drive-down—if he had the arm strength for so to do (and he did worry no little about that). And Anna, for her own, it was obvious that she wanted to *take* direction, or at least to start out that way. She wanted to be a conventional woman—despite her gym maniac-isms for her own gym reasons. She must have fought within herself as much as Arthur did the same. . . So, above her, and with the erection that almost seemed that had begun with at least an hour before, while he wore women's clothing and stared at himself dressed-so in the mirror of his flat, he now entered her, and she was wet. She was wet—*Anna Bass was wet!* Wet with *love?*—yes, it must be, that which he had until now only heard about from books and from guys talking-bragging, and innocent that he was, he feared that she might apologize—for that secretion of sex, that normal wetness that *he* had caused—*hurrah!* . . . And, in a way, how can you discount the amusement?—sex is funny, no?—she laying there beneath him with her strong muscular arms gone wide as if she were reaching for a long barbell and not him, she put him in mind of—well, what could he say? how could he discount his imagination?—she resembled, for an instant, no, more than one instant, a crab. One stranded on sand, on its back and begging, begging to be upturned—so that it might scamper away, to the eternal sea and safety (and he was so sure that she was captured by the same image, or one similar, for her eyes became cats avoid-ing him, absconding from his eyes, falling-away to the sides just as her breasts did, and her cheeks were now so ripe-ish red, as if no other woman had ever looked this way—so vulnerable, so unprotected, so *compromised*!?). . . And he went up-and-back, in-and-out, as nature teaches you (or too much masturbation), but which, unlike in most movies (except for professional-dirty ones), he did this slowly, what some French person, perhaps in Colette, called "rose-petal fucking"—as opposed to sharp-rock-fucking. . . And did she appreciate this?—this slowness, this love, this LOVE, which was also this embarrassed fear. Her crab-reaches had discontinued, and her arms had fallen, they had retracted-inwards, to go round him, as if they taught wrestling as well (his imagining) at Gold's Gym—except for that, with her inexperience (whether she had been ever with Joseph Lerner or not—*no, she couldn't have been!)*, she matched his sweet "rose-petal fucking" with the tenderest of caresses and roundings, of his slender female-hormonic shoulders—and her potent legs carried him to a within-*within*, those strong calves and quads and hamstrings of hers housing his stringy ones, saying *I have got you, oh Remain*—which he did for his orgasm, not-knowing if it was matched by her own, had she had one—and indeed his was minor, no gushing geysers he had read about, he was not depleted, hardly—and he sure was not going to ask her whether or not she'd had one. . . And, as he was not sophisticated, he did not at this juncture roll Anna over, or try to, so that she might now take a chance and be on top, above; he *asked* her to climb over him and be there, looking down. His very polite words were, "Would you, please?"—and with his miming motions of such, she, unsophisticated as she was, fully understood, and perhaps sympathized. And as she climbed over, she was a million miles from the primordial, she was awkward, and he was glad of it, for again it was evidence of her lack of experience and her equality with him: And as she climbed over, their knees knocked, their calves collided, their thighs bumped, unsexually, more like the two of them were negotiating the beginnings of a rock-climb out in the Alleghenies of Western Maryland, and her rear-end had no grace of movement, as it might, it ought, in a dance or in an attempted display that she would have known was needed. And for a man who had been a boy who had idolized the women-dancers' glide-grace in the movies, like Cyd Charisse and Leslie Caron, and he who still couldn't but be this lonesome-idolizer, this klunkiness of Anna's, it had to be toler-ated—no, more than that, it was a serious test of his love that he believed he had. Thus, he stared-up at his love, once she had achieved position, well-centered, steady (fairly steady), and he stared with eyes that were lies but were true in their determination and wished-emotion. He stared up at the taut-large magnificence (in a way) that had allowed "his girl" to win not one but *two* PoseDowns, "his girl" who did have breasts be-tween those T-bone lats and biceps and triceps and super clavicle-bones (*Thank God she had them!*) but whose breasts, although they were the wonderfully female saucer-like (*Thank God again*), they pointed-out like *cones*, as if trained or shaped, as if (who knew?) there were female titty-lifts and adjustable presses at Gold's, maybe there really were machines for that compacted fitting, especially designed? . . . And well *now*: Anna being atop, does he fiddle and phumpher with his "instrument", so recently used, until he might be able to manipulate it into her vagina before it flagged (oh no, not that silly-messy marshmallow-stuffing shit again!) or does he, sincerely, perhaps gentlemanly, definitely sweetly, *ask her* to place *It* in?—which action would require her to hoist herself a bit by quads and hamstrings and glutinous maximus (as if she were [well, this picture did occur to him] shitting out in Nature—did he really truly have to think of *that*— *damn, he loved her!?*) (anyway he was sure she did free-weight exercises for her ass-muscles, so they were strong enough for a less-than-gymnastic, less than sweaty, lift-up); but the asking, and the lifting, it still would not be, as imagined by a neophyte like himself, particularly ladylike—and her resembling then a Romanian or Chinese gymnast might well affect him unwarrantedly. . . So: He decided on the self-asserted manly "grab yourself and plunge-up-and-in" of his own. *Just do it!*—which still required her to lift-up somewhat, *he actually hadn't considered that*; but, he discovered, being the asserter here did indeed undercut the—what he saw as—the fecal-implied—for Puritan him anyway—but maybe that stool-passing "mime" was, for some men, sexy?—that man-unladyness of the necessary squat (and truth was he feared that he might well like to see it). . . And maybe Anna, in her lack of experience despite her being a med student (one after all didn't have necessarily anything to do with the other), maybe she saw it, her lifting-up, in that ladyless way too—for while Arthur worked at his insertion up between her legs and down—in a way—beneath her body, Anna's chin was high, her look was high, not haughty but as if she were scrutinizing for cracks, for dirt, the seldom looked-at ceiling—and she was silent, though it was the sort of silence that told one who listened, one who was close, one who was The Other, that that silence was surely sound, and good—an unuttered squeal and cry, an alas and an at-last. . . And it was for this, this escape, this hiding, which had been his own way for so long, it was for this, for this too, that he loved her, he knew that he did. That softness, rounded in her rounded face, that plea in her eyes, that child plea, that girl-child plea (that he had too—or he could have had), that begging in her eyes and with her extended lips, despite her power by way of the physical, her gentleness despite her physique too, and although this was not a propitious thought to possess of one's sex partner, he had begun in the seeing of her as a saint, all while knowing, being fully aware, that this was the romanticism of a child, of a deprived, of a young man so long mocked but looking looking looking. . . They were they, in their love, they were one, as insipid and naïve as it sounds, its bell tolled all the more, its bell rang within each of them, for them both. . . and as if he were smoking grass on one of those few evenings at Carnegie-Mellon when he had smoked grass, hoping it would help with one of the two coeds he had "dated", while sitting on the edge of a cliff over "Panther Holler"—meaning Panther Hollow—he came to The Vision, the Truth Sight, and its truth could not mate with words: With Anna: He was a He and She was a She, and She was while a She a He (even if not by biology—as was he—but by volition, even if she did not recognize her volition), and He was while a He a She, and so He was a He-She and She was a She-He and round the circle and spinning back again so that She was a She, absolute, and He was a He, absolute.

This journeying, this compound, this crossbreeding of one breed from a two that were a geometric many, off-the-charts, this discovery never-to-be-found-again-should-he-go-searching-for-a-million-years, he was sure of it (he did not recollect that his endocrinologist, some twenty years before, trying to ease his parents' pain, had explained to Arthur and to his father and his mother: "It's estimated that one in every fifteen hundred animal births is anatomically atypical—in fact, in the animal kingdom a full one-third of all species you could consider as intersex, so this shows how varied animals are, and humans are included—it's just socially that we can't bring ourselves to include them, to accept them. To accept what really is normalcy. But there really is an infinite number of ways to be, as we humans are incredibly complex creatures—and gender is just one part of what makes us each so damn unique."), but just now, with Anna, with their compound of compoundings, their variety, when he pressed her neck he pressed as a man, undoubtedly, he felt that and he loved it, but there just was that ineluctable sensing that he was a man being a woman being a man, pressing in an interface with startled fingers, startled because her neck was, face it, so much a man's—and did she even know that now? even with its girl-resistance (and girl-acceptance) that strong neck of hers, it must have been habitual?—as habitual as she must have felt all over herself—and known!—that it was, if any woman's was, as a woman's, the same yielding, if even it was habitual-yieldless as a man's. No she couldn't have known all the twistings, no one could, this bizarre love-moebius that had him kissing her shoulders so many continuous times that it seemed

one endless kiss of those shoulders that he wished he
had as his own, wished he'd had all his life (hers were
like his dad's) but was glad that she was glad that she
had them, she had worked so hard for them at Gold's
(no further mentioning of this, he swore), so this
moving-about moebius of their loving, their *attach-
ing*—and when he remained within her it was she, as a
man, yet, taking him in with a power stronger than his
was, and he wanted to fight it while succumbing to it,
this rolling round sensation that he could not tell where
he left-off and she began (*she was still a woman!*), and
it was so strong a feeling, and one of his power's being
stronger too than hers, that he could not believe that she
did not have it as much as he did, *if she did not*, and it
was so overwhelming as well that Arthur nearly choked
but gasped, as this was the way it should be, should
always be, for two people who—the world thinks—
should *not* be, where it was impossible to tell who was
imposing whose will on whom; yes, this was the *perfect*
way; and a song came to him, which he thought was
one of Leonard Cohen's (who he didn't much care for,
but was Joni Mitchell's (who he cared-for even less
[neither one was jazz])—part of a song:

> I've looked at love from both sides now
> From give and take and still somehow
> It's love's illusions I recall
> I really don't know love at all.

"I love you," he gasped it out.

And she couldn't repeat it because it was too deep
inside, within her, he decided, to be violated by the
vocal outbreath that too often, to save itself, to save The
Other, reached to sound out so easily vacant Lies.

Hyperbole scared this sweet caring girl. As did possible, dreaded, deluding, Empty Ardor.

It was no lie, however, even if delusion, that on his walk home at 2 PM, he had flown himself into the atmosphere beyond selfish, even if it was a munificent selfish, to what you might call a world benevolence, for as much as their togetherness had been himself as Mister Manly, more than he could ever have imagined he could be, he softly in charge of Anna's thighs and her breasts and all of her, it was also *not* him, as he was also *in-the-charge-of* Anna and her arms and thighs and legs, those strengthy bolsterings, he both comfortable and fulfilled and uncomfortable and not, not fulfilled at all, which by the way was too a fulfillment, a joy-despair; and this was why he found himself planning a visit to an endocrinologist, blood tests, whatever, to determine, if his and Anna's child would be burdened by imbalances of the endocrines—what were the percentages, if known? And what could he and his beloved wife, his nobody-else-but, do about it? Need biology be history, be fate? For theirs and their child's sake. . . and he envisioned himself and his woman Anna going together to the Endocrinology Office, in her University building (maybe she knew the man [or woman]). They listening carefully, in love.

XIV

Conspicuously massive at mid-torso, ex-gargantuan who still looked less like a man asking for Welfare than a Daddy Warbucks who ought be bestowing it, Akram Medani walked into Arthur's social-work cubicle. His huge belly was abounce as uncontained jelly—this due to his pronounced limp (which looked, by being over-pronounced, partially faked)—and his full beard pointing downwards towards that medicine ball belly, which forced out of his baggy-shiny pants his stringy-used Hawaiian shirt. His hair was black, long, and thick with dirt-made curls. He sat in the red plastic chair across from Arthur's junior-league nebbish-desk. This Akram had been assigned to *Mister* Arthur Becker, the young social worker of renewed Dwinski-Dwin confidence— who, yet carrying within him his early-years' dual-sex faith and affinity for mime, mimed in his mind a parody of this poor Syrian refugee, this legal asylum grantee who had been, in now devastated Aleppo, could you believe it? a doctor. An internist. So he said.

"You were in jail here—in Baltimore?" Arthur

asked, as he had only been assigned to parolees, not indigents. They were another DSS department.

"I stole. A watch, from Tarjé."

"From who?"

"Tarjé. Isn't that what they call it?"

"Oh, Target."

"I just wanted to say it right, as they do."

"It's Target." From his earliest days, his most-ultimate never-ending mocked days, Arthur hated wise-ass flippant talk.

" 'Target'," Akram repeated, as if to exhibit that he was obedient and good and willing to learn. "Well, I have to say," he said, "it's not that I am needing one, a watch. In all honesty I would have gone to selling it, on a street corner, not that anyone needs watches anymore with all those cell-phones and I-phones—I had one in Syria, and *they* are hard to steal—although mine was stolen. In any case, considering my circumstance, my refugee status, my sufferings"—Akram rocked his head sideways with what he had endured, smiling in a wretched-stretched way that showed smiling was the last thing he ought to do—"the good judge considered all, he warned me, and he suspended my sentence. But officially for the city here I fall into the realm of parol-ee."

"I see," said Arthur, his voice now gone resonant with his new love-authority and love-confidence. With the tilt of his head carrying the same weight as his voice had—and for the same love-reason—he studied Akram's record, which was one printout page on his desk: "And your family, they're all gone."

"Three children, a wife. Need I tell you of Assad Hussain's barrel-bombs? Their Sarin gas?"

"No, I've read, I've seen them on TV. It's horrible."

"Horrible, this murder I've seen a hundred, a hundred *thousand*—as a doctor, I have washed many children's skin, their *hair*."

Akram Medani was now nodding-nodding, as if affirming all the messages of the world media, and of all he had seen. "Perhaps," he said, "my family, they are still somewhere."

"I hope so."

The Syrian nodded once again, this time abstractedly, as if he did not believe his nods or Arthur's hopes. This was an ex-Prometheus presently reduced to Puck.

Arthur forced himself to stare at the man: he felt himself becoming intimidated by those sorrowful black eyes, coated as they were by gray-fleshed sockets and threaded by reddened yolks; it was as if those eyes enforced the authority-in-misery in beard in belly and even in absurdly happy floral Hawaiian shirt. It was as if Abraham in the Bible, after sacrificing one of his sons, had walked away droopily in a fashionable Persian sweatshop shirt. Arthur was also daunted by the man's obvious intelligence—or what was left of it. His vocal tones were already not near so strong and authoritarian-deep as, when he'd entered Arthur's piddling office, they had begun.

What in the world was he supposed to do for this man? What could any mere social worker, equipped with talky-pushy questions, do?

By assigning this Akram Medani to Arthur was Dwinski-Dwin testing him? Usually with his black felons his main question had to do with whether or not the parolee was still in the habit of hanging-out with his old crowd, his "brothers". Obviously such an inquiry was pointless with this Syrian, it was ludicrous. But what was this ex-doctor, alone-in-the-world, well, alone-in-Baltimore, about doing? How would Arthur prevent by talk, by social-worker "trust", this abandoned, educated man from stealing again. Again and again and again—for godsakes the world's average morality, its civic justice, meant nothing. This abandoned doctor's suffering had even put Arthur's young-boy school-suffering to shame. Arthur found himself just about hoping that the man *would* steal again, valuable stuff, saleable stuff, and that he, who had no experience in what blacks called "boosting", would help the man. He fantasized that he could get tips from some of his other clients.

Ridiculous.

"It says here," Arthur said wide-eyed with disbelief, examining Akram's papers, "you're living now in the Men's Shelter provided by the Jewish synagogue, Chizuk Amuno."

"Yes. It is in their old mosque, I mean House of Worship, of years ago, on Eutaw Place, in the black ghetto. It is a scary place in a more scary area. Now they, the Jews, -they perform their worship way out in the suburbs, the Shangri-La—I have never seen it, and I am sure that I never will."

Akram reported this information without a touch of hostility or envy or implication of hypocrisy.

"Yes," said Arthur, "I know where "The Chizzie" is now (which affectionate name was what they called it when he was a boy and people went there frequently). My father owns a seat there."

The seat was for show, a superstitious thing: Sophisticated rich Mark Becker was not religious in the least.

He almost never went to the new Chizuk Amuno, which was architected in what might have been described as the winged-domed air-harbor style of Dulles Airport or a Martian landing colossus—even on the High Holy Days of Yom Kippur Mark Becker seldom attended. And this was not unusual among the nouveau riche of the city's Jewish populace. They supported the new palatial prayer-haven, with their dollars, not with their bodies. . . And apparently they kept-up support for the old Chizuk Amuno, apparently not for worship but to offer succor and house the poor. Admirable, you can't not say.

Akram said: "It is not so wonderful there, however. It is rows of cots. Many, close-clumped—I'm sorry if I insult—blacks, as here at the Welfare."

Arthur offered, "I can imagine."—and then he regretted what he said, as it could be construed as an insult of blacks. And so, what happens!—

An inspiration comes to the now Anna-blessed man, the god-worthy who had been finally allowed to find his true Love—*one out of a billion*—and at the same time has lost his (supposed) betraying best friend Joseph. Well, you win you lose. The inspiration:

"You know, Akram, you might stay at my place."

"I . . . What? Is this legal?"

"Sometimes, for justice," said the revamped-proud Arthur Becker, "legality ought be stretched to be truly legal."

I am such a good man!

Akram grinned-out a bass-throated "I agree." His black eyes lit as if an electric charge had shot down from some redoubt way beyond this planet; they brightened his gray sockets.

"My place," said Arthur, "is just an efficiency, it's no mansion, believe me, but there is a sofa."

"Heaven."

But: the speed, the impulsive lack of hesitance, on both men's parts, coupled with the filth and the girth of his new roommate, immediately had Arthur clutched in the gut by some taut hard chains of hesitance, of uncertainty and of doubt—and, sure, understandable regret.

What did I just do!?

Well at least, that evening, he did not have to help Akram Medani move in: the Syrian ex-doctor had only to his name a bulging satchel, well-scuffed, pocketflaps hanging—which he tossed onto Arthur's proffered sofa as if dispensing with his pet Chihuawa which he no longer wished to hold. . . The respectless tossing, and not a careful-considerate soft-placing, did annoy Arthur. As did Akram's suspicious-light two-step perambulation of Arthur's mini-flat, as if it contained an IED, covered by loose floor boards, and that might blast your exploded body parts over to the clanking radiator that endlessly sent up geysers of blinding steam, up to the upstairs neighbor's flat and on down to the lower neighbor's.

They got along well, if 'well' meant nothing happened, nothing amiss, nothing really much except on the dangerously implicit level of this subtlety and that, ie. beginningness-control—although what in the world was supposed to, right-off, happen?—accent on the "right-off". Just for sharing his "apartment" with a refugee was Arthur to be short-listed for Baltimore's Best, an award announced yearly in *The Baltimore Sunpapers,* and usually intended for the person, male or female (but usually male) who "exemplifies the most admirable in the public service of citizenship, without regard for fame" (The award was manifest in the miniature form of the clipper ship, first introduced to the world in the War of 1812, when America [again] defeated Britain). . . But, as said, between these two nothing happened: Arthur arose each day into the ever-ascending rancidness of his cramped efficiency-for-one, and the ineluctable truth was that perversely he scavenged for the ineluctable odor that the Syrian had imbued-into Arthur's sofa, probably for perpetuity; but this revulsion served only to justify and reward Arthur more with his immersion into his own magnificent kindness and generosity. He would then walk the six or so blocks to his cubicle at the Department of Social Services, never failing to scrutinize in peasant wonder the absurdly-named Gothic prison on the way, The Maryland House of Corrections; and Akram arose each day into what he considered a normal smell and searched the want ads for any decent job that might accept the services of an ex-internist from Aleppo, Syria—and of course Akram got nowhere ("These want ads alone, they exhaust me as much as does donning the required dressing—and I will *not* clip my *beard*!"). And, of course, inevitably, Arthur began to feel like an annoyed and on the continuous edge of harping, wife. So he swelled (and swallowed) such volatile *cris du coeur* as 'Take *anything*, you're an *immigrant*, a *refugee*, sell *shoes*, load-up and dump-down *garbage* [though even Arthur knew that that plum job was unionized], don't be too haughty to hawk Big Macs.'— and no he never said this. Akram, for his own—and after all he was a doctor, and apparently an especially perspicacious one loaded with preternatural sympathies—perceived, first Arthur's dissatisfaction, and then in no time his house-mate's hormonal handicap—Akram could even see that Arthur's penis was quite the complicated female-adapted-to-male jerry-rigged affair. (And Arthur, for his own, could not bear to observe Akram's penis, so overhung as it was by the Syrian physician's hairy belly). And Akram, had he commanded the rudeness and impoliteness, and not been afraid of being kicked-out onto the anomie of Charles Street and then lord knows where, might well have asked Arthur if he could handle "The Thing", turn it round-and-round in professional inspection and wonderment at Western Science, how, Allah-be-damned, these sons of Abraham and Einstein could create a phallus by way of tinkering-and-puttering with a uterus and clitoris—*Inshalla—in all of Islam such aberrant creatures would be pilloried and pulled-apart for such insults to God, for God is Great!—not Man.* . . And Arthur, ever aware of his situation, of how he might be sex-presenting (without trying-to) to a roommate who was not the lonely-and-impaired Joseph Lerner, was in constant awareness and suspicion of Akram's awarenesses and suspicions—and the fact that he tolerated these without blowing-up had himself praising himself, evermore, for his goodness and his patience (and not his passivity). And he did *not* inform his supervisor, the ever-nosy-intrusive Dwinski-Dwin, of his and Akram's living situation, which was so obviously and tenaciously against the rules and would without doubt have him fired, "let-go", in the time it took to flick-on-by-remote CNN, which Akram did obsessively, so as to get glimpses of the ever-increasing devastations to his Syria—and to moan and swear and wail as if praying, and even cry.

But Arthur, to divert Akram's attention from that disaster (and from Arthur's penis), and obviously for praise, and to exhibit his deepest human generosity to his "girlfriend" intern, and even to show to the beaten-down Arab that he was not embarrassed by his (rather repulsive) residence, invited Anna to meet his "roomie", the Syrian internist. Except that Akram, a physician, an educated man, but equipped with as much Arab-testosterone within him as was female-estrogen (apparently still remaining) within Arthur, sadly mis-understood: As immediately as he—so long deprived of a woman and haunted by the probable death of his own woman, his submissive-decent wife Hannan, and habit-uated to the normalcy of Islamish-reductionist treatment of women, whether in inordinately tidal clothing or inordinate two-step behind-walking, or in quiet (but sometimes violent) sex—as soon as Akram had taken-in, by contrast, Arthur's Anna ('Is this woman *inten-tional*?'), Anna paired-with Arthur's unmuscular and unfaulted misproportion and misbirth, he absorbed Anna's "intentionally" muscled malproportion (Arabic women did not frequent the Middle Eastern version of any Gold's Gym), this on top of her sweetest smile, really come-hitherish to anyone of East or West who (perhaps savagely) wished to be come-hithered, all this as submissive-seeming, and strongly so, to any Arab who had not resided long outside of Arabia, and topsy-turvy as it was, it was certainly a welcome change from the hostile glowers of the money-distributing and food stamp providing female "workers" and short-word lie-challengers at Welfare with their vile anti-Arab algo-rithms that justified their treating him like Arab males treated Arab females—as soon as now indigent, now mourning, now sequestered and lost-in-the-world, Akram, had digested and unmixed all this social-psychology (to his own happy preternatural Levantine demixing), he went on the offense, in both meanings of the word: Sweet Anna had arrived from Gold's Gym in T-shirt that pictured a black woman in boxing gloves, leg-raised as in kick-boxing, and, of course Levi's, and just to be a welcoming American—after the welcoming Arab, as was the Arabian custom, offered Anna tea (which Arthur, a coffee-man, couldn't stand)—after the proffered gracious tea, she had walked to the generous Akram and embraced him wholeheartedly and—ohboy!—kissed him on the cheek, which was about all the invitation even this polite tea-giving internist out of Syria required. Teacups spilling and sloshing (onto a worthless decades-trodden rug), he doubled-up on Anna's embrace, lifting powerful-her off her feet and then body-slamming powerful-her down onto Arthur's stink-ridden sofa, which was so unimagined a response to her genuine good-American welcome that Arthur found himself absolutely frozen, except to holler-out an indignant, "Hey, wait!"—which, who knows?—Akram might well have interpreted as his roomie's declaring Firsts in the (inevitable-assumed) rape. And before Arthur could make his move—whatever that move might have been, his being not remotely a strongman—Anna had strong-armed herself up off the sofa (God it did stink to high hell), punch-fisted Akram in the protuberant hairy belly, and (politely, considerately?) not in the groin-by-knee, as *muscleless* women were taught to do, and her strength was of such impress that the Arab physician fell-backwards onto the tacky wall-to-wall once-orange carpet of Arthur's furnished flat, with Akram's marble-black eyes staring up at Arthur's "girlfriend" as if an M-1 were being aimed straight down at him with the worst of intentions, and his darkened penis yet stiff, perking-out from the pee-slit of his jaundiced underpants like a cartoon of an apologetic Pinocchio (Anna) or the periscopal snout of an opossum (Arthur). . . No, Akram did not get it, and thus he was not daunted, not quite—perhaps this was some American idiosyncrasy—mighty showoff foreplay rightful in the mighty advanced king of nations, *but still only foreplay*: for American ways could not triumph over the universal-natural ways of woman-and-man, eons-old and eons-proven—and Akram now broke a smile, one of the widower's and now childless man's ingratiating simpers that he had allowed himself to this date; and Akram went for the rightful-male-upward-trajectory and stood, breathing heavily, holding onto his big belly as if it were a gift both being bared and being beared, and thus game-and-ready for the challenging act of this weird American love. But Anna, she just plain stuck-out her right hand, which she still, amazingly, generously, meant in friendship—it seemed; which hand Akram took, not sure what to do with, even as Anna squeezed so hard, so *hard,* for there to be no doubt of her intentions, and Akram came down again to his knees. . . And for the remainder of Anna's stay they watched a doctor show which happened to be all-the-rage at this date, where the Englishman playing an American named "House" was the world's greatest diagnostician and the world's worst human being— Akram stewing during commercials over his indignity and the obvious disillusionment of his sojourn in the "happy-safety" of America, and Anna saying to Arthur at the door as she went home: "Darling"—yes she called him darling, which wasn't sexual but did thrill him on down to his toes—"darling, you have such a good heart, I hope it doesn't ruin you—or us."

What did Anna mean?

Otherwise: *"Why?—oh Why?"* Akram would go lamenting when he, at every 6 PM, still in his ever-employed underpants (he wouldn't deign to steal Arthur's "girl-knickers"), Akram snapped-on Arthur's ancient-used cathode-ray Sanyo, to maybe, who knew? get a peek of a glimpse at Something, *Something*, that might indicate the survival of his family or his town or at least a part of it.

"Oh Akram," Arthur tended to say. And that would be it.

And the "It" shown on the Sanyo was so little, so sparse, so news-nothing. Endless devastation, endless crumblings, the endless infinite vacuumizing of your birthplace and your lifeplace. That is, when American News showed any foreign anything.

"Your American News," would go Akram, "it is so Idiot, so primitive parochial. It is just *American*."—the 'American' voiced by him with an unhidden sneer. "Don't you people care about the *world*? On CNN, but Middle East CNN, or European CNN, you get to see the *world*—not which policeman shot which Negro in *Oklahoma* who was only blazoning a cellphone and not a *gun*."

"I know," Arthur's usual words. "America is very provincial."

"They receive more global News in *Siberia*. You all

here are so indifferent. No wonder you are all so *stupid* and Republicans."

But after a while this criticism, although he agreed with it, got to grating on Arthur, and he said: "If I were so indifferent to sorrow and misery as you say America is, why then would I have taken you in?"

Akram, with his narrowed black eyes inevitably sighting in sorrow-search, caught the drift:

"You are regretting."

Arthur lied, "No-no. . . No."

"I know No is Yes."

"You can stay, for as long as you wish." *Do I really mean this?*

"Well Arthur, I will tell you, I am regretting too."

This is gratitude?

"Regretting no, *not you*, but that I came to dumb America, where the men are women and the women are men. It was a mistake."

Arthur didn't *agree* in words but he didn't not agree. How could it have been, for him, otherwise?

"Arthur," said Akram, who was standing, belly in the lead, "I am leaving. I am returning to Syria. I should not have left. Maybe there is still a chance. Maybe there is a miracle." For after all he had prayed to Allah on his knees before Arthur's sleeping-sofa, and in his underwear, every day, sun-up and sun-down. Which Arthur had certainly respected enough to conquer his being put-off and put-out.

Anyway, to Arthur's mind this leaving by Akram might well have been the best decision possible.

And Akram repacked his pathetically shabby one bag and left Arthur's flat. If he might be able to manage to get himself all the way through the mountains and clans and religions of Turkey and then skirt round the inimical fighting Kurds, to Syria, who could ever know? Maybe all this, after the ugly-weak-Christian-Jew pariah confusions of America, the weak-idiocy commercialism of America, this was his way of suicide. Decent suicide. He would not mind achieving suicide, if achieved in this brave way. Arthur hated to think that he, well, when looking at it all through this his ex-roomie's eyes, he couldn't help but understand. . . No, he did not hate to think it or understand it.

But what had Anna meant by her having said on leaving Arthur's flat, "darling you have such a good heart; I hope it doesn't ruin you, or us."? Arthur got a good sense of her meaning when on his next visit to her place (one day) he went to embrace her and she backed back a trifle and said, "You do know, you put me in a terrible place with that Syrian, that sad man."

"I was only trying to be hospitable to him, and friendly."

"Oh, I know you and I know that."

"Well then?"

" 'Well-then'. You had me cornered into where I had to defend myself and"—she began shaking her head as if rejecting a posed question that was ridiculous, her soft facial features in a confusing contest with the powerful-planted pedestal of her body—"do a thing I never want to do."

"Be impolite to a man?"

She stared at him with a sorry-flattened smile—it seemed two dimensional and dissolving in its weary disappointment. "I wasn't impolite. No, I meant, beat-up a man. I've never ever wanted to do that kind of thing."

Such a statement coming as it did from sweet Anna seemed as if it had come from a different person speaking a different language. Until that moment Arthur had never thought in such terms. Had he thought in that way, he might have pictured Anna beating-up himself—which sight he could not bear to envision, with all its consequences upon further consequences. For example, for their marriage; and for greater example, for their children to observe. The consequences just came tumbling down, My God!

"It kills me," Anna said, "to not only do such a thing but to witness such a thing. It isn't right. Certainly there are women who can defeat men in battle, but unlike with men it isn't a triumphant thing, or a proving thing—and I did not want to be defensive, but he forced me. I was justified."

"I know."

Arthur realized that he had only seen such "interactions" of female-defeating-man in the movies, where a woman, schooled in all the Eastern Tai-Chi-Ju-Jitsu moves, like the actresses Angelina Jolie or Sandra Bullock, destroys a man—who is always deserving of the beating because he is foreign and unconscionably bad.

"And," said Anna, "I hated it, hitting that poor man and throwing him down, it grabbed at my insides— because, although you would think I wouldn't think that way because I love to make myself look so strong, the truth is I-am-just-a-girl, and that is how I want to remain—I do not like feeling myself as *coarse* or as a girl-bully."

"Anna, you had no choice. He's an Arab. Different

culture, it wasn't his fault, it wasn't your fault. He was—"

"Another woman would have just run. She would have taken-off and left the two of you. And so preserved the image of the-weak-so-coward-woman."

"Anna," Arthur said, determined to say it as strongly as possible. "I do love you. And that love has not been lessened by my having seen you, uh, handle, that man."

"Arthur," and now she again shook her head as if *she* had done wrong, "but now I'm not so sure of how it has affected me by having seen you see me do what I did to him, and not in any plain old training exercise on the mats. I'm so uncomfortable with it, you can't know. It's as if I don't want to be me, except I *do* want to be me. But I don't want to be a me having seen you seeing me in that fighter-way. It undermines."

"I understand."

"No, you can't." Then her brown eyes seemed to dilute, to wash-away her ability to see, to confront. "You can't understand how women are, even as you were one—or a girl."

Arthur had had enough of that sort of palaver for a millennium, even when it was meant as a palliative: he decided to let it be.

He said, "It'll never happen again."

"It could, Arthur. In the streets. You never know."

"I can fight."

Her entire lower face rose up to close her eyes and thus deny her amusement at that exaggerated claim—his proud belligerence meant in gentleman's decency. Anna saw "her man" popped on the noggin and tumbling in eternal somersaults before her very saddened eyes.

Arthur went again to embrace the woman he still felt was his woman—*and why shouldn't she be!* Anna again backed off, perhaps—to Arthur's mind suddenly transformed by the (false) authenticity of her fears and argument—she was perhaps afraid that she might hurt him, squash him—which was ridiculous, it really was.

It really was!

Embarrassment was another thing, but he'd leave that for another day—and even if it were true, he'd get over it, and it would go away. Maybe embarrassment wouldn't even be embarrassment.

Arthur asked, or stated (but only in the covered quarry of his mind, so as not to come-off too weak) 'You do still love me, don't you.'—and then he answered his own silent question with one of Anna's ambiguous muscle-softness worry-shrugs. He looked 'his woman' over, lord she was so powerful to see, especially when you were focused in that way. Then Arthur asked, or stated (again only in that well-covered silent quarry of his mind), 'The love we felt together in all our many-varied ways just some days ago, and that no one, no one, or *no-two*, could match, it was so incredible, and didn't that *prove* to us that we are meant for each other—and no one else, *no one*, fits?'

"I don't think, until we've thought more all about it," Anna said, backing away now towards her convenient, anti-romantic sink, "we should enter into our love again."

"*Anna!*"

"We have to think, Arthur. Maybe as I did when I was ten or so and decided to start lifting up my little-boy barbells, and changed my looks and life forever, and everyone's who came, who comes, into contact

with me."
   "I love you."
   "Oh Arthur, we'll just have to see."

XV

"Well," said Dwinski-Dwin in his office to Arthur. Sitting-up, arms folded before his chest in Super Caesar mode, but still looking small—as he was small—he still managed to show that he was set to go launching into a super-demeaning consultation. "You sure screwed that Arab one up, didn't you." Comically though he also sounded like Hardy chiding Laurel.

In any case, his presentation was enough to have Arthur shifting about in the red-plastic bucket chair on the opposite side of his boss's desk.

"Akram?" Arthur asked, knowing, obviously, full-well.

"He notified Social Services."

"How could he? He left the country."

"He didn't leave the country. He couldn't get out—he's fucking *Syrian!*"

"But he notified of what? I treated him—"

"You treated him as a *brother*. Arthur, we are not here our clients' *brothers*—you fell to the same fault with that Jamil character of yours. That sort of intimacy destroys the whole process, who knows *how* 'these people' feel about their 'brother' kin, especially case-workers faking it 'for good intention'—they have *contempt* for that. I thought with that Jamil Tandon's playing you that you'd have learned your lesson."

"His family, Akram's." Arthur was leaning his neck about as forward as he could manage without threatening his smug superior that he might dive over the man's desk. "His country. What a loss to live with."

"Be that as it may. We are not *God* here, Arthur."

All I have to do is get fired and that may well finish me off with Anna—though she knows deep-down that We Are One. She being so worried about our future.

"You have such *feeling*, Arthur."

So here it comes, the calm before the storm, the wry sarcastic backhand before the deadly fronthand.

Dwinski-Dwin looked down at some papers strewn-along his desk and began rustling, bent forward to find the apparent One. The implicit weight to Arthur was that this Supervisor of his wanted him to fail—and fail and fail and fail: "Look, Arthur, I think the one-on-one may not be your métier. Your instinct is to get too close, whether it's to help The Other beyond helping or to prove something to yourself—that may well also be beyond helping, you know?"

I don't know!

I do know!

Arthur couldn't argue with such a Dwinski-Dwin observation that he himself had unearthed about himself perhaps one thousand times. And re-earthed the exact same number.

"We're starting a new program here." Dwinski-Dwin held that unearthed paper between himself and Arthur, as if he were hiding or deciding if he ought to inform Arthur of this-new-thing that perhaps the young man might fail at as successfully as he had failed at the-old-thing. Then Dwinski-Dwin lowered the paper, his brown Mexicanish eyes swelling at this-man-who-tried-so-hard.

Arthur expected that The New Program might be on the order of something like Group Therapy—except that Group Therapy was not new, not even at the DSS, and he doubted that Dwinski-Dwin would see Individual Therapy failure him as qualified to run a group made up of Individuals.

"Arthur, have you ever heard of Biofeedback?"

"Yes, sure."

Does he want me to administer it or receive it?

"Have you ever been a party to it?"

"When I applied for the police—you know about that?—that I was a police recruit, short-lived."

"Yes, it's in these papers." He rattled them as if breezing away non-existent heat (this resembled mime). "Your police 'work' was here at the DSS, observing, protecting" (again that sarcastic semi-sidewise tone), "and it was short-lived."

"I wasn't fired," upshot Arthur, as if that was what Dwinski-Dwin was implying. "I decided I wanted to be a part of the Department here. Helping people."

On the 'helping people', Dwinski-Dwin effected an ear-rattling cough.

"Well, anyway," said Arthur, "for police-work I did take a polygraph. I passed it."

"Yes, of your honesty that's one thing of which I have little doubt." Dwinski-Dwin exhaled, the paper he held rattling once again. Was the out-breath frustration?—or was it merely a well-earned innocent exhale? "In any case, polygraph is based on the same principle as biofeedback, the brain, the cardio and muscles and nerves, but they're not the same. The polygraph is feed-out, not feed*back*—which would of course undermine the whole intention of the polygraph—investigation. Bio*feed*back is in the search for truth, and change; poly is in the search for truth, yes, but not for change."

"I know that."

Arthur was getting lost.

"Then *why* did you?—oh forget it." Dwinski-Dwin seemed to feel the visual dislocating need to go at the brushing of his shoes, which he did with his fingers, raising his knees and feet as some kind of psychic buffer. "Look Arthur," he said, "biofeedback can be used for, or rather against, many psychological road-blocks and impediments. Relaxation of course. Lying-aversion. Even as a cure for chronic constipation or diarrhea, how about *that*. But here we want to work on 'ambition', on the positives—helping our clients devel-op some start towards a 'get-up-and-go', so as to work their ways off of the endless drain of the dole."

"I see."

Arthur heard his low-key (artificial-knowing) 'I see' as perfectly competent and manly. He was rather proud of its calm depth.

At just that moment some client went galloping through the DSS halls hollering, "You *mother-fuckers!*—I ain't *never!* . . ."

Truth was he sounded black to Arthur, who rued his prejudice: White men, white recipients, they hollered-out "motherfuckers" too.

"Well," said Arthur's supervisor. "I have the feeling

that, in view of your not especially glorious success as a caseworker in the one-to-one, perhaps because—and I must admit that I'm not necessarily comfortable in saying this—but because you may well make our clients, *your* clients, uncomfortable due to your physical abnormalities, which lead the men that *you* are supposed to lead, into a kind of confusion of identities, i.e. whether to respect you or not, or walk all over you, and I am not trying to hurt or wound you here, Arthur—I have the feeling that you might do better as a kind of 'technician'. As a biofeedback operator you would, for the most part, wrap an electrode strip no larger than a bandaid about the client's finger and the two of you would listen to clicks that would, in their deceleration, if that took place due to your tutelage, your guidance, indicate an improvement in clients' self—"

Damned if I want to do this: I want to work with people, as people, not as fingertips. Not as electronic jolts and clicks. I don't want to be some accountant or bookkeeper of emotions—and anyway it seems to me like a WOMANISH thing to do. Damnit! It's bad enough that now Anna has her doubts and I Love her. Alright, I've had enough of life's frustrations and unfairnesses, I'm going to lay it on the line:

"Why?" Arthur now forced out, staring about as aggressively as he ever had with anybody—"*Why did you Kiss me!?*"

"*What!?*"

"You *Kissed* me, right here in this office. Don't you *remember*!? You hugged and you *Kissed* me."

Dwinski-Dwin settled deeply into his much larger chair than Arthur's; it appeared that he did this in order to think while in a cave, to distance himself as far as was possible from this delusionary homosexual-double-sexual incompetent who seemed now to be coveting him and making up lies, horrendous lies.

"Are you insane?" he went.

"You kissed me." This time Arthur muttered-it-out almost under his breath, as if they were two people who were very close, as in a cell. Perhaps this little Sephardic Mexicanish Jew needed to take a polygraph.

"Arthur," went Dwinski-Dwin, "I'll put this as succinctly and, I hope, as painlessly, as possible, you—"

Arthur knew what was coming, and he could hear himself planning his defense, his manly response, his return-attack.

"You're *fired*. Just go clean out your desk, which I imagine hasn't much in it anyway."

"Unless I'm mistaken, sir—and I've read all the Welfare Department rules, there has to be a hearing. This institution is a *democracy*."

"Arthur, you want a *hearing*?—you want to make what's bad even worse, you want to make it so that you'll never be hired for *any* job, *anywhere*, you're barking here up a very precarious tree."

"You fire me, I'll report that you kissed me."

"*You'll* report." It was obvious that Dwinski-Dwin was threatening that no one in the world, much less the DSS Welfare agency, would believe Arthur, who, for once in his life being on the offense, and enjoying it, countered with the most confident singular nod and listing of his head, accompanied by an overwhelmingly cocky occlusiation of his eyelids.

Said Dwinski-Dwin: "So, you want a Hearing!? So, you're doing me a favor in the getting-rid-of-you department. After what you just said, do you really believe I'm going to back *down*?"

The night before the referendum, The Hearing, Arthur endured the metaphoric dream that he was being put on trial for a murder which he was not sure he committed or did not commit, and he recollected that dream as The Hearing began, with its initial, compulsory-seeming silence, as if a hanging were about to be effected. An Edward Hopper oil painting might have done it justice. That initial silence of The Hearing took place as everyone first found their seats and stared, while street sounds did manage to filter-in, rendering the room even more silent-seeming, more out-of-this-workaday-world, and it was frightening—to Arthur—and yet the fright of it was, somehow, inexplicably thrilling, as, indeed, a hanging might have been in the town square. The Hearing was held in the grayness-drenched lounge meeting room of DSS. An oblong affair with windows facing in one direction the downtown expressway and in the other the miserably decrepit (and tiny) (and restaurantless) Penn station (which had only one claim-to-fame, aside from its being the last stop before arrival in Washington: it was mentioned in the Thirties swing-song *"Chattanooga Choochoo"*). The long conference table was of a wood that was as indeterminate as that of a medieval shack, and like the chairs surrounding it, it was bulging with "ornaments" of lathe-made canyons bumps and ringlike bulges—it was usually used for caseworker brown-bag lunch or for caseworker anytime breaktime forehead to forearm naps. The walls were decorated with photographs, not of retired great social-workers but of clients—or recipients—who had succeeded in making-it off the dole, and had even risen to "high-paying-jobs"—there was only one white person hanging (obviously, thought Arthur, who was seated at one end of the table, head hung, as if awaiting the guillotine), the white "ex-recipient" hanging must have been a case of affirmative action in reverse. The ceiling light was large and poorly shaded, so its glare fell on the papers placed on the conference table as if each and every person seated had aimed a flashlight on the materials—which Arthur came to see in time were only in small part DSS documents and notes but rather copies of *The Nation, Domestic Policy, The New York Review of Books*, etc. The chief hearer and observer at the meeting was the forever unassailable Doctor Lisalotte Benjamin, who at age seventy-five was so grayish in her dress and in her rather long anatomy (five foot ten) it required some dedicated concentration to demarcate where her clothing left-off and her true person began; Doctor Benjamin was certainly on her last legs as far as active social work went, but she had refused retirement—and no one, it was expected, had ever broached such suggestion such for her. It was also well-known that, despite her humorously incisive eyes and perpetually bright smile Doctor (of Social Work) Benjamin had long ago suffered the loss of both of her parents in the *Arbeit Macht Frei* country-club of Auschwitz, and she was unmarried and childless (and of course grandchild-less) so no one ever was comprised of the insensitivity, much less the crude-cruelty that would have been required for forcing her out into what would have been for her the world's emptiness. Without social work to sustain her—and administrating it was obviously her receiving it—she would have succumbed in no time. . .

Seated also round the table were those senior social-
workers who had primacy, who could make organiza-
tional decisions: Frank Young, a paunchy dark-skinned
black man in his mid-forties, a humorous man, a sexual
man, who had once, to make new recruit Arthur Becker
comfortable, taken him aside and pointed out a speed-
walking tight-skirted black secretary in the hallways
who he referred to as regarding her unbelievably protuberant—and sexually so to most men—rump as "Two
bears in a blanket." A good man, Frank Young, who
had once invited Arthur to his home in what Arthur
recognized as an abandoned Jewish neighborhood
(Frank's wife and kids were shocked at Arthur's entrance: for an instant it had seemed to paranoid Arthur
that they were not discombobulated by his being "ofay"
white but by what they perspicaciously discerned as his
transsexuality [he was wrong]); Frank had invited
Arthur to his home so that this nice white semi-boy
(and thus a "semi-brother in discrimination") might
hear segments of his prized jazz collection ("Can't tell
sometimes if Coltrane's made his handled tenor sound-
out like a worrisome alto—that's genious, my good
man!"), and he had once confided to Arthur that had
America not been "the eternal racist co-opt blind-
barbarity" that it was, he, black Frank Young, might not
have had to have "wasted" the past twenty-five years of
his life as a "pussy-shit lifeguard", for that, social-work,
had always been the pretty much "onliest" job available
to college grad blacks in the "card-shark under-the-
deck-deal America-equality three-card-monte double-
cross"—hell, *he'd* had the "skids" to become a PR guy
or a "stocks-stoker" as, as that happened to be what was
Arthur's super-successful father Mark (which inside

info was of course not available to Frank Young), this genial-generous black Frank, who, as with Arthur's onetime felonious client Jamil Tandon, Arthur was rather sublimely effervescent about re black-acceptance (even as he knew it was, sure enough, false-acceptance—and even, for him, frail double-sex him, black understanding and loser-sympathy); Amity Pascoli, who was, like Frank Young, black and friendly, but unlike him light skinned and thirtyish, with the slenderest of nostrils and the slender-sleekest of proportions— she who was married to a white man, Paul Pascoli, a physics prof at Johns Hopkins U, not to be confused with the hospital of the same name; Maureen McBride, a slovenly rotund white lady "of a certain age" who wore paisley tent dresses, usually the same one weekly, to cover-up her bulk (but which also uncovered its well-known smell) and who had been employed at the DSS for a period far longer than had regretful-comedic Frank Young, and who had on any number of occasions sued the city and the state for their politically reactionary delays and rejections on such important "universal" topics as the inveterate naming of Junior High and High Schools with the appellations of southern Civil War generals and bigshots like Robert E. Lee and Jefferson Davis, and their holding-off on the dubbing of racist Baltimore a Sanctuary City for refugees; and, last but absolutely not least in the seniority department was Carolyn Clapp Clogg (surnames unbelievable but true), she who was, if she was a year, was sixty, and was a daughter of Marylanded aristocracy (she often talked about her pet horse, Brownie), and who had attended Vassar College way back when it was all-girls, and who had known at that queen-school of The Seven Sisters

(Smith, Wellesley, etc), Jane Fonda, and who had performed almost as considerable a quantity of noblesse-oblige as had Lisalotte Benjamin herself. Carolyn Clapp Clogg was slender with gray-blonde hair, thin and short and delicate, as if she had perhaps just undergone a series of chemo infusions; but that lay of smooth felt, considering her thin build and her delicate face, was actually quite beautiful—Arthur had more than once wished to walk to her and pet it.

"It has been so long years since we have had to conduct a session on the order of such as this," said Doctor Benjamin in her Germanicly but friendly guttural (Frank Young winked a 'no sweat, my man' at Arthur), "that, I believe, logic would have us dictate our attendance straight at Arthur here's accuser."

"Yes," said Dwinski-Dwin, "I am ready."

On this trial-of-dismissal occasion, the short Mexicanish-but-Jewish social-worker supervisor with that licorice-stick straight black hair of his had worn a black suit, as if he were a preacherman or was attending a funeral. Arthur had chosen a Harris tweed that his haberdash-savvy father Mark had picked out for him at the most exclusive men's "outfitter" in town, The Canterbury Shop (where Mark Becker had once, in the Fifties, for a serious braggadocio lark, stolen a cross-lacrosse-sticks tie)—the tweed jacket was cut deep at the waist, British style. "Don't you think this is a bit too much?" Arthur had asked his father, who prided himself on his knowing people, strength and weakness: "Impressiveness is next to Godliness," Mark had quipped, comic and serious; and Arthur, while doubting the appropriateness of such high-flown attire-knowledge in a dismal-spare Welfare Department setting, had nonetheless been inescapably impressed and taken the suit—because, also, he goddamn loved it. (The Brit outflare at the hips was perfect for his hated hormonic hip-outflare—it camouflaged his "girliness".).

"Are you ready to listen, Arthur?" This was the indulgent-kind Doctor Benjamin, succoring Arthur as if he were a needy-shaky social-work client. (The Brit-suit had had zero effect on her: she likely hadn't even noticed it.).

Arthur said, "I am ready."

"So:"—Doctor Benjamin, looking straight at Dwinski-Dwin.

"As you can imagine," began Arthur's supervisor, "I am averse, as we all here are"—quick scan of his comrades at the long lathe-deadened table—"to bringing charges"—Frank Young jut in a crack-shot of "quit dribblin' like it's military"—and Dwinski-Dwin shook his head as if he didn't understand, and/or disregarded the black-man-fixture's pathetic wisenheimerishness, so he proceeded—"charges against one of our fellow-colleagues who have obviously chosen to work here out of, well, what is obviously a concern for the social welfare of Baltimore's needy."

'Christ', thought Arthur, 'It's Mister Stilted: he sounds as if he's running for office.'

"You're averse to what you're doing here, *but*?" said Amity Pascoli, who had always been nice to Arthur, even introducing him to her husband the physicist Paul when that supposed genius professor had showed up for lunch or whatnot. Arthur did admire Paul Pascoli, not just for being a brilliant Hopkins physicist (sub-atomic or astronomical?—Arthur hadn't had the knowledge [or interest] to inquire), but he admired him as well for having married a black woman. (It had not occurred to him that he might just as well have admired Amity for the same reason in reverse—marrying a "greasy wop-guinea genius who probably, as a diffident spaced-out genius, had Assburger's").

" 'But'," went Dwinski-Dwin, "okay, I'll come right out with it." He dipped his head for a moment, his big round brown head—it was as if he had crib notes tucked into his belt. "We all know here, although politeness and decency has kept us from saying it, that Arthur is—what do you call it?—a, uh, transperson. He is neither male nor female. He can be either one."

"I'm *male!*" Arthur jutted-in, his own voice surprising him with the depth of its catalysis. "I *can't* be either one! Nor do I *want* to be."

"Is this relevant, what you say?" Doctor Benjamin cautioned Dwinski-Dwin. "Can we not dispense with it? These sorts of statements do breed prejudice, even when we do not wish them to. Which in a hearing such as this one is the last injection we should want to hear. Nor in this Department of Welfare."

"I'm sorry," said Dwinski-Dwin, "but it's relevant."

"And Arthur," said Doctor Benjamin, "I know you're eager, I know you do not wish to be what you consider to be—insulted, but try to control: you will have your turn. You know that."

Arthur nodded—a soft slow nod, as it was directed towards the kindly ancient Head of Welfare who had seen more than her own share of sorrows and who seemed at that moment his own protective mother.

"Arthur Becker here," said Dwinski-Dwin, "claims, and he *repeatedly* claims it"—

I did not repeatedly claim it.

"—that in my office I went over and hugged him and kissed him, sensually—on the lips, implying, as if I were, well, . . . "

As he had already been warned, by Lisalotte Benjamin, that prejudice and insult were inappropriate and even slanderous in this egalitarian Welfare setting, Dwinski-Dwin opted for the benign substitute for the accusative word 'homosexual', inserting the words, "you know."

Again Frank Young winked to Arthur. Was the wink a good-buddy communiqué to the effect that Harold Dwinski-Dwin was indeed, if not a fruit, at least a pussy-wimp-wus-snitch-squealer? And/Or was he sending his approval of Arthur's sexual disdain?—or his preferences? Or was Frank Young himself, with a family of five, gay? *No, no way for that. . .* To Dwinski-Dwin's 'you know' all the others dipped their heads, as if that sort of behavior, while the visualization of it could not be suppressed, lay beneath the conference table.

"And . . . ?" asked Doctor Benjamin.

"And?" impertinently asked Harold Dwinski-Dwin.

"I mean, did Mister Becker here proceed further, in what he said, or in what he may have acted? Did he subsequently disseminate his conclusions about the Welfare offices?"

"No—well, I don't know. But—I-am-not-*gay*."

"That," said ancient Lisalotte Benjamin, "is not a proper word."

"And, proper or no, methinks yon' Mister Dwin-Dwin here protests too much."

The above was the observation of Frank Young.

"Oh, and it is—a proper word," contributed the aristocratic noblesse-oblige Carolyn Clapp Clogg, who sat generations-taut high-and-dignified in her crummy plastic Welfare chair. " 'Gay' is now perfectly accept-able, and usable as is the original meaning of the word. As is the behavior." She had not moved a muscle.

Ms. Clogg was not married, and she never had been.

"Oh, 'gay,' this modern world." With disconsoling head-shake from Doctor Benjamin, who had seen-it-all—or thought she had. "Is there nothing remaining not to be mocked and metamorphosized?"

"Well," now interrupted by politically active (and dress-sloppy) Maureen MacBride, "one is accused of gay and one is accused of transism—and both are per-fectly acceptable, they're day-to-day, they're *nothing*, they're about as petty as petty can be—so let's trash the petty imprisonment and go back to our work, shall we—if in point of fact we have any here."

"No!" It was Dwinski-Dwin. "We, you, you have not heard me out, you can't possibly have made any right decision yet."

"No?" It was Frank Young, who was undoubtedly enjoying this break from his job of twenty-five years of tedious and miniscule sad comedy, and who obviously wished to provoke the prolongation of this, what-he-considered, worthless absurdity—which he did seem to find enjoyable, good theatre.

But Dwinski-Dwin, not-to-be denied: "Arthur Becker, he was insinuating, and his insinuation, it was *hallucinating*. And even though I am *not* what he has *implied*, whether he has implied it and transmitted it out *loud* or not—his behavior does not conform to the values of the DSS, and it diminishes it, and it leaves the suspicion, and the expectation, that in future, if he is allowed to *continue* here with his work, if one wishes to call it that, he will make similar mistakes, or worse ones." Dwinksi-Dwin then recounted Arthur's failures with Jamil Tandon and with the Syrian Akram Medani, embellishing only as much as he ascertained his colleagues here might countenance: "That poor deluded Arab is probably lying dead by now on the fields of Syria, as Arthur *drove* him to go back, inadvertently or not, he *drove* him, with his deluded 'kindness', his *hypocritical* kindness—and as Arthur here's *other* client Jamil Tandon is now returned to his cell in prison—*again* by way of this sad young man's deluded 'kindness'."

"I did *not cause*—!"

"Doctor Benjamin told you, Arthur, not to speak until spoken-to, until it was your turn."

"Harold, *Mister* Dwin (the 'mister' leading Arthur to conjecture that Dwinski did not own a PhD), *you* are not leading the discussion here," reminded the weighty consternated no bullshit Maureen McBride.

"I'm his *Supervisor*," reminded Dwinski-Dwin, and hefty Ms. MacBride looked as if she might, after this meeting, whatever the outcome, knock the watery crap out of the little Mexican-looking, socially-concerned, socially-fearing, well, what-can-you-say?, calculating Jewboy.

"Calling names, or implying them," now piped-up Carolyn Clogg Clapp in her modulated tones.

"Yes, Carolyn?" said the Jewish immigrant leader— and the aging aristocrat continued—

"As Harold has, in a way, implied, these sexual questions are not the issue, while they are of course the issue—and in various ways. To my way of thinking, what is the central issue here is respect—or, I have to say, the lack of it—and a kind of concomitant self, well, self-regard, which may have led Arthur, whether he meant it or not, to be, well, seductive. Now, I like Arthur Becker, I do"—and she smiled graciously at him—"or what I have gleaned of Arthur. But, as the Department here is really built on a foundation of trust and benefit-of-the-doubt and even a dignified containment of one's personal attitudes towards another, it worries me that Arthur—Mister Becker (she smiled at Arthur, as if in apology)—Arthur seems to have precipitated a possible dark cloud of hostility between some workers, and perhaps employees, which can make our work much more difficult. For whatever reason, call it what you may, transism or homosexuality"—avoiding 'gay', she smiled benevolently toward her old-revered immigrant boss—"and, it seems to me that we have to investigate more thoroughly the psychological climate sourcing between these two"—and she hesitated strangely—"men." (Frank Young grinned with a happy sadism). To the best of my knowledge, Harold Dwinski-Dwin here has never been engaged in such a precipitous quarrel with any other worker"—Frank Young cleared this throat, fake objectively—"so, beyond the name-calling there must be some essential element in transmission about here, and as much as I dislike suspecting it I have to suspect Arthur here, his being the newcomer. And so, as firing someone, or letting-them-go, is rather a dramatic non-Welfare Department type of action, I would like to suggest that before we proceed down that unpleasant avenue, that last resort, we inquire of Arthur if he would not mind submitting himself to perhaps a test, a written psychological test, to be administered by the department's psychometrist—or, if that seems too unsubstantial and clerical, a series of 'meetings' with the department's psychologist. I don't think that either would be so intrusively terrible—considering the alternative."

She looked, for agreement, towards the Welfare Head, while Arthur, with an abstract gaze of betrayal, wondered *What-in-the-world-did I-ever do-to-HER? I don't want to take any more psych-tests: I took a zillion of them when I went qualifying for all my miserable sex- surgeries, and the Police Department. . . Just FIRE ME, jettison my ass, if all that test crap's what's in the offing! They're going to turn me into the kind of shifty hater that Dwinski is.*

I hate them all.

No, control yourself. You DON'T hate, damnit!

But Doctor Benjamin now seemed to be bored and slumping *towards* what must have been her late morning pre-lunch nap, and she was as well no little annoyed at Dwinski-Dwin's earlier impulsive and bumptious takeover of the proceedings, this before Ms. Carolyn Clogg Clapp had done the same, but unbumptuously and graciously and upper-classedly; so before such diversions manifested into a mild and sleepy chaos, before they became a surreal ballet-dream-scene she wisely jutted in—

"Please Arthur, *speak*."

"I want to *help* people," Arthur said. As he had the night before prepared himself.

"Your 'Help'," went Dwinski-Dwin. "You do have a bizarre unhelpful way of showing it, of *hurting,* with your"—

"Hey, jim, please butt-out now," went Frank Young. "Let the man roll-on. And, my man, if we're going to be fair here, as we say we are, we ought to have *you*, Mister Harold here too examined for your diggities."

His what?—the long-term members looked about, to each other, Maureen MacBride grinning in appreciation towards Frank Young; and with her delicate caramel-mocha fingers Amity Pascoli covered her mouth, which seemed to have gone agiggle, making Frank Young smile at his own fairness of racio-sexuality.

I wonder if those two have ever had an affair.

"I want to *help* people," repeated Arthur. "I've always wanted to—how could I *not!* And this desire should not be surprising at all, when you consider or"— he looked about at the now intensely-directed faces, waiting—"when you consider all of the difficulties, all of the help-needing *I* have, well, uh, needed, in my life—from the beginning on, the very beginning, me with my at the very start, my, well, vagina that was unwanted—I'm sorry, I'm sorry to bring that up, to *use* it, but—." On the '*use* it' he dipped his head in a gesture of apology towards the women, to show that his intention was not to derogate their cunts—but they appeared to understand a boy-infant not having wanted to have what they had and they wanted and they re-lished. "And," added Arthur, "there were the difficulties and disappointments and embarrassments of my *parents*." Now Arthur heard a long sigh or wheeze—he couldn't tell from which auditor that breathing-out was coming, or if it was from his adversary-enemy Dwinski-Dwin, but he felt, strangely and not so strange-ly, that he was a performer once again at Carnegie-Mellon University, he being called-upon to be both graceful and mellifluous and powerful, and unem-barrassed, to be, in a name, Cadeau Courir—who he wished might just magically appear now and dance to the strong-felt wordage of his speech, Cadeau Courir showing that Arthur here was not-acting, except to the extent that good acting was not even acting but was oh so real, the very heart of The Real. "I don't want to be fawning," he went on, "or begging or complaining"— again the breath-wheeze, sure it was Dwinski-Dwin, that better-than-thou worse-then-thou—"but how could you imagine, how could *anyone* imagine, that a kid and a young adult who has been, in a word, kicked and tickled to death, and gawked-at until he could not bear to look at his own body, his own *essence*, for godssake, such a 'freak' could not want to be, in his *person*, a preventive to the same cruelties happening to *anyone*—me, a young man who has had to *fight* to *ward* off (*god don't say 'slings and arrows'*) the inhuman mockeries that have impelled me to do my best and build myself up, my *muscles* (he pictured robust-soft Anna—what had *she* looked-like as a child?—that had impelled *her* to spend every spare instant at Gold's Gym so as not to be what *she* had looked-like as a child—oh he *loved* her!), me, *I*, who has been impelled to build-up, both physical and psychological, my *muscles*, to fight it out against the sadism, the sadism of sadism and the sadism of indifference, cold indifference, and that's why, if anyone *attacks* me I am *one thing*, I am *determined* to be (sharp-angled lit-fuse look to Dwinski-Dwin), and if anyone *respects* me, as for example the Syrian client-refugee Akram Medani did, I *offered* the that poor man Syrian the sharing of my small apartment, for *he* was *me*, he was a, well, a Jean Valjean condemned by-the-law, by ironic law, by human inhuman *moralities*, so to speak, for stealing in a sense his pathetic slice of bread—*that's* why, as I sit here (he wished now that he were *standing*, Mister Potency, not Mister Pittancy, *he* standing and *ruling*, as if *he*, Arthur Becker, were the decider here on his *job* and *on his life*—and he knew that such impulsive "virility" would finish him off for good), that's why I have become a person who has *taught* himself to, sometimes, *break*-the-rules—no, not to lie that a man is a homosexual—*which I did not do!*—nor to *imply* it—that "slander", it is in *his* mind, *that* man's—but I have taught myself to withstand 'the-curiosity-look', and that sense of superiority over me that people naturally come-by without trying, and to look straight into their eyes (he now decided to look into no one's eyes), until I can—"

"Enough!"

It was Dwinski-Dwin, spread-fingered hands hovering at his temples like the Jaws of Life: "I can't *believe* this," he broke in. "Is this some rehearsed speech, so *con*-job, as it were, to divert what Arthur Becker so obviously—"

"Harold," went The Head of Welfare, ancient admirable Lisalotte Benjamin, in the lowest, softest voice imaginable. "Please, we have to let Arthur here continue."

"No!" went Dwinski-Dwin, his head now implying a lumpish sob-bubbling-prepped beanbag.

And perhaps because Arthur was now experiencing a taste of triumph in the racked recountings of his history and his attempts to surmount his history, and his struggled successes at that at times, and by contrast, Dwinski-Dwin was feeling loss and defeat at his own attempts—Arthur's being fired—and his own dignity slipping through his fingertips, that Arthur now offered a confident calm-voiced, "Please, it's okay, let the man continue." *Let him finish the job of sinking his own ship.*

Lisalotte Benjamin nodded to Dwinski-Dwin her go-ahead—and this nod, to Arthur, appeared as if the Aged History-Persecuted Superior here at this Hearing were following *his* directives—which could only mean that he, Arthur, were rising, faster, stronger, more a male than ever (as far as he could recall), rising to the height of Right, and the defeat of that smarmy boss of his who had looked-down on him.

"Look at me," implored Dwinski-Dwin. "Don't look at Arthur Becker for a moment. Look at *me.*

All did.

"Put the embryo in the ashtray," he said.

In confusion, each looked at the other, as if there were a hidden embryo in the conference room (indeed, if there were even ashtrays). Was Dwinski-Dwin insulting poor Arthur Becker? Was this some sort of encoded but vivid refutation of Arthur?—or a surreal-ugly description of Arthur?

" 'Put the embryo in the ashtray'," repeated Dwinski-Dwin. "That's what line at Brown, the highly respected Ivy League university, my fellow students had such pleasure repeating as I walked-by, small in body as I am, or whispering in a classroom."

Frank Young smirked, as if he'd been one of the guilty Brown students.

"And why did they whisper that humiliation? or even shout it out sometimes—well, the answer is so obvious, isn't it?—I didn't even have to say it to you."

Dwinski-Dwin paused, he looked around the room. Even Arthur witnessed eyes closing, heads turning. For his own, he kept up his stare at Dwinski-Dwin, his out-ranker: He was trying to be tough-him, but sympathy—his female side as he saw it—that was rising-up within him. . . and, paradoxically-but-not, he was proud of that, and always had been.

"So why that insult?—that habitual "fun" persecu-tion. The answer is here sitting before you, isn't it. It's that, and I can come out right now and say it, with my dwarf-like height and my dark complexion and my low-class hair (he touched his hair; he did not run his hand through it) I look like some poor Central American trying to sneak his way over the Rio Grande and into America. I look like some shrimp sneak-attacking the 'great' Davie Crockett at the great Alamo. I look like that little dark one-eyed Mexican criminal in *The Treasure of the Sierra Madre* who claims to Humphrey Bogart—"

Just like "refined" persnickety Dwinski-Dwin, thought Arthur, *to say Humphrey Bogart, as if the whole world doesn't just refer affectionately to the movie-supreme as "Bogie", or at least just Bogart. . .*

"—When Humphrey Bogart asks him who he is, and the Mexican bandito claims he is a vigilante, and Hum-phrey Bogart asks to see his badge, and the 'little darkie' (Dwinski-Dwin emphasized those adjectives, as he was making that point about himself and prejudice) that Mexican, he brazenly declaims, *'I don' need no stinking badge.'*" "

No one laughed. Arthur wasn't even sure that any-one understood—beyond the hip Frank Young, that is—who didn't give a shit.

Arthur: *Couldn't this schmuck have at least re-counted the story with some panache—I mean, it's "steenkeen" badge, not "stinking". No wonder my "boss" here has zero rapport with any of his clients, or with me. I can imagine how the black dudes refer to him, and far worse than did his "Ivy League" Brown U. dudes. Shit, I bet he is gay. . . and, to think, I took comfort at first from his hug, and maybe from his—yuch— kiss. . . And I know what I'll do here as I sit: I'll use my mime-taught skills to present what will show-up here as a laudable concern yet also a laudable indifference to Dwinski-Dwin's history, his competing history, of belittlement; after all, the man had still grown-up normal.*

"So," continued Dwinksi-Dwin, "don't you, each of you, my colleagues, think that *I* have as much right to be respected, and admired, for the indignities that I have suffered—I mean they are both biological slights, mine and Arthur Becker's, but I have never, to the best of my recollection, here or anywhere, expected or claimed any special treatment or any special sympathy for *my* . . . "

And what the hell is he then damn doing here-and-now!?—Arthur, with this corrosive gruesome grin, which he made sure that his adversary saw.

Again there were looks about the room, searching looks: I.e.: Has Doctor Dwin ever claimed any special regard or dispensation for nature's putting its fate upon him?

Hey, but what about dignity—damnit!? Has Doctor Lisalotte Benjamin, our leader, ever claimed, *or implied, or sought-out, any sympathy for Hitler's Kampf being laid upon her. Maybe if she hadn't been broken by her family's being broken, she'd have got married and had the grandchildren like the grandchild that she was of the Auschwitz Hell.*

Arthur, the self-bolstered man (he figured) he had now made-of himself (he figured), he did wish to stand and say the above to the gathered Superiors in the conference room. While the truth was, what is deep-within-one remains deep-within-one, and he was sure, without a shred of doubt, that his misery made Dwinski-Dwin's misery like a rifle-wounded lion's hurt to the nothing-pain of a stepped-on cockroach: *There's millions of Mexicans and Hondurans and Panamanians and Costa Ricans and whoever, and I'm sure they don't walk around bent in misery over being short and peasant-haired. Christ, Dwinski-Dwin is at no more disadvantage than is a Sephardic Jew—which is, I guess, what he is—and what chutzpah to use it, there's no disadvantage here.*

"I'm finished," said Dwinski Dwin, "I have said my say."

He stared at no one.

Silence: The mind-filled sounds of special-pleading words, the competing histories wriggling through the muffled sounds of the legs of the wooden and plastic chairs and shuffling shoes, and the eagerness no doubt of everyone in that room to get themselves out.

"Arthur?" said Lisalotte Benjamin.

Arthur, assuming he had won what, among adults, amongst much less social workers devoted to the civilized care of others, what ought not have descended into the uncivilized realm of a loser-contest anyway—Arthur, like Dwinski-Dwin, declined any further historical surveyings of his absorptions of invectives, any he had so far today let slipslide from his mind. He had done what he had done, and with male-power, *his* male power—that was how he saw it, the whining not un-included. He had won what after all was—and the sneaking suspicion hung with him—a loser game. He felt as sorry for Dwinski-Dwin as his lack of empathy leaked-out to allow him.

"We have decisions to be made then," said Doctor Benjamin, "fair decisions, absolutely. But we also have much work to do outside of this . . . situation. So, we shall decide what-is-to-be-done, but not at present." She announced that the next day, the following Wednesday, would be when decisions would be made.

Frank Young gave Arthur fake-punches, buddy-air-punches, to his belly, as they all split up. "You'll be comin' to my house," said Frank, "we'll hear more of heaven's jazz, you ever hear Eckstine do *"A Cottage for Sale"?*—that *voice*, you'll feel like you lost that sweet cottage itself. *Your*self."

Did Frank Young's vague invitation imply that he, Frank, was giving Arthur a booby prize?—for his inevitable plunge into unbelongingness's abyss.

Not being the world's most confident person, that was Arthur found he felt.

For a few moments, until he felt the other, the (somewhat) winner, way.

XVI

Walking home that evening, Arthur passed as always the Gothic deeply filthened-up-filthened-down Maryland State Penitentiary, where by now his "client" Jamil Tandon was perhaps doing pushups in his funk-ridden cell (Arthur could do twenty—after years of compensatory weight-work; a "normal" male with a normal set of triceps and slats could likely do, he guessed, fifty, and "his" sweet Anna Bass, who knew how many— could be beyond one hundred?). The pavement (or in Balamorese the "payment") was so broken into its decades-surviving slabs and chips and gouges that one might have, in traversing it, felt himself a dancer or a drunk, and, at that, one who was heroic—an advancing warrior—or a retreating one (but definitely not a coward, not in this wasted neighborhood). The sky was a low dark gray, rain in the offing. Rain: if one put foretokening in it, what was the foretokening? Was he to be fired? Nah. Demoted?—impossible, he was at the lowest level now. He still expected exoneration and understanding, but certainly warning of some sort, and he was sappy enough, and so contemptuous of Dwinski-Dwin, to see himself as the recipient of "love"—well, some Welfare Department version of it, despite the rain premonition. He fully expected that he would be transferred away from "the embryo in the ashtray", conceivably to "the groovy-depressed" Frank Young.

He would go to Anna. Perhaps they would just go to a movie. That one where the young actor Jake Gyllenhaal played a sensitive, somewhat femalish-fey con man. Afterwards they would make love, they would rise and fall into the full special spectrum that their sex had produced that last time—at least in his mind it had. . . and they would live together, and, who knows, they might get married, and *they might have children!*—he had already investigated that possibility, questioning the endocrinologist who had treated him for all his life: testosterone, sometimes, could stimulate the production of semen: The endocrinologist certainly hadn't promised, but children was not out of the question: he had given Arthur articles to read, from the prestigious *New England Journal of Medicine* and from *The Lancet*: children was possible. And, more likely than possible, Arthur's Curse of androgyny would not be transmitted to their love-child.

As he walked further downtown across the bridge over Falls Way, he was envisioning himself and his wife Anna bending over the crib, lifting their love-child, kissing their love-child, loving their love-child, bringing-up their love-child, their absolutely *normal* love-child, when a dog, a mid-sized mongrel, came up alongside him and crooked its head to look over and up at Arthur; it was obvious what the dog wished by the supplicating look drowning his eyes: *Would you please help me by leading me across the traffic?* Smart dog to have asked for help. Arthur took hold of the dog's scruff—he had no collar, no name-tag—and said, as he walked, "Come."—which the stray dog did, walking alongside Arthur, and occasionally looking up towards Arthur, and then, once safely across the street, running off with not so much as a Thank You, Sir. *Well, I am a good man*, Arthur thought—and *I am a brave man, that mongrel could have bit me—the old damned No-good-deed-goes-unpunished—just like my fate at Welfare?* He had not then walked more than a dozen steps southward when he heard an "Arthur?—isn't that your name?" The woman was coming from the north, from Mount Royal Avenue, where lots of art students lived near the Maryland Institute, and her voice was familiar and also not-familiar. Her clipped and crackling-confident tones were certainly not those of anyone he knew at the DSS. Arthur stopped, he waited for her to catch up—and he did now recognize her. She was Lisa Lattin, the beautiful blonde med student, or internist, he had met—and been intoxicated-by (those riveting cheekbones)—at Anna's flat. "Heading to Anna's?" the woman asked—and Arthur nodded, and he didn't hesitate on that nod.

"She expecting you?"

"No, but—"

"Then," she suggested, "why not come with me."

"Where you going? I mean, you live just down the hall from Anna."

"I'm not heading home. My destination is The Walters Gallery. I'm an art lover." She grinning sarcastically, as if she were not.

The Walters Art Gallery, world famous especially

for its relics and artifacts of antiquities.

Arthur was embarrassed to admit that he had never been there, so he said, "Sure."

No coincidence, The Walters was in the shadow of Baltimore's Washington Monument. It was not a large museum, but it was elegantly constructed with fine-fashioned Renaissance-appearing details like gargoyles and angels above its outside pillars that to Arthur's limited mind here were (what else but) Platonic. Room to room, with no one else in the place (save one guard who resembled John Travolta, and who ogled Lisa) one crossed from millenniums before Christ to art that was contemporary—and there, sonofagun, in the first Renaissance room that he and Lisa entered, just beyond the statuettes of *lares*, ornate household gods from Pompeii (with visible penises [they indicated protection]), there beyond the *lares* was a statuette from, it was said, second century Rome, with a female figurine bearing male genitalia. Hermaphroditus, it was labeled, the transcription carved into a copper sign beneath which explained that said Hermaphroditus was the off-spring of Hermes and Aphrodite, swiftness and wisdom. Arthur was of course embarrassed—his urge had been to cover his groin—and really there were so many fertility figures and figurines about that he, now attached to the attracting Lisa, half suspected that she had made a deal with the museum's curator to exhibit this panoply of the exotic sex of the classical-human for Arthur's entrance and stupefaction—although he doubted that Anna had ever told this Lisa Lattin one word of his biology-story; and he recollected how his classmates had, looking at him, snickered and laughed when at the University of Maryland, in his first year, in the (thousand page) survey course book, there had been during that first (and only) week devoted to Classics, a photo of this selfsame image—the instructor quipping, "Now see what you kids get when you put together speed and smarts, it's just best to take it easy, wise or dumb, go *slow*." A young instructor with sex-innuendo meant to render himself no dull prof but Professor Popular with the kiddies. At Arthur's expense, he was not aware, not even as Arthur *was* aware, despite that *he was not a hermaphrodite*, that he only *looked like one*, or that *he might be one*, so that he had become an exhibition, a subject who might well have been pictured in that humungous-thick-and-shallow survey book. One's abnormality, even when no-fault, when not as abnormal as The Big Abnormal, it can't but make for one's razor-fault-alertness. Paranoia the offending diagnosis.

"You're sure lingering over that one," said Lisa. "Something I don't know?"

I bet you do know, Arthur thought to say, but he didn't say: he avoided responding. He was more busy clambering-up that time-tunnel of his own quintessence—although by now he was well aware of the alternate wisdom of that Hermes-Aphrodite amalgam, it was no baffling mixture to be feared or worshipped, the speed of Hermes depended upon the Aphrodite message, they were intertwined. Still, he regretted having come to The Walters with Lisa—he shouldn't have, this accompaniment was not wisdom: couldn't he conquer, or at least quash, his attraction to this, well, what word could there be? this dynamite, woman? . . . And dynamite she was, this Lisa Lattin—and dynamite she damn well knew she was: the blonde hair, yes, that stark-pale-to-near-white curtain to the sides of her broadish upper face with its cheekbones appearing almost swollen (with Aphrodite wisdom?—on the edge of Aphrodite cruelty?), no purity, no ethereality messaged here, nor about that long-narrow nose which implied intelligence—and knifish contempt?—the gray-blue eyes discerning, assessing, calculating without the slightest appearance of trying-to, paired-with that long aristo nose, both of which seemed to diminish the observed, as if to say that *the* observer, *she*, Lisa, was superior and held sympathy for the observed only when it, or he, or she, recognized her, Lisa's, superiority—and got near twitchy-beinged facing it; the long neck, quite long but not geeky, it had to be how it was, didn't it, to help maintain that superiority, to augment the Lisa height, which was almost Arthur's at five-eleven, that was his guess; the breasts just right—as they should have been, had to have been, with that lengthy slope of theirs, ski-jumpish, porn-movieish—the body, the heart (or the lack of it), dictated that cant, that sway; all such just beneath the shoulders which were thin-broad, like those of a Thirties actress, say Joan Crawford's shoulders (sans the epaulets); the in-swerve at her sides, that bias magnifying the good-width of her hips, which were definite-bossy in the way their swerve and rotation led and dictated—*follow!*—to whoever might be her companion, the way they said *I care about Me, not you*—if he'd touched her she'd be cold steel, but he wouldn't venture touching. And the clothing, perfect in their nothingmuchness: the ski sweater, dark-blue, with antelopes connected by their antlers, that sweater tucked into her jeans; the strap-casual brown sandals exhibiting the haughtiness of her arches and—of course—the arro-gance of her quick-walking steps.

Her great perfection was her so great imperfection.

Greater than what was her grudging crooked smile.

And why does she look this way? Why so much? Right on down to those pinpoint pierce-jab-stabbings of her expressions—she can't always be so withering in-flexible this way, not so totally; I bet she's sometimes nice, she must be—is all this exaggerated? Like theatre. Does my presence, even when I'm not feeling flimsy—as with now (at least I wasn't feeling flimsy until now)—does this me bring out especially the super-bitch in her? I wouldn't be surprised.

"Anna told me," she said, "you live nearby The Walters."

"Across street."

Excited, yes, but he'd immediately avoided showing it—as much as he could.

"Let's go there."

She might just as well have said 'Let's you eat doggie gutter-shit', as took place in that disgusting film by "Baltimore's own" John Waters, *Pink Flamingoes*. He'd have done it—he might well have.

For godsakes why would she want to go to *his* place? He was no George Clooney nor Brad Pitt, al-though unavoidably he was, in his physique, unique. Again that question of Anna's having told her things. . . And this Lisa being a med student or already a doctor, and studious-curious.

Once inside Arthur's little cell of an efficiency, she wasted no time. With her demonic look of voluptuous attention and control, her index-finger wagging in a strange spontaneous chastisement that was both mock and real, murderously real, and her eyes insisting that everything in this crummy furnished efficiency belonged to her, to *her*—this was now *Lisa's* realm!— Lisa Lattin took hold of and turned on the 3-way light at the end of Arthur's sofa, which she sat on to undo her sandals, which she kicked across the room (for some reason: bravado?); she bent forward in process of pulling over her head her antelope-antler pullover, she stood to draw down her jeans.

"You're not going to follow suit?" she asked, or, really, she said.

Trying to come off confident and casually routine, he took off his clothing, the Canterbury Shop Harris tweed jacket his dad had chosen for him, the crossed lacrosse-sticks tie (his dad had chosen for him), the pleated-to-the-belt-loops olive drab slacks (with belt-in-the-back yet) his dad Mark had picked-out for him, as Mark Becker often wore the same. It had not occurred to Arthur at the time that he had donned all this regalia for The Hearing, but now he did realize that he had been modeled after the immoral-sharp-calculating "hotshots" of that popular TV show of Fifties manipulator ad-assholes, *Mad Men*.

He stood before her as she remained seated.

"You are not the greatest of male specimens," she said. "But no doubt you have been advised of that before."

"I never claimed to be Adonis."

She smirked at that ludicrous prospect, her thin lips weaving in exaggeration.

And why does she have to say 'advised of that', instead of just plain 'told'? Does she have to thespian her way to aristocracy? She's more insecure about her-

self than Anna is.

In bold attempt he began walking towards her, but by paradox: slowly, pausing to press-down his fear, and then to build-up his momentum—he hoping that his competing muscles of anxiety will now compete to relax.

She narrowed her eyes, staring at his unmoved penis as if it were a spot, a stain she'd missed on a new-bought skirt. She said "Stop. Sit."

There was only one chair in his flat, a Kennedyesque rocker that he had purchased at a used furniture store on Lombard Street, and that he had had to put together—and the flimsiness of which had led him to not trust, even though the big-bellied Syrian Akram Medani had sat on it many times (while Arthur had waited for it to collapse). In augmentation he had bought an ottoman, plastic, green.

He sat, as she'd directed—on the ottoman. His bent-up knees had his thighs in a weird schoolboy incline.

"I'll tell you," she said, "when to come." She smirked with relished confidence.

She asked, "Are you in love with Anna?"

"I don't know. Maybe."

"She is a fine person."

"I know."

"Then you should love her."

"Okay, I do love her," admitted this naked man seated on his plastic ottoman.

"Then why do you want to be here with me?"

"Who said I do? You asked me."

"Because I saw your carnal itch, cloaked poorly, in your absolute entire being." Again that much-relished weaving smirk.

And he had seen Anna's face, the incubation of betrayal.

"Did my 'carnal itch' mean that *you* had to want to come here?"

"I aim to please." Her gray-blue eyes challenged any and all denials. "No, seriously, I'm not in the habit of competing with the likes of weird-built Anna, especially for a weird-built lover of her own—although I do love her. But I'm also a curious person, an investigator."

"This is not," he said, "very flattering."

"Nor was it meant to be. And, by the way, I'm weird too."

I figured.

"But not in the anatomical ways that are you two."

"Howthen?" Seated on the rock hard ottoman he tried to plant his feet for steadiness: Any motion forward, even a lean, might have indicated something on the order of leap-readiness, which was certainly not his thing.

"My own weirdnesses," Lisa said. "You'll see."

She thinks she's a Mata Hari. But, damnit, I'm fool enough to like it. And she's arrogant prier enough to know it.

"Life," said this Lisa, "it must have been quite trying for you, from jump-street."

She crossed her legs. Her calves and quads, god they were incredible. Not monumental, as were Anna's, but shaped in the sculpted ideal. A teenaged runner at rest—teardrops and long baguettes.

"I," replied Arthur, "I don't feel comfortable talking to you about it all—from 'jump street'."

Christ, we're naked!

"How would you like to be married to me?"

Huh?

"You'd come home from your social-work every day, that tedious endeavor, and there *I'd* be—just like now. My panties are in hanging on the bathroom door-knob, my bra, with its elegant, you know, trusswork—how do you picture it?—salmon? pastel blue?—it's draped over the shower rod." She related this description unseductively, unsweetly; merely matter-of-fact—as if they were indeed long-married.

"Come here, sweetie, and kiss my breasts, make love to them—you can think of me as Mother God. You can say it."

Oh come now. I will not say Mother God.

Bu still he came to her and he bent down-and-over to kiss and suck-on her breasts.

It was difficult, considering the lowness of that much lain-on sofa of his that she was sitting on—he had bought it at the same used-furniture store on decrepit Lombard Street where he had bought the Kennedy rocker. This bending for her breasts made his back hurt. From all his surgeries, from all the anatomical, the spinal, twistings and stretchings and crumplings he had had to endure for his sex-change, his ganglia were always tender—he had, no doubt, disc problems, cervical and thorasic, and probably stenoses here and there, not to mention a touch of scoliosis. *My price to pay for what I figured would be my ultimate happiness.*

"You don't have to bend down like this. You don't like it, *I* don't like it. Go down on your knees and kiss *up*wards, suck *up*. Your knees are okay, aren't they."

"My knees are fine."

Amazingly, some part of me has remained ship-

shape.

"Oh the knees: Glad to hear they're fine. Knees are so religious." She sat up higher, as if to raise her breasts along with her neck (that's become a stalk) and her regal head—now tilted down towards him. "And, please do, call me *Mother God*—you can do it."

"Mother God." His address, being childish, was smothered, embarrassed, mumbled, but no, not lackadaisical.

"Say it *again!*"

This time while it was yet muffled, that Mother God, it had found itself, to even his own surprise, going passionate—for he had also associated the name with pain. His face faced the lips of her vagina, which she had shaved.

"Now, rub your nose, your eyes, rub them all over my breasts, my power breasts—worshipping."

He did it. He wanted to—it had just come into him, that wanting-to. He rubbed his nose, his eyes, and he kept at it, knowing the act was childlike. The touching reached him back to some desire some wish, some prayer-hope very early, very much before he had even thought of being the not-normal specimen that he was.

"Say 'Mother God'."

He did, again.

She was grinning, not in potency but in satisfaction, in what might have been a needed taste of fruition. It seemed as if she were opening her mouth and swallowing something, her rightfully Greatened Self.

And he: He had the sensation that she could experience this "worship" forever, or for as long as he could perform it—in both cases like a puppy rolling onto its back for forever for rubs that will last just as long.

Lisa's breasts were so firm, and so monumental, that they did not retract or stir about as Arthur "worshipped"—they remained as points, projections, aimed elements, and Arthur liked this, he found that he worshipped too this breast adamance, this force of intransigence, this seemed knowing of all that they were about, they reminded him of himself—or his self as he had been at The Hearing, or as he might have been even moreso. Lisa's breasts were teaching instruments, as well as ones for succoring.

"I knew you were right," she said, "the moment I met you. And I think Anna did too. And I know it affected her. I am not a mean woman, though I may look that way—and that is a burden too, you wouldn't believe—I suffer—I *hate* my beauty—yes I *know* it's beauty, it doesn't embarrass me to say it—I hate it because it's ugly beauty, I'd like to look soft, and sweet, like Anna, muscle-Anna—how about *that*! But I saw you, you in your weak-weirdness, your confusion, and your decency, I've seen your types before—I swear this—I felt, alright I'll say it, I could *love* you—and I've been married twice, so I know who *doesn't* work with me—which is just about everybody, every man, every man *being* a man—I *hate* that; so if you could love me—for what I am—for what you'll see in moments now—*I have to show you who I am!*—and neither of us, we can't change."

He came up with nothing but a hard-won, perplexed, "I . . ."

"So, don't hate me now, Arthur, for what I do, now—I am not a monster."

"I didn't think you were."

But he did think she was a monster. Not that that

thought was a deterrent.

"You may think it, soon. I hope you won't, God I hope that. Just remember, I love differently. I am human, but I'm weird. I am as trapped as you—and as Anna is."

He looked up at her as if she were so awesome and confused, the curse and cure of heaven—and he realized that his look was so fake as real, and blankly comical, and he wished an escape that he could not possibly, truthfully, desire.

"We ought to go to your bed," she said.

He went to take her hand, but she withdrew hers, as if holding hands indicated a connection for them that was irrelevant, an imposture, and it might have presented an equality which Lisa had no intention of conveying.

What in the world does she want!

It isn't really Sex!

"Do you ever make your bed," she said when they entered his tiny bedroom.

"No."

"Not even for your darling Anna?"

"We've never been here, made love here."

" 'Made love'," repeated Lisa, as if mocking the timeworn phrase.

"I've been cauterized," she now said, dryly, out of nowhere.

He wasn't even sure what she'd meant.

She lay down and spread her legs.

"Lick."

No request; an order.

Arthur had never in his life performed cunnilingus, and he saw that Lisa suspected as much.

She had spread her legs, and there, like paradoxically a child-girl's, a vulnerable forbidden, a not-to-be-seen, a not-to-be-touched, almost not a true element, was her bare tonsured vagina—and he entered with his tongue.

"Everything," she said. "Mouth too. And go up-in higher, where it is.

"Can you feel 'it'?" she inquired.

"Mmmm," he mumbled, not in delectation, more like a worker to his boss.

He exited, in order to utter a clear "Yes."

"Back in," Lisa said, annoyed or worried.

He went back in.

"It's hard now, isn't it—a clit cock."

"Mmmm."

"Like *your* cock. *Harder* than your cock."

"Mmmm."

He'd wanted to say No—but she was rising, as if she were a shark swimming-up from the deep to take and swallow a seal or dolphin, anything lesser being Nature's Right. Her vagina and his mouth were congealed, near-clotted and spitty-wet, as if they each were fighting each to take full control. He had not the experience however to work her clitoris about with his tongue—he just pressed on it.

Unbelievably he had been so intent on "worshipping" that he had not been aware that he had an erection. But now that he was aware he realized that it was the most exhilarated erection he had ever had—even in the best of his masturbations. And more than with Anna, despite all the unbelievable changes and exchanges of male-female sensualities, male-female *existences*, that they had produced; this fever of agitation with Lisa was certainly from his submission and from her now arching upwards as if she would elevate her center to the ceiling and her vagina hold him there.

"I *love* you!"—he couldn't not say it. He had taken his mouth from her vagina in order to speak, to proclaim his "love", with his lips and tongue now touched to the purest skin where would have grown her pubic hair, and he imploringly looking up. Of course he didn't believe what he said, that outburst that had forced itself to force itself—he even promised within that he would abate, unman, any urge for frenzy: such was to not be a Man.

Confusing.

"I love this too," she said, her eyes downcast in a sort of sardonic superiority that also managed to seem sympathetic—at least in the way that she experienced sympathy.

"You know," she added, "you will not be fucking me."

He couldn't have cared less: He was relieved, because of her power, and because he loved so much what they were doing.

"I own you," she said. "You were born for me." Those words came to him not from her but from the closing-in of the four walls. "*I* will tell you what's-what and what-in-the-world to do."

This statement, too much it struck home—as if he had been waiting for it, had been indeed born for it.

"You *will* be now standing and bending over."

"What?" he asked, and made an expression of not comprehending: he hadn't heard right?

"You'll see."

She reached into her handbag and withdrew what

she called her "Rabbit", but it was not a vibrator—it was more than that.

Although he had never seen one, what she was holding, not before in real life, he did recognize the thing—sort of. He also realized that his whole life until now had led him to submission to a strong female—if he would allow it, countenance it, what with his having been mocked and diminished so much, this despite his hard trying to compensate, to be *manly*, his probably trying harder and more conscientiously than had—he'd have bet—*any* man. . . Yes, with Anna he had gone through all these varieties of their sex-exchangings during sex, and it had seemed ideal; but these "perfections", it struck him now, could not add-up-to this Lisa quintessence, this delirium, of being Brought-Down, the overwhelming ecstasy of it even in its anticipation—if eyes could groan, his now would. By falling-down to what had thrown him down all throughout his life.

"Bend over," she repeated—and he did.

Her "rabbit" was a strap-on, alabaster, or something like ivory, as long as any penis he had ever seen (or imagined)—and at its rear tip a sort of sniggle-hookish nipple-nob which, when she attached the instrument to herself, would obviously stimulate her clitoris when she'd go-at-him up the ass—a getting-good by giving. . . But she did not enter him with her 'rabbit'. She said—

"Turn round."

He did.

And Lisa, in all her fullest beauty, with her long hair draped now like you might picture an Indian medicine man's, with her bone-angular chin just about extruding, as if in a dare or a response to a dare, and her neck presenting its stretched tendons, and her height now over-reaching his as he still remained a bit bent (*as if he wanted to remain that bent way?*), she began slapping his erect penis, up-back up-back up-back, working her way to walloping it (he guessed? he wanted?), her face turning from desire to the torcherous-desire, her lips gone to their tightly cruel, her eyes arrows, her nose retracted in (it looked like) bitterness, in meanness—so that for an instant, within his own felt pain, which was considerable—but only for an instant—he wondered what had happened to her in her life, what unfairness, for her to strike him like that up-back up back up back—even the sheerest most overwhelming dominance by men, that couldn't lead to this, this Punishment, this Joy-Walloping of hers—and most especially, good-god, for him too.

Ecstasies, so human, so needed?—so not the ecstatic person at all, they are so queerly sick?

'*You've got the wrong guy,*' he thought for a moment; '*I've been punished too. You really need to be beating a Charles Bronson, a Lee Marvin, an Arnold Schwarzenegger, an "Italian Stallion" like Sylvester Stallone, and/or The Rock.*'

But he so wanted it. *Goddamn!*

"And hold it," she ordered. "Don't you *come!*"

He held it, the coming, which was not so easy, the squeezing-down and the clamping-in tight on his sphincter, which act was not meant to be, which amounted-to another masochist-punishment in itself. And which brought moments when he did wish to turn the tables and wallop her—and, truth-be-truth—punch her square in her perfect chin and watch her fall back, beaten.

But of course he didn't do that, that "equalizer".

"Turn round again and bend-over."

And now she did enter. Holding onto his ribs from the rear, as one might prevent the escape of a child who was a thief and liar, she pushed The Rabbit in slowly, and without using any ointment, which of course as a physician she would have had the requisite knowledge for resorting-to, such as the infamous (and joke-able) K-Y Jelly, which even *he* knew about; but No!—she aimed at serious pain's defeating pain itself? (or so it seemed was her intention?), and after all they had just run-into each other by chance, and who caries around K-Y Jelly on the chance of meeting-up with someone you can ass-fuck?—and yes anyway he came, he dripped and he dribbled, he did not "shoot", as the contractions she had caused to his sphincter were too tight—so his semen, to most extent within his own genitals, clutched and hidden, remained.

He hated to say it, but he said it again: "I love you."

Or more properly he whined it, as if she were fate's full strength, made for him, made to return to him and make of him, by dissolving him, his beginnings.

And she said, "Lay down on the bed." Then, before he could obediently follow that order, she changed her mind:

"Let's go to the bathroom. Bring a sheet."

Obvious what was in store.

They entered the bathroom, and she became his mother with the rebuking statement, "Godamighty it's funky."

"Yes."

He hadn't much been in the mood to tackle the large job left by the departing Akram.

"Shower more." She pinched her nostrils. "Buy some Glade or something. I can barely stand it to be in here."

'Then let's leave it.' He didn't say this.

"Lay down the sheet on the linoleum."

"Lisa," he said, "maybe we shouldn't go this far."

"You want me to—you know it."

"I'm not denying it. In a way I do."

"It's the primordial. Dionysian. Everyone should experience what it is."

"Have you?—before?"

"I was married, twice."

"And you did that?—this?"

What did her inscrutable roll-eyed shrug quite mean?

"My marriages failed because I did not do this—with those men I couldn't."

"Lisa, I think, don't you think? you're glorifying this all too much."

"Glorifying the Dionysian. You can't glorify what's already a glory—and always has been. The All. And once we do it, you know, you're fixated: you are mine forever."

"That sounds so"—he was a bit afraid to say it—"childish."

"Anyway"—and she jutted-out her rear end like a tomboy playing tough—"anyway, my shit, it's sweet."

"Your *shit*? I just thought we'd . . ."

He had been about to lay down on the sheet; but 'shit'—that had not been what he had imagined. So, when he did lay down it was because he saw her as exciting herself by her own exaggeration, and he by his.

She sat on his face. "You excite me," she said, "by your inherent—I don't know—it's your slightness, while your slightness, it's so fighting that—I see it, God it makes me *cream*." The pressure of her ass, it was surrounding and smothering and overwhelming but— how could he explain this?—comforting. And inti- mate—as if they had been married for years, and knew each other inside-out. But this was while it was still farce to him, still mime, before he felt her efforts at squeezing, squeezing, she was really *trying*—and her shit smell, only that, just the smell, that from her rear's entrance was not what she had said it was, she being funny he'd thought—that claim of "My shit is sweet"— and caught in the whirlpool-depth of it, the imagining, he had almost *believed* in the shit-sweetness; but since it was not any kind of honeyish smell up there but a fecal smell, a reality smell, and that without any *real* shit coming-down, he raised her enough with his arms and took himself out from under.

"You were really *trying*?"

"Think what you wish."

Wouldn't her conscience have stopped her? Her cleanliness? Her immaculate physician sense of the olfactory?—what?—what would have stopped the damned so-called Dionysian?

Out from under, he was relieved of course, and proud, and glad, of his having lifted her off; but to deny a certain smidgeon of disappointment, more than a cer- tain smidgeon, that would be denying, well, that desire- metaphor of, call-a-phony-spade-a-spade, divinity—no, that all was crazy. He was happy to be out, he regretted being-out, who knows, maybe they would try again— *would they really!?*—Lisa's domination had excited him more than had the multi-dimensions of his roll- round similarities and differences with Anna and how they, he and Anna, had come to unite, to mirror the universe in a way, to mirror the subtle hormone-shifts that make for one animal's difference from its other, its closest Other, and its yearning to reach-out and remain attached—and these concurrences and changes, this totality of excitement, it had been in his mind, full-occupying his mind, firing his mind, his long-unfired mind, until now, as such had been the totality of his life's excitement—until now; it had been in his mind until now because all had been Love, all of it, Love Perfect and defined, and it still spoke in his mind—only now, due to Lisa, his mind also spoke The Other—Betrayal.

Can there be two Essences?—one good Right positive for the lasting, the emotional cerebral, and one the good Right Eros that had drawn from your birth-right, your weak-as-a-feather birthright that you're escaping, you're trying to—but it still drew that birth-right right back into you, and—anyone with a brain knows—it therefore drew oblivion.

XVII

After, after—she was gone, that Lisa—and he lay back on the sofa: *But I love Anna, how we are, our jigsaw of our sex that so fits, our vulnerabilities entwined—I think that is love if there is love. It has to be. We belong.*

The bifurcation, though, that split that comes with sex and only sex, aimed-sex at your weakest you: no, it's not love, but it's aimed at your vitals so it simulates and stimulates—a mime: not love, but a chaining, that can't but have me in-crave for that Lisa (and maybe she for me?), it is what we all, we humans, are.

And the weakness of it, considering who and what I was, no excuses but that weakness, it was ingrained in me.

Is fighting it the answer? Fighting the ever-cheating. Fighting the bifurcation. Fighting the ingrain?—the abnormality of Normalcy.

ALAN GOLDFEIN

FIGHT THE INGRAIN
(Bumper Sticker; T-Shirt)

FOR COMMENTS TO THE AUTHOR
PLEASE CONTACT:

americaneditions@aol.com

www.ingramcontent.com/pod-product-compliance
Lightning Source LLC
Chambersburg PA
CBHW022145170626
46807CB00005B/2080